A Sister's Trust

Sisters of Smithville #2

~*~*~

This one is for my sister Ava

~*~*~

Contents

~*~*~

Chapter 1

The Promise

~*~*~

Smithville, Missouri; spring 1840

A gentle breeze blew over the hill, rustling the tall prairie grass. Two young girls in matching dresses ran, laughing, to the top.

"Look, over there! Another daisy!" the younger one exclaimed. She released her sister's hand for a moment in order to add the flower to the bouquet she held in her opposite fist.

"That should be enough now, Eva," said the elder.

"Do you think Mama will like them, Joy?"

"I think that she will love them."

Eva beamed.

The sisters skipped back down the hill into town.

"Why is Mama sick again?" Eva asked once they were nearly to their house.

"I don't know," Joy answered.

"Is she gonna die?" the four year old asked.

Joy released Eva's hand and pushed open their gate.

"Come, Eva. Let's not think about such things."

"But will she?"

"I surely hope not."

"Me too."

"Let's go show her the flowers. They are sure to cheer her up."

Eva nodded eagerly and followed Joy into the house.

Two year old Peter was playing on the floor in the parlor with a couple of spoons. Baby Johnny was crying in his cradle by the rocking chair. Joy rushed to comfort him.

"Where are Frank and Teddy?" she asked Peter.

Peter continued beating the spoons on the floor, completely ignoring her.

Eva walked past her little brother and entered her parents' room. Her mother lay still in the bed.

"Mama?" Eva set the flowers on the bed and climbed up beside them. "I brought you some pretty flowers."

Rose Remington smiled slightly and reached out to touch Eva's cheek.

"Thank you, my darling."

"Are you going to get better soon, Mama?"

"I truly hope so, child. Would you please put those beautiful flowers in some water by my bed so I can see them better?"

"Yes, Mama."

Eva slid off of the bed and left the room. She found a glass jar and poured in a little water.

"Careful you don't spill," Joy admonished from the rocking chair.

"I won't."

Just then, Frank, who was eight, burst through the door with his brother, younger by two years, right on his heels.

"Frank! Teddy! Where have you been?" Joy demanded.

"Gee, sis, you sound like Mama," Frank said. "You're only a year older than me, and you went off by yourself."

"I'm responsible for you while Mama's sick. You could have at least told me where you were going. Besides, I asked you to attend to Peter and Johnny."

"We were just playing with Harvey and some of the other fellas."

"I don't like that Harvey Green," Joy declared.

"He's a fine fella. You can't tell me who to play with."

Joy took a deep breath.

"You're right. I'm sorry, Frank. I have no right to tell you what to do. I guess I'm so concerned for Mama that I forgot myself."

"Oh! I almost forgot to tell you the news!" Frank exclaimed, instantly forgetting the previous subject.

"What news?"

"Mrs. Henning had a baby girl last night. I have to go tell Mama." He rushed into the bedroom.

Eva followed him, carefully carrying the jar of flowers.

Frank quickly repeated the news to their mother and left.

"Eva," Rose said softly once Eva had placed the flowers on the bedside table. "Would you please tell Joy to come in here?"

"Yes, Mama."

"Joy, Mama wants you," Eva said as she stepped back into the parlor.

Joy slowly rose. She placed the sleeping Johnny back in his cradle and went into their parents' room, closing the door behind her.

~*~

"Joy, you know that I have been ill for quite a while now. I know it's been hard for you to take care of the little ones, but I wanted to tell you that you've been doing a good job. I'm sorry that you can't go to school, but you must understand that with your papa at work and me in bed, there is no one to watch Johnny, Peter, and little Eva all day. I know how much you like school." Rose barely managed to finish her sentence before bursting into a coughing fit.

"It's all right, Mama. Soon you will get well, and I can go back to school."

"I would like that very much, my sweet girl, but I must tell you the truth. I am very, very sick. I do not know when - or if - I will get well."

"What do you mean, Mama? Of course you will get well."

"Only the good Lord knows. Listen closely to me, Joy. You are my oldest child. I know this is so much to ask of one so young, but you are my only choice. Joy, I need you to become the lady of this house. You are to take my place as the mother. Watch out for the young ones and show them right from wrong. Teach Eva how to cook and sew."

Rose paused to cover another cough.

"I cannot say how much longer I will be with you all. Joy, I need to know that I can depend on you. That you will keep this family going, no matter what happens. Don't worry, your papa is strong. He can't be here all the time, though, he needs his job. I'm leaving you in charge whenever he's not here. Joy, can I trust you?"

Joy shook her head. "No, Mama. I couldn't do it. I'd never be as good a mother as you are. I can't. I'm too young."

Rose took Joy's hand and looked into her daughter's eyes.

~ 9 ~

"I know you can, Joy. I'm not asking you to become me. I hate to place such a large responsibility on you, but I can't ask Mrs. Lewis to help any longer. She has plenty of responsibilities of her own, being the reverend's wife. I know you can do it, Joy. You have my complete trust."

"All right, Mama," Joy finally agreed. "I'll do my best to make myself worthy of your trust."

Chapter 2

Early Struggles

~*~*~

"Now, Eva, would you please do me a big favor and keep Peter entertained while I wash the dishes?" Joy asked, setting their little brother on the parlor floor. "He's been clinging to my skirt all day."

"I'll help," Eva nodded. She took Peter's hand and led him to the pile of blocks in the middle of the room. Come on, Petey, let's build something."

"Fun!" Peter exclaimed.

"Thank you so much, Eva. You're a big help," Joy said gratefully.

Eva beamed with pride.

Joy quickly returned to the kitchen before Peter noticed her. He didn't like to let her out of his sight - and grasp - for too long. Joy understood why, though. She was the only mother-figure he currently had. Mama was still in bed, even though it had been months since her initial illness. Joy was beginning to worry that their mama would never fully recover.

Joy carefully poured the water she had warmed on the stove into the dishwashing basin. She added a bit of soap and retrieved a fresh cloth.

"Oh, my," Joy muttered, sighing heavily at the sight of the dirty dishes. She hadn't had a chance to wash them after breakfast, and they had just finished the noon meal. "Here we go." She pushed up her sleeves, picked up a plate, and began swiping the cloth across the surface a few times. After dunking it into the rinse water, she set it on the counter to dry later. "One down, one million to go."

It was nicer to do the dishes after supper, when the older boys were there to help. But after a quick dinner at home, they had to return to school. Joy couldn't wait until Eva was old enough to help. Of course, by that time, she too, would be in school. At least she could keep the littlest boys from being underfoot until then.

As she washed, Joy thought over how the past few months had gone with her playing mother. She thought that she had been doing a fair job.

Not as well as Mama, of course.

It was hard to keep an eye on the three youngest at home and not worry too much about how Frank and Teddy were doing at school. She hoped that they didn't spend too much time with that Harvey Green. That boy was born a trouble-maker. He took after his older brother, Jack, for sure. And of course, there was Papa working in the dangerous mill. She wondered how her mama had ever managed to remain in a sane state.

More than anything else, Joy missed going to school. She hated the fact that she was falling further behind on her lessons with each day Mama remained in bed. At least Frank told her what he learned each evening when he came home. But he was a grade younger than she was and had learned his lessons the previous year. Joy also dearly missed her two good friends, Marta and Willa. They did stop by occasionally and tell her about school. However, Joy had noticed the last time they had visited that the two of them seemed closer, and she felt more distant. Joy had promised Mama that she would take care of the children, but was keeping that promise worth risking her friendships?

Will things ever go back to the way they used to be?

Joy sighed deeply.

"Why is life so hard?" she wondered aloud.

"You're only nine," Joy told herself. *Then why do I feel as if I'm forty? Oh, Mama, why did you have to get sick?*

"Please, Lord, make her well so that I may go back to school and no longer have all of this responsibility."

Oh, Joy, what a selfish prayer. You should be happy enough if Mama gets well enough to be up and about.

Joy suddenly realized that she was vigorously scrubbing at a pan. She slowed her hand and scolded herself for getting so worked up.

"I trust you, Lord. Everything will work out all right. I trust that it will." She took a deep breath and slowly let it out, feeling much better.

Finally, all of the dishes were washed and rinsed. Joy found a towel and started drying. She began humming and realized that working was more enjoyable while doing so.

She was nearly finished when she heard a commotion in the parlor.

"That's mine!" Eva cried.

"No, mine!" Peter shouted.

"Give it back!"

"No!"

"Please!"

"No! No! No!"

"Joy! Peter took my block!"

"Let him have it, he's littler than you," Joy yelled into the other room. She tossed the towel onto the counter and picked up a stack of freshly-dried plates.

"Ouch! Joy, Peter just threw the block at me!" Eva wailed.

"Goodness!" Joy exclaimed. She thumped the plates on the counter and marched into the parlor.

"Eva! Peter! You know better than to fight like this. Apologize this instant!"

The two youngsters sat, frozen, on the floor. Both stared at her in shock.

"Come on; tell me what this is all about." Joy planted her hands on her hips.

Peter glanced at Eva.

"Joy mean," he said.

"I am not mean!" Joy declared.

"Are too," Peter responded.

"Peter Remington! Don't talk back!"

Just then a loud crash came from the kitchen. Joy immediately swung around to look at the cradle. It was empty.

"Johnny!"

Joy raced into the kitchen with Eva right on her heels and Peter toddling along behind. She skidded to a stop when she entered the room.

"Oh no! No!" she gasped, covering her mouth with both of her hands.

The plates she had just dried were now lying on the floor, a shattered pile of china. Johnny sat nearby with the towel clutched in his fist, crying.

"Johnny! You could have killed yourself!" Joy exclaimed, rushing to pick up the young boy and checking him for cuts.

"Johnny broke all of our plates," Eva declared, stepping further into the room to get a better look.

"Eva, stay over there!" Joy nearly shouted. "I don't want you to cut your foot on the sharp pieces. Here, take Johnny back into the parlor." Joy set Johnny down next to Eva. "I have to clean this up."

Eva led Johnny out of the room.

Joy went to the corner of the kitchen to retrieve the broom. After sweeping up the pieces, she carefully dumped them into a bucket.

Seeing the drying towel lying in the doorway where Johnny must have dropped it, Joy went to pick it up. As she grasped the towel, a sudden realization flashed through her mind.

"Oh, no. How could I have been so careless?" Joy muttered. She straightened and pressed her palm to her forehead.

"He could have been killed because of me."

~*~

"Oh, Mama! I can't do this anymore!" Joy cried, rushing into her parents' bedroom.

"What's wrong, Joy?" Rose asked softly from the bed. "What was all of the commotion about? Did I hear something break?"

"Yes, that's just it. Oh, Mama, Johnny could have died, and it would have been all my fault!"

Rose's eyes grew.

"Is he all right? What happened?"

"He's fine. Oh, they were arguing, and there was a crash and the broken dishes..."

Rose relaxed slightly.

"Slow down, Joy. Why don't you start from the beginning?"

"Well, I was doing the dishes when Eva and Peter started arguing over their blocks. I went to stop them. And while I was in the parlor, there was a crash in the kitchen. I ran in there, and Johnny was sitting on the floor surrounded by a pile of broken plates. I checked him for cuts right away, and he was fine."

"I'm afraid I don't understand how this was your fault, Joy. Dishes will get broken from time to time, and as long as Johnny wasn't hurt, I really am not concerned."

Joy shook her head frantically.

"But don't you see, Mama? Johnny was holding the towel! I had tossed it carelessly onto the counter and it probably only landed halfway on. And then when I set the plates down, I put them on top of the towel. I was so annoyed by Eva and Peter's arguing. I was so careless! Don't you see? Johnny grabbed onto the towel to help himself stand and pulled the plates nearly on top of him with his weight. How could I be so careless!"

"Joy, stop saying that! It was an accident!"

"But Johnny could have been killed!" Joy shook as tears filled her eyes.

"But he wasn't, and we can thank the good Lord for that. Come here, darling." Rose held out her arms. Joy fell into them, sobbing.

"Hush, sweetheart. It's all right. I know you were scared." Rose stroked Joy's hair.

"I don't think I can do this anymore," Joy cried. "Please get well, Mama!"

"I'm trying to, but I'm still weak and..." Rose was interrupted by a series of coughs.

"You get some rest, Mama. I'll... I'll do my best to get along until you get well."

"That's all I'm asking, Joy. Don't push yourself too hard."

Joy quietly left the bedroom, closing the door gently behind her. She closed her eyes and took a deep breath.

What is my best, if I can't even keep my little brother safe? Joy wondered. *How will I ever be able to go on after this?*

~*~

Eva watched as Joy leaned against the wall with her eyes closed and her lips moving slightly. She had heard her sister and mother speaking but didn't fully understand want had been said. Johnny was fine, so what was all the fuss about?

Peter stacked four blocks, then promptly knocked them down. He picked one of them up and held it out to Eva.

"Share," he said.

"Sure, *now* you want to share," Eva muttered. "No thank you, I don't want it anymore." She pushed the block away.

"Share Johnny," Peter declared. He patted over to the cradle where their brother now lay sleeping, and tossed it inside.

Johnny awoke with a loud scream.

Joy's eyes flashed open.

"Peter Remington! What did you do?"

Peter looked terrified.

Joy marched over to Peter, picked him up, and planted him several feet back. She knelt down to comfort Johnny.

"Um, Joy," Eva said nervously, knowing it was a bad time. "I have to go to the outhouse."

"Go by yourself," Joy waved her away as the baby continued to scream.

Eva stared at her sister in shock. She was never allowed outside by herself.

"But, Joy..."

"Just go, can't you see I'm busy."

Unable to wait any longer, Eva rushed through the kitchen and out the back door.

She was in such a hurry that she forgot about the loose board on the step. The toe of her shoe caught, and she tripped, landing face to face with a copperhead.

~*~

"Joy, did I leave my primer here?" Frank asked, bursting through the front door.

"Yes, you did. It took you long enough to notice." Joy said sarcastically from the rocking chair.

"Well, Mr. Walters didn't ask me to read until right now."

"Couldn't you have shared with somebody?" Joy asked as Frank raced into the kitchen.

"Nope. Joe's primer is missing that page."

"Oh, Frank, before you leave, could you check on Eva please? She's been gone for a while. And I don't want to wake Johnny up."

Frank glanced at his youngest brother sleeping in Joy's lap. Peter lay on the floor nearby, also asleep.

"Where'd she go?"

"To the outhouse."

"By herself? You know that..."

"I know, I know," Joy huffed. "Just go and find her please."

"Sure, I'll go. Anything to stay out of school longer."

Frank opened the back door and stared at Eva who was lying on her stomach at the bottom of the steps.

"What are you doin', Eva? Joy's worried about you."

Eva lay completely still.

"Eva, get up. Stop fooling around." Frank thumped down the steps and reached down to grab hold of her arm. He froze when he saw the brightly colored snake lying in the grass.

"Now don't move, Eva," he whispered.

"What do you think I've been doing?" Eva hissed through her teeth.

"You stay right there. I'm going to get the hoe."

Eva continued to stare at the copperhead, who stared back at her with cat-shaped eyes.

Frank slowly backed up and eased along the step until he reached the far end. The lean-to door was just a few feet away. He stepped down and walked along the house to the small door. Opening it carefully, Frank reached inside and grasped the hoe.

Making a wide loop around, Frank crept up behind the snake.

"Don't move a muscle," he warned Eva.

Eva remained frozen on the ground.

Frank raised the hoe high above his head and carefully aimed, knowing that he had to hit his mark the first time. He was suddenly grateful that his father had taught him to chop wood last summer.

In one quick motion, Frank brought down the hoe. It landed several inches behind the snake's head. The creature tossed violently about. Frank immediately slammed the hoe down upon it again.

Eva scrambled back.

Frank kicked and stomped the snake.

"I think its dead now," Eva whispered. She was huddled in a ball on the bottom step.

Frank looked down at the copperhead, cut in three pieces with its insides now on the outside.

"I think you're right," he agreed.

Holding out his hand, Frank helped his sister to her feet. Eva clutched his hand so hard it turned white.

"Where have you two been? Couldn't you find her, Frank?" Joy demanded.

Frank quickly told her what had happened.

"Oh, my. This is too much for one day." Joy sighed. She covered her eyes with the hand that wasn't supporting Johnny. "You were so brave, Frank. I couldn't have ever done what you did."

"It was nothin'," Frank said with a shrug. He couldn't help but grin with pride, however. *Just wait until the fellas at school hear this. They'll never believe me. Speaking of school...*

"I gotta go, Joy!"

"Don't bother, the bell rang a few minutes ago."

"Oh."

"My, Frank, you actually sound disappointed."

"Very funny, sis. You know I love school."

Joy raised an eyebrow doubtfully.

"Don't you believe me?" Frank put on a puppy-face.

"I know you just want to tell your friends about your act of heroism. It'll have to wait for tomorrow."

Frank shook his head and grinned. Who knew his sister was so good at reading minds?

The door slammed shut.

"What happened to you, Frank?" Teddy asked. He hung his hat up by the door.

"Frank saved me!" Eva announced.

"From what?" Teddy demanded.

"A snake!"

Frank related the story to his brother, using great detail. He enjoyed watching Teddy's eyes grow larger in suspense.

Once he was finished, Joy rolled her eyes and shook her head.

"Honestly, Frank. You elaborate too much. Don't you know how dangerous that was?"

"'Course. That's what makes it so exciting. Oh, I have to go tell Mama!"

"Frank!" Joy exclaimed. "I know that you're excited about this, but you and Eva were in real danger. If one of you had gotten bit, I wouldn't have known what to do."

"Relax, sis. Everything turned out fine. Hey, you were the one that let Eva go out by herself."

Joy's face fell.

"You're right. Another major mistake I made today." She closed her eyes and sighed deeply. "I knew I wasn't worthy of Mama's trust," she murmured.

"What was that?"

"Nothing. You wanted to tell Mama about the snake."

"Oh, right!" Frank instantly forgot about Joy's words. He rushed off to tell of his adventure once again.

Chapter 3

A Great Tragedy

~*~*~

Early the next morning, Joy woke to the sound of coughing, but it wasn't her mother's. She slid out of bed, careful not to disturb Eva, and crept out of the room.

She strained her ears, but the coughing had stopped.

No, there it was again. It's coming from my room.

Joy glanced at Eva. Her younger sister was sleeping soundly.

The faint cough sounded again. It was coming from the cradle at the foot of the bed.

Johnny.

Joy quickly knelt by the cradle. Johnny stared up at her with watery eyes. Feeling his forehead, Joy found it to be burning with fever.

"Papa! Papa!" she cried, jumping up and racing into her parents' room. Only her mother lay in the bed.

"Your father had to go to the mill early today. He already left," Rose told her.

"Mama, Johnny has a fever!"

"Wet a cloth with cool water and try to lower his temperature. Send Frank to get Midwife Stevens," Rose instructed.

Joy dashed out of the room and up the ladder to the loft.

"Frank, wake up!" Joy shook her brother.

"What is it?" Frank moaned, half asleep.

"Go fetch the midwife. Johnny's ill."

Frank jumped out of bed and pulled his trousers on over his underwear.

"I'll run as fast as I can." He was gone by the time Joy reached the ladder.

Joy poured some cold water into a bowl and grabbed a cloth. She entered her room and found Eva sitting up in bed.

"What's going on?" she asked.

"Please leave the room, Eva. Johnny's ill with a fever."

Eva obediently left.

Joy dropped the cloth into the bowl, then wrung it out and began gently wiping her little brother's face. Suddenly, Johnny began coughing up his dinner. Joy held him upright so he wouldn't choke.

"Please hurry, Frank!"

Johnny started screaming. Joy saw that he had also coughed blood.

"Lord, help me. I don't know what to do."

Joy sat on the floor, holding Johnny in her lap. He continued to vomit and was still burning up. She did her best to clear his face with the cloth, but the effort was pointless.

The front door slammed shut. Frank bust into the room.

"The midwife's neighbor says she's out of town delivering a baby."

Joy stared at Frank in horror.

"But he said that he'd tell her to come here as soon as she returns," Frank added.

"That could take hours. I don't know how to care for Johnny. Tell Mama about his symptoms. Maybe she knows how to help." Joy briefly explained Johnny's condition.

Frank left to repeat the news to their mother.

"She says it almost sounds like cholera. But other signs are diarrhea and sunken eyes, so it shouldn't be that. She said that it could be the flu."

"What's cholera?" Joy asked.

Frank shrugged. "I don't know, but it sounds terrible."

Joy nodded.

~*~

Eva sat on the parlor floor, playing with Peter. Frank and Teddy had left for school hours ago, and Joy was still in the room with Johnny. The midwife hadn't arrived yet, and Joy hadn't even made breakfast.

"I'm hungry," Eva said to her brother.

"Hungry," Peter agreed with a nod.

"I'll see if there's any bread left over."

Eva stood and walked to the doorway of the room she and Joy shared.

"Joy," she said softly.

"I told you to stay away so you don't get sick," Joy snapped. She was still sitting on the floor, rocking Johnny back and forth. Eva could tell that she was tired and feeling helpless.

"Peter and I are hungry."

"I can't make you anything right now."

"I was just wondering if there was any bread left over."

"There is, but it's moldy. That's why I told you not to eat any yesterday. Don't touch it."

"I won't." Eva went to the kitchen to find something else. A block of cheese was all she could find. Being too young to use a knife, Eva took a bite out of the whole block and carried it back to the parlor to share with Peter.

After a short while, Joy emerged from the bedroom. She solemnly walked to their parents' room. Eva stared after her with wide eyes.

"Mama," she heard Joy say. "He has all the symptoms for cholera. What is the cure?"

Their mother sighed softly.

"Joy, there is no cure."

~*~

Eva's young legs carried her quickly across the grassy prairie to the mill. She slowed as she neared the building. Men were everywhere; unloading sheaves of wheat from the farmers, loading sacks of freshly-ground flour onto wagons, going in and out of the building, yelling at each other. The mill sure was a noisy place.

Joy had sent her to school to tell her brothers to get their father, but she had decided that it would be quicker if she went straight to the mill. Now she wasn't so sure she had made the right choice.

"Hey! You there! What do you think you're doing here?" a tall, dark-haired man yelled at her.

"Umm..." Eva nervously shifted from one foot to the other. Maybe this wasn't such a good idea. "I'm looking for my papa."

"And what might your papa's name be, sweetie?" a kind-looking man asked, stepping up beside the first man.

"Umm…" Eva couldn't remember ever hearing his name. He was just "papa".

"Can you tell me your name?" the kind man asked.

"Eva."

"Do you know your last name?"

"Remington."

"Oh, so you're Harold's little girl?"

Eva nodded, hoping that he was right.

"Remington!" the man called into the mill. "You've got a visitor!"

Just then Eva's papa stepped outside with a sack of flour slung over his shoulder.

"Eva!" he exclaimed. "What on earth are you doing here?" He dropped the sack on the ground and raced over to her.

"Oh, Papa!" she wailed, flinging her arms around his neck. "Johnny's gonna die!"

~*~

Joy was crying when Eva and Harold returned. She looked up at them with red eyes.

"He's dead, Papa!" she wailed. "I didn't know what to do. It's my fault he's dead!" She still clutched little Johnny in her arms.

Harold set Eva down and knelt next to Joy.

"No it's not, Joy," he said firmly, stroking her disheveled hair. He carefully removed Johnny from her arms and placed him in his cradle, covering the body with a quilt.

Joy leaned into her father's chest and burst into fresh tears.

"He had cholera, Papa. Mama said that there's no cure, but I kept trying."

"That's all you could do, Joy. Mama's right, there is no cure."

"How did he get it? Are we all going to die?"

"We'll give you a nice hot bath. That might help. And maybe you should stay away from the others until we make sure you aren't going to get it. I'll ask Mrs. Lewis to stay here for a little while. As for how he

~ 23 ~

caught it, I'm not sure. I heard that if you drink contaminated water or eat moldy food, you might get it, but we should be safe from that."

Eva had been watching the scene in tears. She couldn't believe that her baby brother had just died. But when she heard her father's ending words, she was filled with a sense of dread.

She had given Johnny a piece of bread the day before - after Joy had told her not to eat it.

~*~

For the next few weeks Joy couldn't sleep. The cries that she had once found so annoying were now replaced with a silence that rang louder than the church bells.

Chapter 4

A Friend

~*~*~

Time passed. Life went on.

Eva was relieved that she was finally old enough to go to school. It was hard to stay at home all day, with Mama still sick and Joy blaming herself for Johnny's death. Eva knew the truth; however. She was the one to blame. *If only I hadn't given him that bread.*

At least with me starting school, Joy will only have Peter to look after now, Eva thought as she walked alongside Frank and Teddy to the schoolhouse.

The autumn morning sun shone brightly in the east, promising beautiful weather for the day. It had rained the previous night so the ground was wet. Eva stepped closer to Teddy to avoid a puddle in the road.

"Not so close, you're embarrassing me," Teddy said, nudging her away.

"Stop it, Teddy," Frank said. He gave his brother a shove. "What's the matter with you? This is Eva's first day."

Teddy stared at the ground. "Sorry. I just don't want the fellas teasing me about a tag-along little sister."

"That's all right, Teddy," Eva said, wounded by his remark. "I won't stay by you anymore." She ran up ahead.

"Eva, wait! I'm sorry!" Teddy called to her.

Eva ignored him.

"Now you've gone and hurt her feelings," Eva heard Frank say.

"Hello, I'm Violet Baker."

Eva looked to her right and saw a girl running up to her.

"What's your name?"

"Eva Remington."

"Are you walking all by yourself? Can I walk the rest of the way with you?" Violet asked.

Eva grinned. "I would like that. I was walking with my brothers, but they were embarrassed by me."

Violet nodded knowingly. "The same for my brothers." She paused and pointed over her shoulder. "There they are, back there, talking to those other boys."

Eva looked.

"Those are my brothers, Frank and Teddy."

"Daniel and Joe are my brothers. I also have an older sister and one younger brother. Do you have any other siblings?"

"Your family sounds a lot like mine. I have an older sister named Joy. She has to stay home from school and take care of Peter because my mama's sick. Peter is my little brother. I used to have two little brothers, but... Johnny... died."

"Oh," Violet murmured.

Eva wondered if she should tell Violet about what had happened. *But if I do, will she hate me because I killed my little brother?* Eva could see Violet becoming a good friend. If Violet knew, that would surely ruin everything.

"Well, are you just going to stand there or come inside?" Frank asked. He walked past the two girls who had come to a halt at the bottom of the steps to the schoolhouse.

Violet held out her hand.

"Come on, let's go. I'm nervous, too."

Eva took Violet's hand, and they entered the building together.

~*~

Eva was surprised to find that she truly enjoyed school. She was quick to learn the alphabet and her numbers. Mr. Walters, the teacher, said that she would be learning to read in no time.

Her growing friendship with Violet made her days extra pleasant. Every day Violet would wait by the Remington's gate for Eva. Violet's brothers would often join her to walk with Frank and Teddy, but the boys never walked alongside the girls. They always followed from a distance. Eva didn't mind, though, as long as she had Violet to talk to.

Eva and Violet never seemed to run out of anything to talk about. Violet told Eva about her family, her dog, and life on the Baker's wheat farm just out of town. Eva told Violet about Joy and Peter, the sampler that she had just started, and what little she knew about her papa's job at the mill. But she never, *ever* talked about Johnny. And Violet didn't ask questions. It was as if there was a silent agreement between them that he was not to be mentioned. Either that or Violet didn't even remember that Eva had lost a brother. Eva preferred that they didn't speak of him. Even though it had been over a year since his death, she still blamed herself.

"Why don't you eat dinner at my house tomorrow?" Eva asked one chilly day in mid-October as the girls walked home. Since the Baker's lived out of town, Violet and her brothers brought their noon meal to eat at school instead of going home as most of the other children did.

Placing her hand on the gate to her house, Eva waited for an answer. She didn't have to wait long.

"I would like that very much!" Violet answered excitedly, clasping her hands together. "I will tell my mother not to put anything in the pail for me tomorrow." She giggled, then added, "On second thought, maybe she should add my normal portion. My brothers usually beg me to give up my food. They eat more than our horse!"

Eva joined in her friend's laughter. Swinging open the gate, she waved goodbye and started down the walkway.

"Eva!"

Turning around, Eva saw Frank standing in the street with Joe Baker and Harvey Green.

"Would you tell Joy that I'm going fishing with Joe and Harvey?" Frank yelled.

Eva nodded. "Just be sure you're back for supper. You know that Joy doesn't like us to be late."

Grinning, Frank responded, "Even if I'm late, she'll be glad to see the dozens of fish I'll catch." With that, he waved and raced after his friends.

Eva sighed as she entered the house. She wished that she was old enough to go off and play with Violet by herself.

"Eva, would you please come and help me in the kitchen?" Joy urgently called.

Eva dropped her books on the chair and walked into the other room.

Joy was covered from head-to-toe in flour. Peter stood on a stool nearby giggling uncontrollably.

"What happened?" Eva asked, unable to keep from laughing.

"It's not funny," Joy said, frowning first at Eva, then Peter.

"It is funny," Peter snickered. He reached out and patted her cheeks. Flour billowed up around her face. The result sent both Peter and Eva into hysterical laughter.

"Stop it!" Joy scolded. She turned to Eva. "I was kneading bread dough when Peter decided to dump the entire bin of flour onto my head."

Peter sent Eva an innocent grin.

"My, Joy, how you have aged," Teddy said from the back door. The corners of his lips were turned up in a teasing grin.

"Yes, and the lot of you is the reason my hair has turned white," Joy shot back.

Teddy chuckled. "Come on, Joy. You know I was just teasin' you. Do you know how ridiculous you look? You must see the humor in this."

"There is no humor in this situation!" Joy declared, pounding her fist into the bread dough for emphasis. She hit an air bubble in the dough, and the loud pop made them all jump.

Gradually, a smile began to form on Joy's lips. She glanced up at her siblings, who were watching her carefully.

In one quick motion, Joy scooped up a handful of flour and flung it at Teddy. It hit him square in the face.

Teddy gasped.

Joy burst into laughter. Eva joined her until she found herself to be Joy's next target.

Peter squealed with delight and clapped his hands.

"Now for you..." Joy turned to her youngest brother.

"No! No!" Peter cried. He jumped off the stool and landed right in the pile of flour on the floor. A cloud of the white powder billowed up around him. When it finally settled, he was as messy as Joy.

By now all of the children were laughing uncontrollably.

Once they had settled down, Joy declared that she needed to get cleaned up and start supper.

"Teddy, would you help Peter wash? Eva, please sweep up this mess. Where is Frank, anyway?"

"He went fishing with Joe Baker and Harvey Green," Eva reported.

Joy frowned.

"I told him to be home in time for supper."

"He better be," Joy said, and then she muttered something about Harvey Green. Eva knew that she didn't like him. Why not though? Eva had no idea.

Eva didn't mind cleaning up the flour mess one bit. Perhaps because it had created such a surprisingly wonderful, carefree moment. It had been a long time since she had seen Joy smile - really smile. Joy hadn't been very joyful since...

Chapter 5

Long Delayed Conversation

~*~*~

"Joy, this is my friend, Violet."

"Eva talks about you all the time," Joy said to Violet. She was surprised when Eva led the little girl into their house during the noon hour.

Violet smiled. "I hope it's not too much trouble for you to cook extra for me."

Joy sent Eva a confused look.

"I'm sorry, I forgot to tell you. It is all right if Violet joins us, isn't it?" Eva looked expectantly at Joy.

Joy knew that she couldn't say no with Violet standing before her. She hadn't made enough food for a guest, but they would have to manage.

"Of course it's all right," Joy declared. "Just be sure that you're quiet; Mama is sleeping."

Violet nodded solemnly.

"Mama sleeps a lot," Eva said to Violet.

"Eva," Joy chided. She didn't want her sister sharing too much information about their private lives. Even though everyone knew that their mother was sick, didn't mean that they needed to know what a poor replacement she was. No doubt Eva had already shared this fact with her friend. Not to mention the flour incident yesterday.

"Come on and eat," Joy motioned for the girls to enter the kitchen. Frank and Teddy had snuck in through the back door and were sneaking frosting off of the cake she had just finished making.

"Frank! Theodore! You take your dirty hands off my cake this instant!" Joy exclaimed.

"Gee, sis, our hands ain't dirty. We washed 'em real good."

"Frank Remington! Where on earth has you grammar gone?" Joy placed her hands firmly on her hips and scowled at the boys.

Frank shrugged.

"Don't know. Maybe China." He nudged Teddy and snickered at his joke.

"That wasn't funny. Now leave my cake alone. I made it special for Papa."

"Yes, ma'am." Frank gave her a mock salute, and Teddy followed suit.

"Would you like me to help set the table?" Violet asked from behind her.

Joy smiled at the little girl and nodded. She decided that Eva had made an excellent choice in a friend.

Unlike me, Joy thought with a frown. Marta and Willa hadn't come to see her since April. And since she rarely left the house, she didn't see them about town.

Joy would have loved to leave home for a while, even if it was just to get groceries. But her mother didn't think that she could handle young Peter on the streets by herself. The only time Joy went out was for church on Sunday - not that they went very often. Although a believer, Harold Remington wasn't strict about going to services. Most of the town folk said that he wanted to spend his day off with his wife - which was a good thing, but also agreed that he should set an example for his children by attending regularly.

After the meal, Eva led Violet into the bedroom so that she could introduce her friend to their mother. Joy began clearing the table.

"See ya later, sis!" Frank yelled as he raced out the front door, letting it slam shut with a bang.

Joy jumped then shook her head. *Won't that boy ever learn to close it quietly?*

"Eva, Violet! You'll be late returning to school!" Joy called.

The two girls emerged from the bedroom.

"Your mama is very nice," Violet said. "Thank you for dinner, Joy."

Smiling, Joy replied, "I'm glad that you liked it. You'll have to come again."

Violet beamed. "I would like that very much."

"Bye, Joy," Eva waved. The girls headed back to the schoolhouse.

As Joy washed the dishes, her fingers trembled. She dreaded this chore every day. The memories that it stirred were painful. Although Johnny hadn't been hurt when the dishes broke, the events of the next day were fresh whenever she thought of that disaster. She wished that she could forget - not Johnny - just the fact that it was her fault that he had died.

Taking a deep breath of relief as she put the last dish away, Joy went to the parlor to check on Peter. She was pleasantly surprised to find him asleep on the floor in front of the fireplace. The boy rarely took naps anymore.

"Hmm" Joy wondered what she should do. She had done the laundry the previous day, and the house was relatively clean.

She glanced at the closed door to her parents' room, wondering if her mama was awake.

"I could talk with her for a while," she mused aloud. She was ashamed to admit that she didn't visit her mother very often, other than to bring her food and make sure she didn't need anything. When was the last time she had a long conversation with her mother?

Joy quietly opened the door and peeked inside. Rose appeared to be asleep.

"Come in, dear."

Tentatively stepping into the room, Joy whispered, "I thought you might be sleeping."

"No, darling, I'm quite awake." Rose pushed herself into a sitting position and patted the bed. "Sit and talk with me for a while."

Joy moved to the bed and perched on the edge of it.

"Eva's friend Violet is a sweet girl," Rose commented.

"She is," Joy agreed.

"How is Peter?" Rose asked.

"Fine. He's sleeping right now."

"Does he give you much trouble?"

Joy hesitated. She wanted to be truthful, but she didn't want her mother to worry. She had been given the job as caretaker of the family, and she knew that Rose trusted her.

"He can be... difficult."

Rose smiled slightly.

"Most three year olds are. Don't worry, before long, he'll be a great helper to you."

"And then he'll have to go to school," Joy added, somewhat bitterly.

"Yes, but then you won't have to watch him all day, and you'll be able to go out some and visit your friends."

"What friends?" Joy asked sharply. "I have no friends!"

Rose lowered her eyebrows and frowned.

"What do you mean? Willa and Marta…"

"Willa and Marta haven't come to see me in months! How can they possibly be my friends when they don't even want to see me?"

Rose took Joy's hand in her own.

"Oh, my dear, I'm so sorry. I didn't know. Maybe if…"

Joy leapt up from the bed.

"I know what you are thinking. Maybe if I came to see you more, you would have known about this problem and could have helped me before it was too late. Well, it is too late! I'm sorry that I never come in here, but it is hard! Hard for me to be the mother. You have given me more than I can handle. Peter is always making a mess, and Frank and Teddy spend their time with the likes of Harvey Green! Eva tries to help, but she is too little."

"Joy! Joy!" Rose cried. "Calm down. Tell me all of you troubles. I want to understand and help you. Pour your heart out."

"Mama! Don't you understand? I can't do this anymore! It is my fault that Johnny died. It hurts me just to wash the dishes. And what if the others get sick?"

"Joy! Do you really still believe that? I told you that it was not your fault. You know deep down that it wasn't. You just say those things because you are scared, child - afraid that you will make a mistake. Joy, you *will* make mistakes. We all do. You need to let go of your fears and trust that God will help you with everything that you need to do. You are not in this alone, Joy. God is with you. Do you believe that?"

Joy nodded, unable to look Rose in the eye.

"And I'm right in here whenever you need advice. I'm not completely useless. I would like it very much if you would bring Peter in here to see me every day. I'm afraid that he's forgotten me. I know that you don't want him to be a bother to me. But he is my son, and I want to see him ever so much. After all, I'm not contagious. I really don't understand why you don't let him in here."

Joy shrugged. "Like you said, I don't want him to be a bother."

Rose smiled and shook her head. "He wouldn't be a bother. Not in the least. I wish that all of you children would visit me more. I love you all so much. Teddy comes in after school and tells me about his day - every day. I wish you'd remind the others to do so."

Joy nodded.

"I will."

"Good."

Joy sat back down and took up her mother's pale hand.

"You won't be sick forever, will you, Mama?"

"Only the good Lord knows, child. I don't know when my time will come, but it gives me great relief to know that I have someone I can depend on, should that time come soon."

Chapter 6

A Day at the Baker's

~*~*~

"Tomorrow is my birthday!" Violet declared on the way to school a week later.

"Mine is in the summer," Eva commented.

"My mama said that I can invite one of my friends over to spend the day with me, and I'm asking you. Do you want to come?" Violet was overcome with excitement.

Eva's eyes lit up at the invitation. She had never been to the Baker's farm before.

"I would like that very much!"

"Hurray!" Violet clapped her hands. "Papa will come into town in the morning and drive you out to the farm. Oh, we're going to have such fun!"

Eva was quiet the rest of the way to school, wondering what she could give to Violet as a present. They arrived just as the bell was ringing, and she still had no ideas. She would have to ask Joy.

Classes went well. And before Eva knew it, Mr. Walters was dismissing them.

"Oh, Eva!" Mr. Walters called as she stood up.

"Yes, sir?" Eva looked at the teacher in fear.

Mr. Walters chuckled at her expression.

"No need to be concerned, Eva. I just wanted to compliment you on your ability to understand letter sounds and word structure. The fact that you're already reading continues to amaze me."

Eva blinked in surprise. She had never heard the teacher offer such praise.

"Thank you, sir," she muttered. She hurried out of the building after Violet.

~*~

The next day was Saturday. Eva put on her play dress and sat impatiently while Joy braided her hair.

"Hold still, Eva. Do you want to look like you haven't brushed your hair in a month?" Joy complained.

"Sorry. I'm just so excited! I can't wait to spend the day with Violet."

"I know, but you'll be ready soon if you sit nicely. There," Joy said as she finally tied the ribbon at the end of the uneven braid. "That will have to do."

"Thank you." Eva jumped up from her chair and rushed to tell her mama that she was ready.

"Have a fun time, sweetheart," Rose said cheerfully. "Be good."

"I will," Eva nodded. "Mr. Baker should be here any minute." She raced out of the house and sat down on the front steps, watching for Mr. Baker. It was then that she realized that she had never met Violet's father.

It turned out that she didn't have to worry. In a few minutes a wagon came to a halt in front of the Remington's house. The medium height, dark-haired man waved to her.

"I'm guessing that you're Eva. I'm Violet's father. Hop in! Violet's eager to see you."

Eva called into the house that she was leaving. She ran down the path and climbed into the wagon.

"Nice to meet you, Mr. Baker. I am Eva. Is it a very long ride to your house?"

"Only 'bout half an hour. We'll be there before ya know it. In the meantime, we can get ourselves acquainted. I have the feeling that we're gonna be the best of buddies. What do ya think?"

Eva grinned. "I would like that very much, sir."

Mr. Baker winked. "No need to call me 'sir' or 'Mr. Baker' if we're gonna be pals. You can call me Michael."

"All right," Eva agreed. She believed that she and Michael would be very good friends indeed.

~*~

Violet was waiting at the end of the Bakers' drive when they arrived. She was hopping from one foot to the other in excitement. She waved when the wagon came into view.

"Hello, Eva! I'm so glad you're here!"

"Good morning, Violet!" Eva called. "Would you please stop the wagon?" she asked Mr. Baker.

Michael signaled to the horse and set the brake so Eva could jump down.

"Thank you for the ride, Mr. Baker... I mean, Michael."

Mr. Baker tipped his hat in her direction and grinned.

"My pleasure, ma'am."

The two girls giggled as Violet's father drove the wagon to the barn.

Violet grasped Eva's hand.

"Come on, Eva. I want you to meet my mama, and then we can go play."

"All right. Let's race." Eva made a dash for the house, Violet right on her heels.

"You're a much faster runner than I am," Violet declared as she reached the front steps where Eva was waiting. Eva grinned in response.

The door opened and a small, blond woman stepped out onto the deck with a pot full of vegetable scraps.

"Oh, my!" she said. "You must be Eva. Violet talks about you all the time. I'm Ellen Baker, Violet's mother."

"Nice to meet you, Mrs. Baker," Eva said politely. She could tell that she was going to like Violet's mother just as much as her father. "Thank you for letting me spend the day here."

"I'm so glad that our Violet has such a good friend. You two better run along and play now. I'll have dinner ready in about an hour and a half. Oh, and, dear, would you please feed these scraps to the chickens?" Mrs. Baker handed Violet the pot, and waved them off the deck.

"Yes, Mama," Violet said, accepting the scraps. She skipped down the steps and motioned for Eva to follow. "Come on! I want to show you around."

"I've never been to a farm before," Eva admitted as she hopped off of the deck and trotted to catch up with her friend.

"We'll go give these to the chickens, and then I'll show you the inside of the barn. There's something special I want to show you."

Violet led Eva around to the side of the house where a chicken coop sat. Most of the birds, however, were roaming freely about the yard.

"Watch," Violet said, tossing a few bad pieces of lettuce on the ground. The hens made a mad dash for the food. "Here, you feed them some," Violet offered once the lettuce was gone.

Eva grabbed a handful of the scraps and threw it to the chickens. She chuckled as she watched the birds fight each other for the food.

"There's my older sister, Mary," Violet pointed to a girl coming out of the coop with a basket full of eggs.

"Hello," Mary greeted Eva. "You must be Violet's friend. I'm Mary."

"I don't remember seeing you at school," Eva said. She didn't think that the girl was much older than Joy.

"I don't go to school. Being around a lot of people makes me nervous. My mother teaches me."

"Oh."

"Well, I have to bring these eggs in to Mama. Here, I can take that pot," Mary offered, holding out her hand for the empty dish. "You girls have fun." She walked towards the house, gently swinging the basket.

"She seems nice," Eva commented.

"She is," Violet said. "This way, Eva, I want to show you something in the barn." Violet grabbed Eva's hand and led her up the hill to the upper level of the enormous barn.

Violet pulled the door open just enough for the girls to slip through. Inside, Eva found piles of corn, grain and wheat along one wall. In the far corner barrels, crates, and boards were neatly arranged. In another corner was a huge stack of hay. Hanging from a rafter in the middle of the pitched roof was a thick rope.

"Hey, girls, watch this!"

Eva startled at the shout. She had been so interested in seeing what was inside the barn that she hadn't noticed Violet's brothers.

Daniel, the one who had called to them, stood on top of the haystack.

"All right, Joe, I'm ready!"

Joe took hold of the end of the rope and gave it a good hard swing. Daniel easily caught it.

Grasping onto the rope about five feet from the end, Daniel jumped off of the pile.

"Yee haw!" Daniel yelled. "Look at me!"

Eva watched in amazement as Daniel swung back and forth several times before letting go and landing near the bottom of the hay pile.

"Wow!" Eva exclaimed. "That looks like fun."

"It is," Daniel said. He jumped up and brushed the hay off of himself. He grabbed the rope and looked expectantly at her.

"You wanna give it a try?"

"Me?" Eva asked, pointing to herself. "Isn't that kind of dangerous?"

"Not at all," Daniel assured her.

"Yeah," Joe added. "Unless you let go at the wrong time. And fall through that hole." He pointed to a hole in the floor. "That's where we throw the hay down for the animals."

"Don't go scaring her, Joe," Violet said. She turned to Eva. "Don't worry, Eva, I've done it lots of times, and I've never gotten hurt. But if you don't want to try, you don't have to."

"Well..." Eva glanced at the top of the haystack. "That looks awfully high. How would I get up there?"

"I'll show you," Daniel offered. He trotted over to a ladder built into the wall. Quickly, he scaled it.

"But you're too far away from the pile," Eva said.

"You just kind of push yourself off the ladder, like this..." Daniel bent his knees and then launched himself onto the haystack. "And there you are."

Eva shook her head in doubt. "I don't think that I could do that."

"I just climb up the side of the hay," Violet informed Eva. She got a running start and quickly scrambled up the side of the pile. In order to get out of his sister's way, Daniel slid down the hay stack and landed with a thud on his bottom.

Eva giggled.

Grinning at her, Daniel stood and brushed himself off again.

"Daniel Baker! What on earth are you doing?"

Eva jumped at the sound of the voice. A tall, skinny girl stood behind her with arms crossed and a scowl on her face.

"Just playin', Nora," Daniel replied with a crooked grin.

"Violet Baker, you get down from that haystack this instant!" Nora yelled.

Eva thought that Violet was about to cry, but Joe smiled slyly and flung the rope in Violet's direction.

"Come on down, sis," he said.

Violet caught the rope and pushed herself off the pile of hay.

"You don't listen to anything I say," Nora huffed. She marched over to the center of the barn and grabbed onto the rope, pulling Violet to a halt.

Violet dropped to the ground and grinned at the frowning girl.

"You told me to get down, Nora."

"I meant in a safe way."

"That's the safest way there is," Joe declared.

"No it's not. I bet that your papa doesn't even know you're up here."

"He knows, and he is just fine with us swinging on the rope. He's the one that put it up here after all."

Nora crossed her arms again with a "humph".

"Eva, this is my cousin, Nora. She is living with us for a while." Violet said.

Nora saw Eva for the first time.

"Hello," she said stiffly.

"Nice to meet you," Eva said politely.

"Aunt Ellen says for you to come in for a snack," Nora informed them. With that she marched out of the barn.

"I apologize for my cousin's behavior," Joe said. "She's naturally cranky."

"Oh." Eva hadn't ever met anyone who was cranky by nature before. She glanced over her shoulder at Nora's form thumping down the hill.

"Come on, let's go eat," Daniel said, waving for them to follow.

"Mama makes the best snacks," Violet said proudly.

"I *am* hungry," Eva replied. She and Violet raced down the hill to the house.

Chapter 7

Gain and Loss

~*~*~

"Mama! What are you doing out of bed?" Joy exclaimed when she entered the kitchen from the back door, returning from the outhouse.

"I feel quite strong all of a sudden. It's so wonderful to be out of bed."

"But you shouldn't be doing any work, Mama!" Joy took the bowl out of her mother's hands. "What are you planning on making?"

Rose snatched the bowl back with a grin.

"Bread. It's been too long since I've gotten my hands into a nice, smooth dough. Now you scoot and let me take over my kitchen again. Go have some fun."

"But what about Peter?"

"He's still sleeping, but don't worry. I can take care of him when he awakens. You just run along. It's been too long since I've been the mother. You go be a child for a while." Rose set the bowl on the counter and began getting out the ingredients.

"But what if you start to feel weak again?" Joy pressed. Although she would love to have some time to herself, she felt that she shouldn't leave her mother. What would Papa say?

"Stop worrying about the 'what-ifs', Joy dear. I'll see you after a while." Rose dumped some flour into the bowl, and looked at Joy out of the corner of her eye. She coughed suddenly. "Flour dust. It always makes me cough."

Joy crossed her arms and raised an eyebrow.

"If I didn't know any better, I'd say you were trying to get rid of me," she said with a sly grin.

"I sure am," Rose declared, flicking some flour in Joy's face.

Joy held up her hands in defense and grinned. "All right! All right! I'm leaving."

Joy hurried out of the kitchen and snatched her shawl off the peg by the front door. Wrapping it around her shoulders as she walked down the path, Joy began humming. The mother she had remembered before the illness had finally returned. Maybe things would go back to normal now, and she could become carefree again.

Joy headed three houses down the street to see if Willa was home. She was delighted to see both Willa and Marta sitting on the front steps of her friend's house.

"Hello!" she called with a wave.

"Look, Willa, there's Joy!" Marta waved back.

Both girls jumped up and met her at the gate.

"Joy, don't you have to be at home with your brother and sister?" Willa asked.

Joy grinned.

"Eva is at the Baker's house today, and you'll never guess!"

"What?" Marta asked.

"Mama is feeling well enough to be out of bed. She's watching Peter and making bread. She told me to go have fun for a while!"

"That's wonderful!" Willa declared, touching Joy's arm. "I'm so happy for you."

"Come on, Joy. We were just about to play with our dolls," Marta invited.

"Dolls?" Joy asked. It had been a long time since she's played with dolls.

"You can run back home and get yours quick," Willa suggested.

Joy hesitated, wondering how long it would take to unearth the doll from the bottom of her trunk down in the cellar. *No, it wasn't worth the trouble.*

"That's all right if you don't get yours, you can share mine," Marta offered.

"Thank you," Joy replied. She wondered how exactly that was going to work.

Marta picked up her wooden doll from the top step and handed it to Joy.

"Here, you can use it first. When I think of something to say, it will be my turn."

Joy accepted the doll and turned it over in her hands. Their fathers had conspired with each other one Christmas and carved the three girls nearly identical dolls. They used to play with them together all the time - until Joy's mother fell ill. Joy supposed that her friends had never stopped.

"Um... hello there, Sally," Joy spoke for the doll. She walked it along the steps towards Willa's doll. "Did you finish your schoolwork?"

Willa frowned at Joy.

"Her name is Suzette, remember? And let's not talk about school."

"Oh, right. I forgot." Joy stared at the ground for a moment, trying to think of what to say. "Did you finish all of your chores?"

Both Marta and Willa gave Joy a strange look.

Marta took her doll back.

"Joy, you are clearly out of practice. Watch." She danced the doll about and said, "Suzette darling! How ravishing you look in your lovely new ball gown. That shade of blue certainly becomes your eyes."

"Why, thank you, Marbella darling. I see that you are also ready for the ball. That pink gown is simply divine!"

Joy watched her friends in surprise. She didn't remember that being the way they had played. It was so unrealistic. Joy didn't hesitate telling the other girls that fact.

Marta frowned at Joy.

"You're supposed to use your imagination, Joy," she said. "You've been acting like a mother for so long you forgot how to play."

"Yes, you aren't any fun anymore, Joy. Why don't you go back home to your kitchen and tend to your little brother," Willa added.

Joy felt tears prick her eyes.

"Fine!" she said with a huff. "I don't want to play with dolls anyway. They're for babies!" Joy jumped down the steps and burst out the gate. She ran back to her house and slammed the front door.

"Joy! What's wrong, dear?" Rose asked, hurrying out of the kitchen.

Joy fell against her mother and wept.

"Marta and Willa don't want to play with me. They said that I'm not fun anymore because I'm like a mother now."

"And mothers aren't any fun?" Rose asked. There was a hint of a smile on her lips.

"They aren't going to be my friends now!" Joy cried. "I can't do it, Mama! I can't be a child anymore!"

Rose pulled Joy close and stroked her hair.

"Oh, Joy, I'm so sorry. This is my fault. I knew it was too much to ask you to take over the house. I've made you grow up too fast. You've lost your childhood."

"No, Mama." Joy pushed back and looked into her mother's eyes. "It is not too much for me to handle. You put your trust in me, and I intend to keep my promise. Besides, it was not your fault that you became ill. We can't go back and change the past."

"That is so very true, my dear. You speak much too maturely for a girl your age. Still, I wish that you could have had more of a childhood. And I'm sorry that I pressured you to leave before. I didn't know that your friends would act that way."

"Neither of us did, Mama. It was mostly my fault anyway. I acted too grown-up, and I've forgotten how to use my imagination."

"Nonsense! I'll bet that you can imagine up an amazing supper for us to prepare together. We want tonight to be special, don't we?"

Joy squeezed her mother tightly.

"We sure do, Mama. Today is very special."

Closing her eyes, Joy leaned against her mother and thought. *I guess sometimes you have to loss something in order to gain something. This time it was surely worth it.*

Chapter 8

Christmas with the Bakers

~*~*~

Rose's health continued to rise and fall throughout the next few months. Harold forbade her to leave the house on the cold winter days. And though she longed for fresh air, Rose complied.

Even though Rose was out of bed for the rest of October and most of November, Joy chose to stay at home to help, rather than attend school. Although her parents had allowed her to make the choice, her father had explained to her in private that he'd rather she stay home in case Rose had a sudden case of weakness. Joy had been quite willing to stay home. Not only for her mother's sake, but also because she didn't want to face Marta and Willa. She hadn't spoken to them since that day. She even avoided them in church - not that they had been trying to get her attention. Her former friends seemed to be avoiding her just as much as she was them.

"You should really try to patch things up between you and your friends," Rose said one day.

"It's too late for that, and they're not my friends," Joy replied stiffly.

"It's never too late to repair a friendship."

But Joy ignored her.

~*~

The Bakers invited the entire Remington family to Christmas dinner that year. After much persuading from Eva, Harold finally relented. Rose had been doing quite well. And he figured that if his wife bundled up enough, she shouldn't come to any harm. The air wasn't nearly as cold as it had been previous Christmases.

So Eva busied herself making presents for her family and Violet's. She had recently begun knitting. And with her mother's help, she created tiny trinkets for her loved ones.

When Christmas day finally arrived, Harold prepared to load his family in a sleigh borrowed from the livery. Most of the townsfolk didn't own a horse, much less a wagon or sleigh, since they rarely left Smithville.

Eva was so excited that her fingers shook as she buttoned up her coat. Then Joy wrapped a scarf around her head and neck and helped Eva into her mittens.

"I can't wait to have a snowball fight with Joe and Daniel," Frank shouted as he launched a ball of tightly packed snow at Teddy.

"Hey!" Teddy yelled, flinging one back at his brother.

"Missed me!" Frank exclaimed, easily dodging the snow.

"Everyone in the sleigh!" Harold called. He helped his wife onto the bench in front, then he swung Peter into the back next to Joy.

Frank helped Eva up and hopped on leaving his legs dangling off the end.

Teddy couldn't resist the urge to throw one more snowball at Frank before jumping on beside his brother.

"Don't fall off now, boys," Rose called over her shoulder.

"We won't!" Frank yelled back. He grinned and pretended to push Teddy off the edge.

"Frank!" Joy exclaimed.

"Just having a little fun, sis. You know I wouldn't really do it." Frank held up his hands innocently.

"You behave," Joy admonished him.

"Of course." Frank shot her a lopsided grin.

Joy just shook her head.

Eva tucked herself in the corner under a thick quilt and gazed out at the snow-covered prairie. It was beautiful and mostly untouched since several inches had fallen the night before. It was times such as this that she wished there was always snow on the ground. But then she would think of the lovely green grass and the flowers of spring and wish it would all melt.

When her cheeks and nose grew cold, Eva pulled the quilt completely over her head and dreamed about the wonderful time she would have with Violet that day. She heard her parents call out "Merry

Christmas!" to a passing sleigh, and she poked her head out to see who it was.

It was the Hammond family. Eva didn't know them very well, although the youngest two were still in school. But they were in the higher grades and probably didn't even know Eva's name.

Snuggling back under the quilt, Eva patted her coat pocket to make sure Violet's gift was still there. It was. Eva had carefully drawn a picture of the two of them. *Friends forever* was written on the top.

"Here we are!" Harold's voice startled Eva awake. She pulled the quilt off of her head, surprised that she had fallen asleep.

"Violet!" she exclaimed, flinging the quilt aside and jumping out of the sleigh when she saw her friend standing on the front porch of the Baker's house.

Violet laughed at Eva who had landed in a deep drift. She ran down the steps and jumped into the snow pile as well.

The girls burst into giggles and embraced each other tightly.

"Frank, Teddy! Over here!" Joe called from the top of the barn hill. "You can share our sleds!"

Frank and Teddy raced to their friends.

"Hello! Come in, come in!" Ellen Baker called from the doorway. "Warm yourselves up by the fire."

Harold helped Rose down and carried Peter to the house on his shoulders. Michael Baker came out to help Joy carry in the food they had brought.

Eva and Violet finally climbed out of the snow drift, still laughing.

"Do you want to go inside and warm up, or shall we sled for a while?" Violet asked.

"Let's sled for a while."

"Race you to the top!"

The girls ran as fast as their snow-covered, heavy wool clothes would allow them - which wasn't much faster than a brisk walk - and made it to the top at the same time.

"Where's my sled?" Violet asked her brothers.

"Frank's using it right now," Daniel said. "Since there are six of us and only four sleds, we'll have to take turns."

Violet turned to Eva. "Papa made us two sleds for Christmas last year and one this year. It is nice to have my own sled, and I don't mind sharing."

"I wish I had a sled," Eva said longingly, and she watched Teddy and Joe race down the hill.

"Some time I'll bring it along to school, and we can sled together during recess," Violet offered.

"I would like that."

"Children! Time for dinner!" Michael called

"Be right there!" Joe yelled from the bottom of the hill. He and Teddy headed towards the house.

"Here," Daniel held his sled out to the girls.

Violet accepted it.

"Get on," she instructed Eva.

Eva climbed on the front and Violet sat behind her and held onto Eva's middle. Daniel gave them a mighty shove, and they went racing down the hill.

Eva shrieked with delight as snow blew up into her face. Violet squeezed her tighter and laughed in Eva's ear.

The sled came to an abrupt halt when it plowed into a drift. Eva and Violet were sent head-first into the snow.

Eva scrambled to her feet and reached down to help Violet up.

"That was wonderful fun," she said.

"Look out below!"

The girls whirled around to see Daniel rolling down the hill. He barreled into them, knocking both girls down. The three of them lay piled in a hysterically laughing heap until Frank pulled them to their feet.

"Dinner!" Michael yelled again.

"Coming!" Frank called back.

Daniel and the girls did their best to brush the snow off of themselves.

"Violet! Daniel! What on earth have you been doing?" Nora met them at the door. "Rolling in the snow?"

"Yep," Daniel replied cheekily, flashing a grin at his cranky cousin.

Mrs. Baker instructed the children to remove their wet clothing then place it by the kitchen fire.

Eva found Joy in the kitchen talking with Mary at the table. She couldn't help but smile at the two. They seemed to have become friends. It was the first time she'd seem Joy truly smile in months.

The two families somehow managed to all fit around the table. Mr. Baker said the blessing, then his wife began serving the food. Eva took a little of everything. There was turkey, potatoes, gravy, jellies, biscuits, pickles, cheese, corn, and a great big cake for dessert.

Once the food was gone, the families exchanged gifts. Violet nearly cried when Eva gave her the picture. Eva was absolutely delighted with the bag Violet had made for her to carry her school books in so that they wouldn't get wet.

The children - even Joy and Mary - went out again to sled some more. Peter had wanted to join them, but Mrs. Baker occupied him by playing with blocks with Violet's younger brother.

With Mary and Joy making eight, it became harder to share the sleds. So the boys decided to have a snowball fight until the girls tired of climbing the hill. It took about a dozen times down the hill - half of which they fell off their sleds - before the girls decided that they had had enough.

"All right, boys, we're done," Mary called. She received a face-full of snow in response.

"'Bout time," Joe said teasingly.

Mary flung a snowball back at him. She hit her mark and then handed her brother the sled.

The two older girls returned to the house, but Eva and Violet decided to play a little while longer.

"Let's make snow angels," Violet suggested.

The girls found some untouched snow and lay down on their backs.

"It's going down my dress!" Eva exclaimed with a giggle as she extended her arms to make the wings.

"Mine too," Violet giggled.

They each made four snow angels, all in a row, then decided that they'd better head inside.

"It's getting dark," Violet said.

"Yes, I suppose that we'll be leaving soon," Eva sighed.

"Maybe you can come back for New Years," Violet suggested.

"I'd like that, but it was hard enough to convince Papa to let us come today. He doesn't want Mama to get sick again."

"Maybe just you and your brothers and sister can come," Violet thought aloud.

"I'll have to ask Papa," Eva said.

"Don't you remember?" Joe said, coming up behind them. The boys also had decided to return to the house. "There's always a big New Year's party in town. We'll probably all be going to that."

"That's right," Daniel added.

"I guess that will be fun too," Eva said.

"And you can always walk home with me sometime," Violet offered.

"Frank, Teddy, Eva! Time to leave!" Harold called from the front porch. "You can warm up a little by the fire first."

After the children had warmed up, they bid farewell to the Bakers and climbed back into the borrowed sleigh.

"Bye!" Eva waved to Violet as the horse began trotting away from the house. "See you tomorrow!"

Violet waved back.

Eva snuggled under her quilt once again. It wasn't long before she fell asleep, dreaming of the wonderful day she'd had.

Chapter 9

Lessons

~*~*~

The next day Rose took to bed again. As they walked through the snow to church, Eva thought that if she hadn't pressured her father so much to spend the day with the Bakers that her mother wouldn't be ill that morning. But thinking back to the previous day, Eva knew that she wouldn't have traded the wonderful time she'd had for anything.

Well... maybe except for Mama's full recovery.

The Remingtons squeezed onto their wooden bench, placed approximately in the middle of the left row of the church building. Eva smiled at Violet who sat between Mary and Daniel two benches behind them.

Reverend Lewis stepped behind the pulpit and smiled warmly at the congregation.

"Good morning, everyone, I hope that you all had a delightful Christmas yesterday. We shall begin the service by singing *Joy to the World*. I know we sung it at yesterday's service, but it is one of my favorite hymns. So I hope you don't mind singing it again."

Eva grinned. She also loved the hymn. She knew it by heart and readily burst into the song.

"Joy to the World! The Lord is come..."

~*~

"Joy, Eva is nearly seven now, I think it's time you teach her basic sewing skills," Rose told her daughter early spring. "It may be hard for her to learn, but once she has, I know you'll appreciate the help with mending and making clothes."

"Yes, that would be nice," Joy agreed. The boys were especially hard on clothing, and Joy struggled to keep up with patching holes and repairing tears. "I'll begin working with her right after supper tonight."

"Remember to be patient with her, Joy. One step at a time."

Joy nodded. She tried to remember how her mother had taught her but couldn't recall at the time.

It will come to me as I show Eva, Joy figured. She smiled down at Peter, who was sleeping next to Rose, then quietly left her parents' room, closing the door behind her.

"Let's see…" Joy muttered to herself as she stood with her back leaning against the door, looking at the room before her. "What should I do now?"

Earlier that day she had washed the laundry, dusted and swept, baked four loaves of bread, and finished a shirt she'd been making for Teddy.

Joy glanced at the clock on the mantle.

"And it's only two-thirty."

School would be out shortly. Maybe Frank and Teddy would actually come straight home for once, instead of going off with the other boys. Joy didn't mind them spending time with Joe and Daniel Baker, but that Harvey Green was a troublemaker.

~*~

"Psst, Frank,"

Frank tilted his head toward Harvey Green, who was sitting behind him.

"What?" he hissed back, eyes carefully trained on Mr. Walters.

"Let's me and you go fishing."

"After school?"

"Yeah. The snow's finally melted and the river's overflowing with salmon. We'll catch us a mess of fish in less than an hour."

"Well…" Frank hesitated. "I promised my sister that I'd come straight home today."

"Promises are meant to be broken," Harvey responded.

Frank raised an eyebrow but didn't speak.

Harvey leaned forward and whispered in Frank's ear, "Well, how 'bout it?"

"Harvard Green!" Mr. Walters called from the front of the room. His back was turned to the class, but Frank couldn't help wondering if the teacher had eyes in the back of his head, for Frank knew that he couldn't have heard their whispers.

"Yes, sir!" Harvey snapped to attention.

When Mr. Walters finished writing something on the blackboard, he turned to face the class.

"Read this word for me," instructed the teacher.

Harvey stood and squinted at the writing.

"Um... ab... abol... abolsent!"

Mr. Walters looked at the word on the board, then back at Harvey with wide eyes. He frowned and shook his head. "I'm not even sure how you figured that, Harvey. Can anyone else tell me this word?"

Frank knew what it was but felt that Harvey wouldn't appreciate him saying.

"Obeisant," Marta Jones declared. She tossed her head and threw a snobbish grin in Harvey's direction.

"And do you know what obeisant means, Marta?" Mr. Walters asked.

"Of course, Mr. Walters. It means respectful." Marta looked smuggly at Harvey.

"Very good, Marta." Mr. Walters swept his gaze over the entire class, then rested it on Harvey. "I expect all of my students to be obeisant. Understood?"

"Yes, Mr. Walters," the class chorused.

"Yes, Mr. Walters," Frank heard Harvey echo.

~*~

Mr. Walters dismissed the children about ten minutes later than the usual time. Eva wasn't sure if it was because of Harvey's disturbance, or if he had lost track of time. The teacher was getting quite elderly and had been speaking of retiring for many years now. However, he hadn't seriously discussed resigning with the school board... yet.

"Would you like to play with the other girls for a while before we go home?" Eva asked Violet.

"I would, especially since it's such a lovely day," Violet replied. "But Mama wants me home to help with spring cleaning."

"I suppose we'll be doing that around my house soon as well. Joy usually doesn't let me help with too many things. I think she wants to prove to Mama that she can handle everything by herself. I know she could use the help though. Pretty soon she'll probably have me mending clothes. I'm eager to learn how to sew."

"My mama has been teaching me; I really enjoy sewing," Violet said happily.

"Frank, where are you going?" Eva called to her brother. Frank and Harvey were headed north instead of towards home.

"Harvey and me are going fishing," Frank yelled over his shoulder.

"Hey! Wait for me!" Teddy shouted, racing after them.

Eva ran after the boys and grabbed hold of Frank's shirtsleeve.

"Frank, Joy told you specifically to come straight home."

"I will... once I'm done fishin'."

"Good one," Harvey said with a grin. He nudged Frank with his elbow.

"She said after school," Eva persisted.

"That's right," Frank agreed. "It is after school, and it still will be once I'm done fishin'."

Eva crossed her arms and glared up at her brother.

Frank shifted uncomfortably.

"Aw, come on, Frank. You're not gonna let your baby sis bully you out of a good time, are ya, Frank?" Harvey taunted.

"C-course not," Frank stuttered. He looked hesitantly at Teddy, who had stepped closer to Eva.

"I uh... think I'll just go on home," Teddy muttered.

"You weren't invited anyway," Harvey said, waving the younger boy away. "We wouldn't a sissy mama's boy... or should I say; sissy *sister's* boy comin' along, would we, Frank?" Harvey looked over at Frank for confirmation.

"No..." Frank mumbled.

Teddy threw his hands up in the air.

"Frank! How could you? He just insulted our family, and you're still going with him! I don't believe you! Come on, Eva, let's go home." Teddy grabbed Eva's hand and marched off.

"Teddy, Eva, wait!" Frank called.

Eva sneaked a glance back as Teddy dragged her along. She saw Frank stare after them for a minute, then he turned in the opposite direction and followed Harvey.

Eva sighed. She had never been as disappointed in her brother as she was at that moment.

~*~

"Where's Frank?" Harold asked later that evening as they sat down for supper.

Eva and Teddy glanced nervously at each other.

Joy sighed.

"Eva and Teddy told me that he went fishing with Harvey Green after school. I don't know why he hasn't returned. I'm worried about him."

"We kinda had an argument earlier," Teddy admitted. He related what had happened to their father.

Harold nodded silently and rubbed his chin.

"I see," he finally spoke. "Well, he's probably cooling down and will be home within the hour. If he's not, I'll go out looking for him."

Joy nodded in agreement.

The meal was a quiet one. After the dishes were washed and put away, Joy sat Eva down in the parlor.

"Mama says you're nearly seven, and you should know how to sew," Joy began.

Eva's eyes lit up.

"You're going to teach me to sew? Oh, how wonderful!"

Joy was surprised by her sister's reaction. She didn't think that sewing was such a delightful task, but she supposed that Eva would see that as time went on.

"First, I guess I'll show you how to thread the needle."

"Oh, I can do that," Eva declared.

"Show me, then." Joy handed her a spool of blue thread and a needle.

Eva pinched the thread between her thumb and finger and squinted at the eye.

"It's so tiny!" she exclaimed.

"Yes, it is." Joy chuckled.

Eva attempted threading several times but was unsuccessful.

"Try wetting the thread," Joy suggested.

Eva briefly stuck the thread in her mouth and straightened the end. Three more tries and the needle was threaded.

"I did it!" Eva cried proudly.

"Good job," Joy congratulated. "Now pulled enough through so that it doesn't fall out easily."

Eva pulled nearly two feet of thread through the eye of the needle.

Joy shook her head. "That's too much; it'll get tangled. Try about six inches."

Careful not to pull out the whole length, Eva adjusted the thread.

"I'm going out to look for Frank now," Harold interrupted from the front door." I should be back before long."

"All right, Papa, be safe," Joy said.

Harold smiled at her and placed his hat atop his head.

Turning back to Eva as the door closed, Joy picked up two quilting squares.

"You can start by sewing these together," she instructed.

Eva's eyes grew wide.

"You want me to make a quilt!"

Joy laughed.

"No, just use these to practice your stitches. It will be a while before you are good enough to make anything."

"That's a relief." Eva took the squares. One was light blue and the other yellow.

Joy picked up a dress she was hemming and showed Eva how to make neat even stitches.

"Like this?" Eva asked after pulling the thread through the fabric several times.

Joy glanced at the squares and tried not to grimace at the loose, uneven stitches. She remembered what her mother had said about being patient.

"Almost. Try making them tighter and closer together."

Eva nodded and went back to work.

"Peter finally fell asleep," Teddy said as he climbed down from the loft. "Papa find Frank yet?"

"No," Joy shook her head.

Teddy wandered over to the chair Eva was seated in and dropped down on the arm. Leaning over, he studied Eva's progress.

"Hey, that's not bad, little sis!"

"Really?" Eva beamed up at him.

"Better than I could do, that's for sure!"

Joy smiled to herself, glad Teddy had chosen to be kind instead of honest.

The door opened, and Harold entered. Frank followed, head hanging.

"Oh, you found him!" Joy exclaimed in relief, dropping the dress in her sewing basket and rising from the rocking chair.

"He wasn't too far," said Harold with a slight smile. "I found him sitting on the front steps."

"Of our house?" Joy asked in confusion.

Harold nodded.

"Whatever took you so long?"

"We had a nice long talk."

"Oh..."

Frank finally looked up at his siblings.

"Sorry," he began. "I'm sorry, Teddy and Eva, for speaking rudely to you and not listening when I knew what you said was right. I'm sorry, Joy, for not coming home when you asked me to. It wasn't very... obeisant of me. That's a word we learned today. It means respectful."

Joy nodded and smiled. "I know. And I forgive you." She went over to embrace her brother.

"Me too," Eva declared. She threw aside her project and leapt up to join in the hug.

"And me," Teddy added.

"And me!" Peter called.

Everyone looked up and saw young Peter's face sticking out of the hole which was the loft's entrance.

Teddy sighed in exhaustion.

"It took me a dozen books to get him to sleep!" he exclaimed.

Harold chuckled as he helped Peter down. Then he wrapped all of his children up in his arms.

"I guess we learned a lesson today, didn't we?" he asked.

"Yes, I learned how to thread a needle," Eva piped up.

"I leaned the meaning of obeisant and that you should always listen to your siblings!" Frank added.

"And I learned that it's very hard to get your little brother to fall asleep, and that he doesn't sleep very long!" Teddy exclaimed.

Everyone laughed.

Harold looked at his oldest daughter.

"And what did you learn today, Joy?" he asked.

Joy grinned and tightly embraced her father.

"I learned that I have the most wonderful family in the whole world!"

Chapter 10

Tests of Patience

~*~*~

Eva continued to improve with her sewing. After two days Joy let her help with the mending. And before she knew it, Joy declared that she was ready to make a dress.

"I'm so excited!" Eva cried when Joy told her. "I'll make it green to match my eyes - with lots of frills and ribbon!"

Joy smiled and shook her head.

"Let's start with something simple, shall we?"

Eva immediately frowned. "But it can still be green, right?"

At the pleading look in her sister's eyes, Joy hesitated.

"I would say yes, Eva, really I would, but you must understand. I think you should make your first dress brown with simple, straight seams."

"Why?"

"Because if we used green and you made a mistake, it would be a waste of fabric. We wouldn't want that." Joy thought that that was a reasonable explanation.

"So you don't think I'm good enough? Is that what you're saying?" Eva asked, crossing her short arms.

Joy held her hands out and waved them to stop Eva's accusations.

"No, Eva. That's not what I meant at all."

"Well, what *did* you mean then?"

"It's just the brown fabric is cheaper... and it won't matter quite as much if you..."

"If I mess it up?" Eva interrupted.

Joy smacked her palm against her forehead, wondering if Eva would ever understand.

"Mama would let me use green," Eva said with a sigh.

"Let's just start cutting the fabric, all right?"

"Fine," Eva said with a huff.

Joy held the scissors out to Eva.

"You're letting *me* cut it?" Eva asked sarcastically.

"Honestly, Eva!"

"Sorry," Eva said meekly. She accepted the scissors.

Joy spread the brown cotton fabric on top of the kitchen table and laid Eva's work dress on top of that.

"Cut it carefully," Joy cautioned. "Don't pull on the fabric, or else it won't be cut right. Be sure to make it an inch bigger all the way around for the seams. Add a couple of inches to the bottom of the skirt, since this dress is nearly too short for you."

"Yes, ma'am," Eva replied, a hint of sarcasm left in her voice.

Joy just rolled her eyes.

By the time Eva was done cutting the pieces, it was time to make supper. It was a Saturday, Frank and Teddy had taken Peter to the Quant's house down the street to play. Frank had promised that they would be back in time for the evening meal, and Frank was quite good at keeping promises these days.

"I'm going to start supper now," Joy said.

"May I help?"

"No."

"Mama would let me help," Eva murmured.

Joy hesitated.

"I was planning on making baked potatoes with beef for supper," she finally spoke. "Would you like to help make the biscuits?"

"Sure!" Eva exclaimed. Joy could tell that her sister was surprised by the offer, but she supposed that she usually insisted on making the meals by herself.

Why do I do this to myself? Joy wondered. *I insist on doing things by myself simply to prove that I can, and here is someone obviously so eager to help. Maybe I should have her do things with me more often when she's home. She's already been a tremendous help with the mending, and it would be nice not to have to do everything alone.*

"And I'll show you how to cook the meat so that it's perfectly tender."

Eva's eyes lit up, and she clasped her hands together.

Joy grinned. She could see that she had just recruited a very willing assistant.

~*~

Dumping another handful of flour into the bowl, Eva giggled as the dust billowed up.

"This is fun!" She exclaimed.

"Mm-hmm." Joy murmured from the other end of the kitchen where she was placing the potatoes in the oven.

"What's next?"

"A pinch of salt."

Eva reached her little fingers into the salt dish and removed a small amount. She rubbed the salt between her thumb and finger, enjoying the gritty texture.

"Next?" she asked once the salt had been added.

"A spoonful of all of the other dry ingredients."

"And then?" Eva asked a couple of minutes later.

"Mix everything together. Then it's time to cut in the lard."

"How do you do that?"

Joy retrieved the lard and came over to where Eva was standing.

"You take about this much..." Joy took a knife and cut of a section the size of her fist, placing it in the bowl. "Then with two knives, you cut it apart, like this, until the mixture is all crumbly. You try."

Eva carefully took the knives and copied her sister.

"There you go. That's how you do it!" Joy exclaimed proudly. "There now, stop. That's perfect. Now pour in some milk, and mix it until you get the right texture."

"How much milk?" Eva asked.

"Oh about so much. I don't know. I usually just sorta guess. Oh, I know. Fill that glass over there about half full. That should be about right."

Eva poured the correct amount of milk into the glass and transferred it to the bowl.

"Good, that's perfect," Joy declared with a nod as she watched Eva mix in the milk. "Now you'll have to knead the dough."

"Oh, I know how to do that!" Eva exclaimed. She sprinkled flour onto the counter and coated her hands and went to work kneading.

"We're home!" Teddy called, just before he slammed the front door.

"You sure are," Joy muttered. "You finally get one to stop, and the other one does it."

Frank entered the kitchen with Teddy on his heels. Peter had gone into their parents' room to visit with their mother.

"Whoa!" Frank cried when he saw the mess of flour. "Let's not do this again."

"What?" Joy asked in confusion. "You don't like biscuits?"

"No, I mean have a flour fight."

Joy chuckled. "Don't worry, we won't be doing that again. Will we, Eva?"

Eva looked at her older siblings out of the corner of her eyes and grinned. She scooped up a handful of flour and raised her arm.

Frank and Teddy both dove for cover.

"I was just teasing you," Eva giggled. "I wasn't really going to throw it."

"*Sure* you weren't," Teddy said, slowly peeking around the kitchen doorway.

"I think you've kneaded the dough enough, Eva. Use that same glass to cut the biscuits."

"All right." Eva turned the glass upside down and pressed it into the flattened dough, making a perfect circle.

"Say, that looks like fun; can I help?" Teddy asked.

"Sure." Eva handed him the glass.

Teddy carefully cut out the biscuits while Eva placed them onto the pan.

"Thank you," Eva said once they were finished, and Joy had stuck the pan in the oven.

"I think I like to help in the kitchen," Teddy announced. "Maybe I'll do it again sometime."

"I would appreciate that, Teddy," Joy said, smiling at her brother. "It's nice when we all work together."

"Sure is," Frank said from the corner of the room where he was leaning against the wall, watching them. "I'll help by eating."

"You're ridiculous," Joy told him with a laugh. "But that's fine with me if you eat a lot. Next Saturday I want to clean out the cellar. It's a disaster down there, and I'm going to need your strong muscles to help carry some of that junk up here."

"Aye, aye, captain," Frank replied with a mock salute. "I'll be shipshape next week… if you feed me properly."

"Do I have to help as well?" Teddy asked. "I told Daniel Baker that we could go rabbit hunting next Saturday."

"Sorry, all hands on deck. Maybe you can go after school on Monday."

"That'd be swell!"

"Sorry I'm late," Harold said, entering the kitchen. "I had to cover for another fella who didn't get there in time."

"That's all right, Papa. Supper isn't quite finished yet," Joy told him.

Harold inhaled deeply.

"Mmm. Smells delicious, Joy. What did you make? Wait a minute - let me guess. Beef… um…. potatoes… and biscuits."

"Correct, but I didn't make the biscuits. Eva did."

"And I helped cut them out," Teddy added.

"Well, well, well. It looks like we have some extra kitchen workers around here," Harold said proudly.

"We do indeed," Joy replied, sending a grin to her siblings.

"I like to make biscuits!" Eva announced.

"I'm eager to taste them, my dear," Harold told Eva, giving her a hug. Looking around, he asked, "Where's Pete?"

"Telling Mama about his day at the Quant's," Frank answered.

"I'm going to tell Mama about my day, too," Harold said with a slight chuckle. He released Eva and went into the bedroom.

Peter entered the kitchen a few minutes later.

"I'm hungry!" he announced.

"That's good because supper's ready," Joy told him, as she pulled the biscuits out of the oven, along with the potatoes.

"Hot," Peter said, pointing to the cook stove.

"That's right, Peter, don't ever touch the stove. You don't want to burn yourself," Joy reminded him. "Teddy, would you please tell Papa supper's ready?"

"Sure, sis." Teddy left, returning momentarily with their father in tow.

Once the family was seated and the blessing said, Harold eagerly reached for a biscuit.

"Got any butter?" he asked Joy.

"No, but Mrs. Lewis brought over some berry jam yesterday. I'll get it."

"They taste wonderful by themselves," Frank declared. "You did a good job, Eva."

Teddy simply nodded since his mouth was stuffed full.

"They are delicious," Harold agreed, having taken a bite before Joy returned with the jam.

Eva blushed slightly at the praise.

"This beef is cooked to perfection, Joy," Harold complimented after trying the meat.

"Thank you, Papa. I could have never made it that well, had Mama not shown me how."

"Your mama's a good cook, and you certainly take after her."

Joy beamed in pleasure.

Once the meal was completed and the dishes taken care of, Joy and Eva returned to working on the dress.

"So what do we do next?" Eva asked, lifting up the cut pieces.

"We sew them together. Or I should say, you do."

"What do I sew first?"

"I usually sew the front pieces together, then the back, and then attach them to each other. But I suppose everyone does it differently."

"So I should sew these two together first?" Eva asked, holding up a couple of pieces.

"Sure," Joy nodded. "I'm going to let the hem out a little on my Sunday dress; it's getting a little short. I'll be right back." Joy went into the room she shared with Eva and grabbed the dress off its hook. She returned to the parlor, picked up a scissors, and began removing the stitches at the hem of the skirt.

"How am I doing?" Eva asked after twenty minutes. She held up her work for Joy to see.

"Eva!" Joy exclaimed with a gasp.

"What?" Eva looked at the dress, wondering what was wrong.

"You're sewing the bottom of the skirt to the bodice!"

Eva's eyes grew wide as she stared at the dress.

"Oh my!"

"You'll have to take the stitches out and start over."

"But it took me forever to get this far!" Eva complained.

"No it did not. You learn from your mistakes, Eva. Try again."

Eva let out an exaggerated sigh. She pulled the needle off of the thread and began tugging out the stitches, which wasn't too hard since they were fairly loose.

The evening wore on. Joy had long finished her dress and was now knitting a pair of socks for Frank.

Harold was talking with his wife in their bedroom. Frank and Teddy were in the loft playing checkers, and Peter was supposedly sleeping.

Joy glanced at the clock.

"It's getting late, Eva. We should go to bed."

"Please, can't I work on it a little bit longer?"

"No, we have church tomorrow."

"It's only seven-forty."

"By the time we put our nightgowns on and brush our hair, it will be nearly eight."

"Please, Joy," Eva begged.

"No, Eva. It's time for bed," Joy said firmly.

"Fine," Eva said with a huff. She threw her dress on the floor and stomped towards their room. "Mama would have let me stay up longer," she muttered.

"Well, I'm not Mama!" Joy cried in exasperation.

Eva turned and looked at her sister, and Joy was surprised to see tears in her eyes.

"Isn't that obvious!" she exclaimed, and slammed the door in Joy's face.

Chapter 11

Patience and Perseverance

~*~*~

Eva had changed into her nightgown and was pretending to be asleep when Joy entered the bedroom five minutes later.

"Eva, I'm sorry for what I said. I should have been more patient with you."

No response.

"Eva, I know you're awake."

Nothing.

Joy sighed and went about preparing herself for bed.

"The Bible says that you shouldn't let the sun go down on your anger."

"I'm not angry," came the soft whisper.

"You're not?" Joy asked in surprise, sitting on the edge of the bed.

Eva rolled over to look at her sister. She shook her head. "No."

"But I thought you were."

"Not with you anyway. I'm angry with myself."

"Why?" Joy questioned.

"Because I've been very hard on you all day. I'haven't been very cooperative, and I keep comparing things you do to how Mama would do them. I'm ashamed of how I've been acting. You work very hard to take care of us and Mama - along with running the house. I only make things harder for you. I'm terribly sorry. Could you ever forgive me?"

Joy looked at the tears in her sister's eyes, which she was sure mirrored her own.

"Of course I can forgive you, Eva. You're the best sister I could ever hope for, and I love you very much."

"Oh, thank you, Joy!" Eva cried joyously, embracing her sister. "I love you, too!"

Joy held the young girl tightly for a moment, treasuring the moment. Finally she pulled herself away, saying, "We'd best get to bed now."

Eva nodded and snuggled back under the covers.

Sliding in next to her sister, Joy smiled to herself. She felt as if they had just had a wonderful bonding moment that she would remember for the rest of her life.

~*~

After getting dressed the next morning, Eva helped Joy make breakfast, which consisted of their usual Sunday fare of eggs, sausage and pancakes.

"That was wonderful, girls," Harold announced once he had finished. "Eva, you're getting to be a very good cook."

Eva beamed. "Thank you, Papa. I have a good teacher." She smiled at Joy.

"And I have a good student," Joy responded.

"You children best head on to church now," Harold told them. "I'm going to stay home with your mother today. She had a rough night."

"Are you sure you don't want me to stay?" Joy offered.

"No, no, Joy. You're stuck at home all week. I know how much you enjoy church. Run along now, and be good."

"We will, Papa," Joy promised. "And thank you."

The Remington children walked properly down the street to the church.

The Baker family arrived in their wagon the same time as Joy and her siblings. Eva rushed to embrace Violet. Frank and Teddy called a greeting to Joe and Daniel.

After a moment's hesitation, Joy sent a wave and a smile in Mary's direction.

"Good morning, Joy!" Mary called to her with a grin. She walked over to where Joy was standing. "It's nice to see you again. I missed you the past couple of Sundays."

"Mama hasn't been doing very well lately," Joy responded.

"I'm sorry to hear that," Mary said sincerely.

Mrs. Baker joined the two girls.

"Good morning, Joy. How is your mother?"

"Still quite ill, Mrs. Baker. Papa is staying with her today so I could come to church."

"I hope she gets well soon, dear. It must be terribly hard on you to care for your family at such a young age. And no doubt you miss school."

Joy nodded.

"Yes, ma'am, I do miss school. As for caring for my family, I suppose I've grown used to it and even enjoy looking after my loved ones."

"Of course you do, darling. God created women as natural caregivers. I believe that when you grow up and have a family of your own, you will be a wonderful mother."

"Thank you, Mrs. Baker," Joy said, blushing slightly.

Reverend Lewis called them into worship just then. Joy followed the Bakers inside the building. She found Peter, Teddy, Daniel, Eva, and Violet sitting in their pew. Frank had joined the Bakers. Joy was used to such an arrangement so she slid into the empty space next to Peter.

"Good morning, everyone," Reverend Lewis greeted the congregation warmly.

"Good morning, Reverend," the worshipers echoed.

"Today I'm going to read from the book of Hebrews," Reverend Lewis announced after they had sung a hymn.

Joy had a hard time following the reverend as he read, but one verse stood out from the rest;

"You need to persevere so that when you have done the will of God, you will receive what He has promised."

Persevere, Joy repeated to herself. *That is what I need to do. Persevere. For taking care of my family must surely be the will of God, or else, why am I doing it? But what has God promised me that I will receive once I've finished carrying out His will? Nothing that I can think of.* Joy scolded herself. Of course God hadn't spoken to her or left her a note that she should know what He might have in store for her.

But I will persevere, she told herself firmly. *I'll continue doing my best, whether that is sufficient or not. And I'll try to be more patient with Eva.*

A verse from Ephesians that she remembered from long ago came to mind; *Be completely humble and gentle; be patient, bearing one another in love.*

Chapter 12

Cleaning the Cellar

~*~*~

Before Joy knew it, it was Saturday again. After making a hearty breakfast with the help of Eva and Teddy, she gathered up her siblings to explain her plans for cleaning the cellar.

"Frank and Teddy, I'm putting you two in charge of moving heavy things around down there and bringing things we don't need up here."

"Aye, aye, captain," Frank said with a salute.

Teddy grinned and mimicked his brother.

Joy rolled her eyes.

"Eva, you're going to be helping by dusting the shelves and the canned goods. You'll also be in charge of keeping the oil lamps burning so that we aren't left in the dark down there. Peter will be with Mama for a while. Eva, you'll have to check on them every so often. If he becomes too much of a trial, or Mama gets tired, you come get Frank to take him over to the Quant's house. Mrs. Quant said that she wouldn't mind if he stayed there for a spell. Does everyone understand?"

"Yes, *ma'am*," Teddy said.

"What are you going to be doing? Bossing us around the whole time?" Frank asked.

"No, I'll be sorting through everything. Seeing what needs to be thrown out and what is worth keeping. I also will be taking inventory of how much we have left of canned goods."

"Oh," was all Frank said.

~*~

Eva watched as Frank lifted the trapdoor to the cellar and slowly descended into the darkness, carefully holding an oil lamp in one hand.

The cellar was the one place in the house Eva absolutely hated. It was cold, dark, and dusty down there. The dirt walls were damp and there was always an abundance of cobwebs hanging from the ceiling. She was certain that rats also resided amongst the stacks of crates in the far corner.

"Eva, you're next," Joy said, giving her sister a slight push.

Eva felt as though she was about to walk the plank. She pulled the hem of her old work dress out of the way and gingerly placed her foot on the top rung of the ladder. Landing her other foot on the second rung down, she froze with both hands planted firmly on the kitchen floor.

"Frank and Teddy are already down there, and they both have lamps," Joy said. "There's no need to be afraid."

Eva remained frozen in place.

"Come on down, Eva," Frank called. "Don't worry; there aren't any rats down here. I'm waiting at the bottom in case you slip."

"Slip?" Eva exclaimed in horror.

"Thanks for scaring her, Frank!" Joy yelled to her brother. "Eva, you know that the floor is only six feet down. That's not even twice as tall as you are."

Eva finally started moving again, and before she knew it, was safely on the hard dirt floor.

"See, I knew you could do it," Frank congratulated her with a gentle slap on the back.

Eva smiled weakly at him in the dim light.

"Alrighty," Joy said as she landed on the floor next to Eva. "Let's get to work."

Frank and Teddy each set their oil lamps on a shelf and began opening crates to check their contents.

Joy moved over to a shelf that held all of the preserves she had either made last year or had been given as gifts.

"Eva, come and dust these off," Joy called. "I would say that if we use them sparingly, we should have enough to last until the berries along the Little Platte River are ripe again."

Eva took a rag out of her pocket - she had stuffed several into each one - and began doing as Joy had asked.

After a few minutes, Eva noticed that the cellar had grown darker. She hurried to check the lamps, and saw that one was nearly out of oil.

"Where's the extra oil?" Eva asked.

"On the shelf just above the one the lamp is on," Joy informed her.

Eva looked up and saw the cans of oil. She stood on her toes but still couldn't reach it.

An arm came from behind her, and a hand grasped one of the cans.

"Here you go," Frank said with a smile, handing it to her.

"Thank you, Frank." Eva opened the can and carefully poured some oil into the lamp. With the room once again brightly lit, Eva went back to her dusting.

"You should go check on Peter, Eva," Joy suggested ten minutes later.

Eva set her rag down on the shelf where she was currently dusting the canned pickles and began the ascent to the kitchen, which was much less scary than going down.

"Is Peter still being good?" Eva asked as she entered her parents' bedroom. She halted and a smile spread across her face when she saw that both of them were asleep, Peter curled up in Rose's arms. A book lay nearby. Eva wasn't sure whether her mother had read Peter to sleep, or if it was the other way around. Peter was just learning to read and was quite proud of it.

"They're both sleeping," Eva announced as she climbed back down into the cellar.

"That's good. They both need it," Joy said.

"Look at all of these baby clothes!" Teddy exclaimed, holding up a tiny dress.

"Oh, my! It's so little!" Joy cried in delight. She went over to where the boys were working and poked around in the crate. "I didn't know that Mama saved all of these."

"Why shouldn't she?" Eva asked.

"Well, I suppose that she's never going to have another baby so she might have given them away to someone else."

"Oh," said Eva.

Joy held up a small white garment and stared at it for a moment. Suddenly, she clutched it to her chest and began crying.

~ 73 ~

"Joy, what's the matter?" Frank asked.

Joy squeezed her eyes shut and shook her head.

"Nothing. It's just that I remember Johnny wearing this."

Both Frank and Teddy stared at their older sister for a moment. Eva came to put her arms around Joy's shoulders; she began crying as well.

"I'm sorry to bring back bad memories, Joy. We should have never opened this box," Frank said. He reached out to take the garment from Joy.

Clutching the soft piece of clothing a moment longer, Joy spoke softly, "That's all right, Frank. Sometimes we need to remember things - even if it's a bad memory." She released the garment to Frank and slowly rose to her feet.

"It's time I make dinner," she said. With that, Joy climbed the ladder and disappeared from sight.

Eva and her brothers all looked at each other.

"I guess we should keep working," Teddy finally spoke.

"I guess so," Frank agreed. He placed the cover back onto the crate with the baby clothes and carefully pounded the nails back in. With Teddy's help, he shoved the crate into the farthest corner of the cellar, where it hopefully wouldn't be found for a long time.

~*~

Johnny's memory flooded back stronger than it ever had as Joy went about warming last night's supper. His face she could clearly picture, smiling and gigging in his own silly little way, and then the look of horror on his face when the dishes had crashed to the floor. Next came his face just before he died from cholera. The sunken eyes. The pale skin. How clueless she had been to help him.

"Oh, Lord, why did Johnny die?" Joy cried out. Tears rolled down her cheeks. She wiped at them angrily with the back of her hand.

"Stop crying, Joy!" she told herself firmly. "You're supposed to be strong for your siblings. Remember? You're supposed to persevere."

Taking a deep breath, Joy let it out slowly and willed the tears to stop. After a short while they did.

"See now? That wasn't so hard."

Joy quickly set that table and called her brothers and sister up to eat.

~*~

Eva was the first one up the ladder. She immediately saw that Joy had been crying again but didn't say anything. Instead, she quietly sat in her chair and waited for Frank to bless the food.

"Teddy and I went through the vegetables," Frank told his sister as they started eating. "There's a bushel basket we filled with the rotten ones. Most of them are still good, though."

"That's good," Joy said with a nod. "Thank you for doing that."

Frank and Teddy both nodded and smiled slightly.

"And I cleared away all of the cobwebs with the broom," Eva added.

"Wonderful. Thank you, Eva. I think that's about everything. Frank, did you put out the oil lamps?"

Frank's eyes wet wide.

"Nope! I'd better go do that right now!" He leapt up from his chair and scurried back down the ladder, returning a moment later carrying both lamps.

"Thank you, Frank. We wouldn't want to start a fire," Joy said.

"That's for sure!" Frank agreed as he set the lamps on the counter before he shut the trapdoor.

"You all worked so hard on cleaning the cellar that I think I'm going to make a chocolate cake. How does that sound?" Joy asked.

There was a hearty response.

Joy chuckled. "Fine! I'll make it just as soon as the table is clear."

Eva and Teddy both rushed to empty the table of dirty dishes.

"I'll wash," Frank offered.

"And I'll dry," Teddy added.

Eva looked hopefully at Joy.

"Can I help make the cake?" she asked. Joy had been quite willing to let her help in the kitchen the past week, and Eva was eager to learn to bake a cake. Perhaps she could even surprise Joy by make one for her birthday in a month.

"Of course you can, Eva. You're my best helper."

Eva beamed.

"Hey!" Frank exclaimed. "Don't us boys get any appreciation?" He held up his sudsy arms.

"Yeah!" Teddy snapped the flour sack towel in Joy's direction.

"Sure you do. But I know you're only so willing to help today because I mentioned the cake. Now yesterday…"

Frank held his bubble-covered hands out in defense.

"Never mind! Never mind!" he exclaimed.

Both Joy and Eva chuckled.

"What do we need first?" Eva asked, looking to Joy.

"Well, I suppose you can get out the flour, sugar… Oh shucks! We're out of sugar!"

Both boys moaned.

"You mean you can't make the cake?" Teddy asked.

"And we're doing these dishes for nothing?" Frank added.

Joy raised an eye brow at her brothers.

"I never consider doing the dishes to be *nothing*. I believe that there is some money in the grocery jar. We can surely spend a few pennies on some sugar."

Teddy grinned.

"That's a relief," Frank said with an exaggerated sigh.

"Who wants to run and get it?" Joy asked.

"Oh, please may I?" Eva asked. She knew that Violet and Daniel often brought eggs and milk into town on Saturday and was always eager for a chance to see her friend.

"Well…" Joy hesitated.

"Please?" Eva begged. "It's a short walk to Luke's Mercantile. I promise I'll go straight there and come straight back. Please?"

"I'll go with her," Teddy offered.

Joy smiled slightly and shook her head. "No, I need you here to do the dishes."

"Aww," Teddy moaned.

"Besides, I think that Eva's old enough to go by herself. I believe that she'll keep her word and go straight there and back."

Eva's eyes lit up.

"Really, Joy? You're letting me go? Oh, thank you!"

"Yes," Joy chuckled as she retrieved the money. "But remember, I trust you to keep your word and not lose this money."

"I will, Joy. You can trust me."

But as Eva headed down the street, she wondered, *would she still trust me if she knew I fed Johnny the moldy bread?*

Chapter 13

Second Thoughts

~*~*~

Time passed. Life went on.

Eva blushed at the loud applause that erupted as she ended the last verse of *Joy to the World*. She stepped down from the front of the school room and sat in a chair next to Violet. She couldn't believe that she had actually done it without making a mistake.

Mr. Wessington, their new teacher, had insisted that each child have their own part for that year's Christmas program. He told Eva that she had a beautiful voice and should sing a solo. Eva had been so nervous. She refused to do it at first. Then her mother had promised that if Eva would try and do her best, she would try and do her best to make it to the children's Christmas program.

Eva looked over her shoulder to smile at her mother. Rose grinned back. Eva had never seen her mother look so proud in all of her eleven years.

"I knew you could do it," Rose mouthed.

Eva settled back in her chair to watch Angelina Henning sing *Silent Night*. That little girl was just the sweetest thing, with her lovely blue eyes and charming personality.

A few chairs down from Eva, Maria Henning sat with her arms crossed, glaring at her little sister. Eva could tell that Angelina was trying not to look at Maria. But when the girl did, she cringed and missed a line. A smug grin settled onto Maria's face.

Next to Maria, Adelaide Haynes let out a muffled snort. Her expression matched Maria's. Eva had never cared much for either of the two girls.

On the boys' side of the room, Matthew Black chuckled at Angelina's mistake. Eva watched as Thomas Crews gave his seatmate a nudge and a frown and send an encouraging smile in Angelina's direction. Thomas and Angelina had become good friends shortly after a little incident with a sled and Mr. Wessington earlier that month. Eva knew, however, that Thomas had always been protective of her.

On the other side of Violet were the Kline twins, Grace and Emma. They were quite shy and rarely spoke to Eva, but at least they were polite when they did. Mr. Wessington had allowed them to supply cookies for the event instead of recite.

Eva didn't care if none of the other girls in town wanted to be friends with her, as long as she had Violet. She couldn't ask for a better friend.

Harvey Green read the first few verses from Luke chapter two. Shortly after Mr. Wessington had begun teaching, he really cracked the whip with the boy. Now, with the help of a pair of glasses, Harvey was an excellent pupil.

Peter, now nine years old, recited the next few verses from Luke. Eva grinned at the way he spoke, voice full of enthusiasm. Maybe one day he would become a pastor.

Glancing over her shoulder to see if her family was as impressed with him as she was, Eva noticed Joy didn't seem to be watching the program at all. Joy had become rather sullen and didn't talk nearly as much as she used to. For a while she had been so strong, always encouraging herself with words like *perseverance* and *patience*. But Eva heard those words less and less. Instead, Joy used words like *hopeless* and *failure*. Eva wondered if caring for their mother was taking its toll on her sister.

Mama is trusting her to care for us while she's sick, Eva thought. *If Joy decides she doesn't want to do that anymore, then what happens?*

~*~

Joy was trying to pay attention, she really was, but she was so terribly tired. The previous night she had stayed up late in order to ensure her mother would be well enough to attend the Christmas program. Rose had been weak of late, and Joy hadn't wanted her to go out in the cold. But her mother had insisted that she had promised Eva and would not disappoint. Joy had said that she was sure Eva would understand, but Rose was determined.

~ 79 ~

Looking over at her sister, Joy frowned. *Why does she have to be so persistent? Doesn't she know what's best for Mama? No, how could she? She's only a child.*

She's older than you were when you started caring for Mama, a little voice reminded her. *But she doesn't have to tend to Mama. So she isn't as mature as I was at her age.*

At fifteen, Joy was as mature as someone twice her age. She had grown bitter over the years, as well - a result of self-pity. She complained continually about her lack of friends and life outside of the house.

Darting a glance in the Bakers' direction, Joy saw Mary smiling at the children in the front of the school. She and Mary had been friends for a while after that Christmas years ago, but then Rose had a bad spell and took to bed for several months. Mary had visited Joy often. But finally Joy had sent her away, feeling that Mary was only coming because she felt sorry for Joy. Now Joy was too ashamed of herself to try to make amends.

Mary happened to glance at Joy. Their eyes met for a moment. There was a pleading look in Mary's eyes. Embarrassed at being caught staring, Joy quickly turned away.

A short while later, Joy felt someone watching her. She peered at Mary, but the girl's attention had returned to the front. Looking over her shoulder, Joy saw that it was Jack Green watching her.

When he saw her looking at him, Jack grinned crookedly. Joy groaned and immediately turned back around. Jack was the most horrid boy in all of Smithville; Joy had never liked him. He was terribly hard to look at, with his yellowed teeth, blemished face, and greasy hair. His only good feature was his green eyes - and even those were hidden under bushy eyebrows.

Why, out of all of the boys in Smithville, does Jack Green have to be the one to like me? Joy wondered, shaking her head. *Because you don't deserve anyone better than him,* she decided. *You're not much to look at yourself, Joy Remington. At least Jack looks his age - sort of. You look like an eighty year old woman.* That wasn't completely true, of course, but the strain of caring for her mother had indeed aged her. There were permanent circles under her eyes, and her face was drawn. She felt weak and was tired all of the time. Just the other day, she had discovered a white hair. Thankfully, it was by her ear where she could easily hide it.

I need to take a break. I can't handle this anymore. I've done my share; it's time someone else took over, Joy told herself. *I need to be free.*

Chapter 14

An Interesting Proposal

~*~*~

The Christmas program ended with all of the children singing a special "thank you" song they had written themselves, thanking both the guests for coming and God for sending His Son.

Eva and Violet helped Emma and Grace clean up the refreshment table. As she was setting a stack of leftover cookies in a basket, Eva saw Mr. Wessington approach her parents out of the corner of her eye.

"Violet, look," Eva whispered, nudging her friend. "What do you think he's talking to my parents about?"

"I don't know." Violet shrugged.

"Maybe you're in trouble," Frank teased from behind her. His hand shot out, and he snatched a cookie from Eva's pile.

"Maybe you're in trouble," Eva shot back, slapping her brother's hand.

"I don't go to school anymore, and that hurt," Frank complained, massaging the back of his hand.

"It was supposed to," Eva replied with a scowl. "Stop stealing cookies.

"I can't help it; they're good."

"Of course they are," Eva replied. "Emma and Grace made them."

The twins blushed at the praise.

"Well, obviously *you* didn't, sis."

"Frank, you're so mean," Eva said with a huff.

"Aw, I was just teasin' you, sis. That's what brothers are for."

"My brothers tease me all the time," Violet whispered to Eva. "But I don't let it bother me, and pretty soon they stop."

"I'll try that next time," Eva whispered back. Noting that the teacher had moved on, Eva spoke to the group, "Now if you'll excuse me, I'm going to go see what Mr. Wessington talked to my parents about."

"You're in trouble," Frank hissed as she walked away.

Eva ignored him.

"Eva, Mr. Wessington was just talking to us about you," Harold said when he saw Eva approaching.

"What about, Papa?"

Harold beamed proudly.

"He said that our Eva is the smartest girl in her whole class! He wants you to move up to the seventh grade!"

"Really, Papa?" Eva asked in delight. She loved learning and knew that she was doing well in her lessons. But she hadn't known that she was doing *that* well.

"It will be a lot of hard work, Eva. He asked us to talk it over with you and see if you want to make the switch. Your father already said that it would all right with both of us," Rose informed her. "But of course, we want your opinion."

"I would love to, Mama, Papa! I'd love to move to the seventh grade!" Eva paused for a moment. "Will I still get to sit next to Violet though?"

Rose smiled and her father chuckled.

"I'm sure that that can be arranged," Harold said.

"Then that's a for sure 'yes' on my part," Eva declared.

"Good! We'll go tell Mr. Wessington right now." Harold took his wife by the arm, and they wove their way through the crowd towards the teacher.

"Yes, I do agree that the children did a wonderful job with the program, and they worked so hard," Mr. Wessington was saying to Jacob Henning.

"Angelina has become especially fond of you," Beth Henning commented. "I hope that you shall be our teacher for years to come."

"As do I, Mrs. Henning," Mr. Wessington responded with a smile.

"Rose! How wonderful to see you up and about!" Beth exclaimed when she saw the Remingtons. She wrapped Eva's mother up in a warm embrace. "It's been such a long time since I've seen you. How have you been doing?"

"A lot better, thanks to my Joy," Rose replied with a smile.

"Jacob, good to see you outside of work," Harold said, shaking Mr. Henning's hand.

"That's true," Jacob replied with a chuckle.

"Eva, my, aren't you growing up!" Mrs. Henning turned her attention to the girl after chatting with Rose for a few minutes. "You did an excellent job singing. Lovely voice you have. I don't get to see enough of you; you should come over and play with Maria more often. It certainly would do her good to spend time with girls other than..." Mrs. Henning hesitated and seemed to change her mind. "...with other girls."

"Yes, ma'am," Eva replied politely with a nod.

Mr. Henning glanced at the teacher then the Remingtons.

"Beth dear, I think that Mr. Wessington would like to speak with the Remingtons."

"Of course. I'm sorry for holding you up," Mrs. Henning said. She took her husband's arm.

"It was wonderful to see you both," Rose called after them.

"You as well," Mrs. Henning called back with a wave.

"Now, Eva, have your parents told you the news?" Mr. Wessington inquired.

Eva nodded, a huge grin spread across her face.

"Can I take that as a 'yes'?" Mr. Wessington asked with a chuckle.

Eva nodded again.

"Excellent!" exclaimed Mr. Wessington, clasping his hands together. "I have more good news for you. I wanted to wait until you had made up your mind, though."

"What is it, Jonathan?" Harold questioned.

Mr. Wessington could barely manage his excitement.

"Well, I think that Eva is quite intelligent and should continue her education beyond the eighth grade."

"What are you saying?" Rose asked, although she felt she knew.

"I think it would be a good idea for Eva to attend an academy once she's finished here."

"An academy?" Harold hesitated. "Do they even take girls?"

Mr. Wessington held up his hands to slow the questioning.

"It is indeed quite rare for colleges to accept girls, but there are a few female academies back east, that, as stated, take only girls."

Harold and Rose glanced at each other, then Eva, and turned their attention back to the teacher.

"Aren't they awfully expensive, though?" Harold asked. "Even if we would want to send Eva - if she is interested - we could never afford it."

"I was coming to that. If Eva is as smart as I believe she is, I think she has a good chance at winning a scholarship."

"Do you really?" Eva exclaimed in delight. She had never considered going on to a college before, but the thought intrigued her.

"She may have a good chance if she's competing against the girls in this town," Harold spoke. "But there must be dozens of girls across the country who are much more intelligent than Eva, and much more likely to win a scholarship. Isn't that so?"

Mr. Wessington nodded.

"That is true. However, I have a good friend whom I went to collage with. He is now an important professor in a girls' academy in Georgia. I could write to him about Eva - given your consent - and he might be able to pull a few strings."

"I don't know," Rose said, hesitating. "Isn't that sort of, I don't know, cheating?"

"Not really," replied the teacher. "So, what do you think?"

Harold and Rose looked at each other again, then to Eva.

"What do you think, dear?" Rose asked.

"I think I would like to further my education," Eva told the adults.

"That would mean leaving home, you know," Rose informed her.

Eva wrung her hands together and stared at the toes of her shoes peeking out from beneath her green skirt.

"I know," she whispered.

"It wouldn't be for a couple of years, yet, and we can't even guarantee you'll win a scholarship," Harold said.

"You don't have to make up your mind right away. Think it over," suggested Mr. Wessington.

"We will," Harold told him.

"And we'll pray about it, too," Rose added.

"Take your time with your decision," Mr. Wessington advised. "There's no rush."

"Of course. Thank you for everything." Harold shook the teacher's hand. "Good night, Jonathan."

"Good night, Mr. Wessington," Eva called to the teacher as he left. "And Merry Christmas!"

Chapter 15

Wise Words

~*~*~

"Didn't Joy seem rather sullen tonight?" Rose asked her husband as they lay in bed that night.

Harold shrugged under the covers, pulling the quilt up past their feet.

"I guess I didn't notice. She seemed to be just as she always is." Harold sat up to fix the quilt.

Rose frowned in the darkness.

"I wonder how long she's been like that. Strange I didn't notice sooner. I think she must be depressed. Do you suppose we've placed too much responsibility on her?"

"She's been doing a fine job."

"I know she has, but I believe that the strain is finally catching up on her. I knew right from the start that this situation wasn't fair to her, but I couldn't think of any other solution." Rose sighed deeply.

Harold found her hand and squeezed it.

"Don't beat yourself up about it, dear. We both agreed that Joy taking over was best for all involved."

"For all except Joy! I don't think I thoroughly thought out how much this would affect her. Harold, maybe it's time we find someone else. Do you suppose we could afford a hired girl?"

Harold shook his head.

"Not with my salary. I barely make enough to keep food on the table. I don't mean it the way it's probably going to sound: but what would Joy do if we hired a girl? She's so used to doing all the work."

"That's true," Rose mused. "She wouldn't completely drop her responsibilities. Just lighten them. Then she could have some for herself. Maybe go courting."

"Rose darling, I'm not really sure how to tell you this, but most of the boys her age have already claimed a girl. There's not really anyone left for her."

"Oh, but there must be!" Rose declared, sitting up with a sudden burst of strength. "My baby can't grow up without love."

"She has a family who loves her very much," Harold comforted her. Rose smiled sadly.

"That's not the same."

"I know, darling. I'm sure love will come along for her when the Lord says she's ready." Harold kissed her forehead. "Go to sleep now. You need rest. Don't worry any more about Joy. She'll be fine. She's a strong girl."

Rose settled back under the covers, but she couldn't sleep.

No wonder Joy's been so depressed. Not only does she have more work than she can handle, but she also probably fears that she'll never marry.

For several minutes Rose lay still, staring into the blackness, mulling over the problem.

"Harold," she broke the silence with a soft whisper. "What about that Westfield boy? He's nice."

"I hear he has his eye on Willa."

"Oh, that's too bad. I suppose Marta has a fella as well?"

"So says her father."

Rose sighed. "That must make it even worse for Joy, knowing that her former friends have potential suitors."

"Rose, you're worrying too much about this."

"I know. I'm sorry."

"Just try and go to sleep."

There was a long silence.

"How about Mark Black?

~*~

"Joy, your mother wants to speak with you," Harold said, entering the kitchen the next morning.

Joy turned from the stove to look at her father. She wondered what she might have done wrong.

"I'll go in just as soon as theses eggs are done."

Harold stepped forward and removed the spoon from her hand.

"I can take care of those. You go on."

Now Joy was really worried.

What have I done?

Knocking softly on the door, Joy nervously entered the room.

"Good morning, Mama. Papa said you wanted to talk to me?"

"Good morning, Joy. Yes, I do. Please sit near me."

Joy perched on the edge of the bed.

"I couldn't help but notice you looked quite sullen last night. I now realize that you've been that way for a while. I'm ashamed that I haven't noticed before."

"You're in bed most of the time so how could you?" Joy responded flatly.

"Yes, I know. That is another way I have failed you. Being in bed is no excuse for not noticing my children's problems."

"Oh, Mama, I didn't mean it that way."

Rose patted her hand. "I know, dear, but it's true."

"You can't help that you're ill, Mama."

"No, I can't. I'm not unconscious, however. I should be more aware of what's happening in my own home. Now tell me, Joy, do you feel overwhelmed by your responsibilities? Be honest."

Joy hesitated. Overwhelmed was exactly how she felt, but what good would it do to confess that to her mother?

"No," she finally said.

Rose raised an eyebrow.

"Are you sure?"

Joy nodded firmly.

"Then is there something else bothering you?"

Joy paused to mull over the question and the possible answers. There was something bothering her, but she couldn't place her finger on it.

Slowly, Joy shook her head no.

"Are you sure?" Rose asked again.

This time Joy didn't respond.

"Is it because there are no boys who seem interested in you?"

Joy looked at her mother in surprise.

"Who told you that?"

"Your father and I were talking last night."

"How do you know that no one is interested in me, though? Did you ask all the boys?"

"You needn't get defensive, Joy. I'm not saying that there's any reason that a boy shouldn't like you. You are a very pretty girl with a lovely personality and multiple talents."

"You're just saying that because you're my mother," Joy grumbled.

"Does that make it less true?"

Joy ignored the question.

"I don't get out enough that a boy would notice any of those things - even if they were true," she said instead. "I honestly think the only boy that might possibly like me is... Jack Green." She spit out the name as if it were poisoned.

Rose frowned thoughtfully.

"Jack Green. That's strange. I don't believe I've ever heard you mention him."

"That's because he's not worth mentioning," Joy said bitterly.

"So you don't like him?"

Joy looked at her mother in horror.

"Mama! Have you ever *seen* Jack Green?"

"That bad?" Rose asked with a chuckle. "I suppose that I haven't seen him in quite a while. I remember him to be a fine-looking young man."

"Maybe it's your eyes that are sick, Mama."

"Joy," Rose said in a strange tone that instantly caught Joy's attention. "Sometimes you see people how you want to see them - with your mind. Eventually, that's how they really look - to your eyes."

"What does that mean, Mama?"

Rose smiled and patted her hand again.

"You'll know when you're supposed to, Joy."

Chapter 16

Harshly Accused

~*~*~

January of eighteen forty-eight was especially cold and snowy. There were many school days cancelled. Eva grew bored of sitting in the house all day; she missed Violet dreadfully. However, she spent much of the time visiting with her mother, something both of them enjoyed. Eva knew that Joy was also relieved to have the extra help around the house.

"Do you get lonely in here by yourself all day?" Eva asked her mother one day as a blizzard raged outside.

Rose smiled. "I do get lonely at times. I am grateful, though, for these past few weeks. I know that you don't like to miss school, but it is so wonderful for me to have you here all day."

"I enjoy being with you also, Mama," Eva replied, smiling back. "Will you tell me a story about when you were a little girl?"

"I would love to. Hmm, let me think…"

"Where did you grow up?" Eva interrupted. "Have you always lived in Smithville?"

"No, my papa was a baker in Boston. That's where I met your father."

"Why did you move out here?"

"I've always been rather sickly. Your papa thought that living out west in the fresh air would help me."

"Did it?"

"Yes, for a while. Before we moved to Smithville, we lived in St. Joseph. Joy and Frank were born there."

"Really?" Eva asked in surprise. She had always assumed that she and her siblings had all been born in Smithville.

"Yes," Rose answered with a grin. "Your papa lost his job as a carpenter during the time I was pregnant with Teddy. We lost our house and began traveling around. Papa did odd jobs here and there for a couple of years. We basically lived in our wagon. When I found out I was going to have you, we decided it was time to find a stable place to live. We happened across this little town. Papa heard that Mr. Smith was looking for extra workers at the mill and was hired right away. The company gave us this house, just like they do for all the mill workers, and we finally had a real home again."

"And that's when you became sick again?" Eva asked.

"Not right away. It wasn't until that summer when I began to feel ill."

Eva sat in silence for a moment as realization set in.

"That was the summer I was born," she murmured.

"What was that, dear?"

Eva looked up at her mother.

"It was me. I'm the reason your sick. You were just fine until I was born."

"Oh no, Eva. That's not true at all!" Rose exclaimed. She pulled her daughter into her arms.

"Yes it is!" Eva sobbed.

"No, darling. Remember? I told you that I've always been sickly."

"But you were better until I was born. I made you weak again. Now you'll never get well, and it's my fault!"

"Eva, Eva! Don't blame yourself!" Rose held her at arm's length and looked her right in the eyes. "I don't want you ever to blame yourself. It's not one bit true. And even if I am sick because of you, I want you to know that you're completely worth it. Even if I cough continuously, and never get out of bed. Every cough, every minute I lie here would be completely worth it, just so long as you are here with me."

"Is that the truth, Mama?" Eva asked, tears streaming down her face.

"Every word. I love you, Eva. Don't ever forget that."

Eva tightly embraced her mother.

"I love you too, Mama."

~*~

"Harold, did you notice that our children have a terrible problem of blaming themselves?"

"What do you mean, dear?"

"I told Eva of how we came to Smithville, and she discovered that it was during the time she was born that I became sickly again. Now she blames herself for my illness. And Joy, well, I believe that she still blames herself for Johnny's death."

"Are you sure of this, Rose?" Harold asked with concern.

"Quite positive," Rose replied, nodding.

"I will speak with them."

Rose smiled.

"I was hoping you would, dear."

~*~

"Joy, Eva, I would like to speak with the two of you," Harold announced after supper. "Boys, you go on up to the loft."

The sisters glanced at each other nervously.

"Yes, Papa," the three boys chorused.

"Let's go and sit in the parlor," Harold suggested once the boys had left.

"But the dishes..." Joy waved her hand around the kitchen.

"Can wait."

Joy wondered what he had to tell them that was so important.

After the three of them were seated, their father began.

"Your mother has recently pointed out to me that the two of you," Harold gestured to the girls, "seem to have a habit of blaming yourselves for things you possibly couldn't have done. Might either of you know what I'm speaking of?"

Both Joy and Eva shifted uncomfortably.

"I suppose she told you what I said the other day, about me being the reason she's ill," Eva finally spoke.

Harold nodded. "That she did."

"Why would you be the cause of Mama's sickness?" Joy asked in confusion.

"Because the summer Eva was born, your mama's sickness returned."

"Returned? You mean that she had it before?"

"Yes." Harold looked sternly at Eva. "Your mother explained to Eva that she had always been sickly, even when she was a young girl living above her father's bakery."

"Our grandpa owned a bakery?" Joy was learning things she'd never known.

"Yes," Eva said with her eyes lit up, "in Boston. Can't you just imagine smelling the breads and cakes all day long! It must have been delightful!"

"It was," Harold agreed, a distant look in his eyes and a grin on his face. "Your mama was always sneaking me some kind of a treat. That's why I'm so fat!" He laughed heartily and patted his stomach. "Anyway," the serious look returned to his face, "back to the subject at hand."

Both Eva and Joy sighed.

"Eva, you do know that Mama's sickness isn't your fault, don't you?" Harold questioned.

Eva hesitated, tilting her head to one side.

"Eva, look at me." Harold gently took hold of his younger daughter's chin and tipped her face up so that their eyes met. "I want you to say, 'it's not my fault', and I want you to mean it, all right?"

Taking a shaky breath, Eva whispered, "It's not my fault."

"There now, that feels better, doesn't it?"

Eva nodded slightly.

"Good," Harold said with a small smile. He dropped his hand.

Glancing at her sister curiously, Eva asked, "What does Joy blame herself for?"

Joy stared at her hands in her lap, refusing to meet her sister's gaze.

"Why don't you tell her, Joy?"

"Does it even matter?"

"It does if you still do."

Joy peeked at her father out of the corner of her eye.

"Still do what?"

"You know what I mean."

Joy let out a long sigh.

"I don't believe there's anything you could possibly blame yourself for, Joy," Eva spoke.

"Shows how much you know," Joy snapped.

"Joy!" Harold exclaimed. "That's no way to talk to your sister!"

"Fine!" Joy shouted, leaping from the rocking chair. "You really want to know what horrible thing I've done! Then I'll tell you! I killed Johnny; that's what I did!"

"Joy!" Harold cried again.

"Oh, no!" Eva exclaimed. "No, Joy. That wasn't your fault."

"What makes you so sure about that? Huh, Eva? I was supposed to care for him, but I just let him die!"

"I know it's not your fault, Joy... because it was mine," Eva finished in a whisper.

"What?" both Harold and Joy cried.

"How so?" asked their father.

"Because..." Eva began crying. She hiccupped before continuing, "Because I fed him the moldy bread - after you told me not to eat it, Joy." Eva looked up at her sister, tears streaming down her face.

"Eva, how could you!" Joy exclaimed. "After I told you not to!"

"But you hadn't told me it was moldy, Joy, not at that time. Only later."

"What difference does that make, Eva? You didn't listen to what I said! Don't I have any authority? Don't I get any respect?" Joy grasped Eva's shoulders and gave her a rough shake. "You made me believe that I was the reason Johnny died all of these years, when it was really your fault? You poisoned him! You know that, don't you?"

Eva shook her head. Her cheeks completely wet with tears.

"I didn't know, Joy, not at the time. But thank you for telling me."

"Joy!" Harold pulled his elder daughter away from the younger one. "Get a hold of yourself! Don't you realize what you're saying?"

"Yes, I do, Papa, and I don't care!" Joy reached out to give Eva a shove.

Eva stumbled back, tripping on a footstool. She fell, her head narrowly missing the mantel. Harold rushed to wrap her in his arms.

"She let me believe it was my fault all these years when it was really hers! She never said a word. Never told anyone she fed him the bread. She killed Johnny, Papa! You hear that, Eva! You're a murder! I hate you!"

Eva let out a wail and buried her face into her father's chest.

Harold stared at Joy with a look that frightened her.

"Get out." he said quietly. There was a firmness in his voice.

"With pleasure!" Joy turned sharply on her heel and snatched her cloak off its peg. She opened the front door and stepped outside, completely unfazed by the gusting winds and whirling snow, pulling the door shut behind her with a satisfying slam.

Chapter 17

All things for Good

~*~*~

"You told her to leave?" Rose asked in horror. "Harold! How could you?"

"She had turned completely insane, Rose. I won't repeat the things she said. But if you had seen the look on poor Eva's face, you would have done the same thing."

"Send my baby out into a storm? Never! And I did hear some of what she said. I am ashamed that she said them, but I still wouldn't have sent her away in the middle of a blizzard!"

"Don't get yourself worked up, darling. She just needs some time to cool down and think things over. Once she settles down, she'll come back. Don't you worry."

~*~

Too angry to cry, Joy wandered blindly through the storm, in what she hoped was a western direction. She would find shelter until the storm stopped and head to the nearest stage coach station. She was leaving Smithville - and never coming back.

~*~

Eva wept bitter tears as she lay curled up on her bed, the quilt completely covering her. She had known for years that Johnny's death had been her fault. But murder? She had never thought of it that way before. Joy was right, though, she was a murderer. How else could you define her actions of years ago? Hadn't she given Johnny the poisoned bread? Hadn't he died?

How will I ever live with myself? Eva wondered. *How can I ever look anyone in the eye again? Violet won't want to be my friend anymore.*

Joy will hate me forever. What do Mama and Papa think of me? And the boys when they are told?

Eva squeezed her eyes shut, willing the tears to stop. The effort only resulted in increasing the flow, however. She rubbed at her eyes, but that only made them sore.

Flipping the covers off of her head, Eva stared at the ceiling.

"Lord," she prayed aloud. "Please forgive me. I didn't mean to kill Johnny."

"Eva, don't talk like that."

Eva sat up at the gentle voice.

"Mama?" she said in surprise.

Rose moved slowly from the doorway and sat down on the edge of the girl's bed.

"Darling, you shouldn't believe the things Joy said to you. She was confused in her feelings and didn't realize what she was saying."

"She certainly wasn't thinking too much about *my* feelings."

"No, sweetheart, she wasn't." Rose smiled softly and stroked Eva's rumpled hair. "But I'm sure she is now. She's probably regretting the things she said, and is trying to figure out how to apologize."

"So she hasn't come back yet?"

"No." Rose shook her head.

Eva frowned.

"How long has she been gone?"

"For about half an hour. Don't worry, though. Your papa says that she just needs some time to cool down, and then she'll be back."

"It shouldn't take her very long to cool down in that weather," Eva said with a sigh, "although she was pretty angry."

"Yes, she was," Rose agreed. "Eva, I know that Joy really hurt your feelings, and that you probably aren't ready to forgive her. But will you try to? For me?"

Eva smiled slightly.

"Sure, Mama. I already forgave her... in my heart."

Rose beamed and wrapped Eva up in a warm hug.

"That's my girl," she said into Eva's hair.

Eva leaned into her mother's embrace, enjoying the comfort she found there.

"Do you feel better now?" Rose asked, holding Eva at arm's length so that she could look her in the eyes.

"Yes," Eva nodded. "But, Mama, wasn't it my fault that Johnny died? I feed him the moldy bread. What do you think of me now, Mama? Are you ashamed that I didn't tell you at the time?"

"Oh, Eva darling! I'm not ashamed of you in the least! Papa explained that you didn't even know the bread was moldy, although Joy *had* told you not to eat it. It might not have even been the mold that caused him to get cholera."

"But that is a cause," Eva interjected.

"True, but it might not have been in Johnny's case. Sometimes God does things that we don't understand, and we end up either blaming Him or ourselves for them. The truth is, however, that everything that happens is part of God's plan for us. He works all things for good. Something good will come of this."

"What, Mama? I don't remember anything good happening because Johnny died. How long do we have to wait?"

Rose smiled gently.

"We don't always see the good God does, child, perhaps because we're not looking hard enough." Rose eased off of the bed and leaned over to kiss Eva's forehead. "Try and get some sleep now, darling."

"Good night, Mama." Eva snuggled back under the covers.

Rose quietly left the room, closing the door behind her.

Eva looked heavenward and clasped her hands together tightly.

"Alright, God, open my eyes nice and wide so that I might see the good."

Chapter 18

A Rash Decision

~*~*~

Joy didn't know how long she'd been wandering about. Her face was ice cold, along with her hand and feet. She decided that she should find shelter before she froze to death.

It had stopped snowing. But the wind was strong, and it blew the fallen snow up in a whirlwind, making it just as hard to see as when the blizzard had been raging.

A piece of paper came out of nowhere and slapped Joy on the face. She angrily crumbled it up and threw it on the ground. However, the wind picked it up and carried it along again. Stomping her foot in annoyance, Joy continued pressing along.

It was a short while later when Joy smacked into the side of a building. She could tell it was one of the company houses but couldn't tell whose it was since they all looked alike.

Deciding that it didn't matter, just so long as there was a hot fire inside, Joy began to work her way around to the back door. She banged loudly, hoping whoever was inside wasn't sleeping.

What if this is my house? The thought struck Joy rather suddenly. *What on earth will I say?*

An idea came to Joy. She ran her hand along the doorframe until she reached the lower half of the left side. She had once caught Frank carving his initials into the frame when he was supposed to be bringing in wood. When her hand came to the spot, she was relieved to find that it was completely smooth and initial-free.

No one had responded to her knock so she banged again, causing a strange tingle to run through her numb knuckle.

After a few more minutes there was the sound of sock feet patting across the kitchen floor. The door opened, and there before her, stood Jack Green.

~*~

"Harold, it's been hours, and Joy still isn't home. Shouldn't you go and look for her? She may have gotten lost," Rose fretted.

"You're right, Rose, she might have. She also might have found shelter. For all we know, she's next door, sleeping in front of the Black's fireplace."

"And what if she's not?" Rose pressed. "She must be freezing."

"I'll go in the morning, dear. Now don't go thinking that I don't care about our daughter. It would be pointless for me to go out in this storm. I'll get lost myself. Last I looked outside, it was pitch-black, and snow was blowing in every direction."

"Well... I certainly don't want you to get lost, darling. Please go look for her first thing in the morning. And take some of the other men along. I'm sure that Jacob Henning would be quite willing since you helped him look for Angelina earlier last month."

"I'm sure he would. I've no doubt that the others will be just as willing to help search. Frank and Teddy can round them up for me while I begin."

"Good plan, darling," Rose whispered; she was finally beginning to drift off to sleep.

Harold leaned over to kiss his wife.

"Get some rest, sweetheart. This is putting too much strain on you."

Rose had already fallen asleep, but there was a gentle smile on her face.

~*~

Jack was just as shocked to see Joy as Joy was to see him. Of course, why one shouldn't be shocked to find someone at their back door in the middle of the night in a blizzard is the real question.

"Why, Joy!" Jack stuttered. "I sure am surprised to see you here. What in the world are you doing out in a storm at this time of night?"

"Can I p-please c-come in?" Joy asked through chattering teeth.

"Sure." Jack held the door open wider and helped her inside and into a chair by the hot stove. He sat down next to her and stared at her quizzically for several minutes.

Joy rubbed her hands briskly together and then held them against her frostbitten cheeks.

Seeing that Joy had warmed up a bit, Jack posed the question again.

Hesitating, Joy wondered how much she should tell him.

Why should I tell him anything? she wondered to herself. *After all, this is Jack Green.*

For some reason, however, the Jack Green sitting opposite her didn't look much like the Jack Green she knew. This Jack Green was watching her with a concerned look on his face. His eyes held a kindness and were almost tender.

He does deserve some kind of explanation, Joy told herself.

"My papa kicked me out of the house," she finally spoke.

"What?" Jack's eyes opened wide in surprise. "I always respected you father, thought him to be a fine man. Why would he do a thing like that?"

"Because... because..." Joy took a deep breath. "Because I yelled at my sister and... called her a ... a murderer," she admitted sheepishly.

"I assume there's more to the story?" Jack pressed.

Joy nodded meekly.

Jack surprised her by reaching out and taking her hand.

"You don't have to tell me if you don't want to," he said, looking softly into her eyes.

This hidden side of Jack Green confused Joy. And she found herself pouring out the whole story, taking note that Jack held her hand the entire time.

"I think," Jack spoke once Joy had finished, "that your papa asked you to leave so that you might realize what terrible things you were saying, and apologize."

"Really?"

Jack nodded. "I don't think he really expected you to go."

"I can't go back, not now - not ever," Joy said firmly, shaking her head. She finally pulled her hand free of his. "They'll never forgive me now."

"I'm sure that they would. Like I said before, your father is a fine man. I'll bet that they're worried sick about you right now."

"Let them worry," Joy snapped, "serves them right for treating me this way."

"Aw, that's no way to talk, Joy. Your family loves you."

"Sure! They love the way I wait on them hand and foot. I'm sick of caring for them. I've taken my turn. I've served my time. Let Eva be the mother for a while. For the last six years I've given up everything just to take care of my mother and siblings. And what have I gotten out of it? Nothing!"

"I wouldn't say that, Joy. From what I've seen, you've grown into a fine young woman, and you're prepared for most anything. You'll make a great wife and mother one day."

"That day will never come if I go back. They'll just make me continue doing as I have been. I'll never be free. Who would marry me anyway?"

"I would."

Joy looked at Jack sharply.

"What did you say, Jack Green?"

"I said I'd marry you, Joy Remington."

Joy felt her face turn red. She wrung her hands together, which were suddenly quite sweaty.

"I...I..." Joy didn't know what to say.

Jack chuckled. "I've always liked you, Joy. I tried you show you, but you always ignored me."

"That's because I... I thought you were a rather horrid boy to look at," Joy suddenly blurted.

Jack was taken aback. Then he laughed again and ran his hand through his hair.

"I guess I'm not all that much to look at," he admitted.

"I used to think that," Joy agreed.

"Used to?" Jack raised an eyebrow.

Joy nodded and blushed.

"My mama once said that you often see people how you want to see them, and I guess that's how I saw you. But in just this little while that I've spent here with you, I've seen a different side of you that I've never seen before. Maybe because I didn't want to, or I wasn't looking hard enough."

"And it's a good side?" Jack asked, smiling.

"Yes," Joy replied, returning the smile.

"You know, Joy, I saw a different side of you tonight, as well. I've seen that you have a bad temper."

Joy dipped her head in embarrassment.

Touching his finger to her chin, Jack tipped her head back up so that she was looking him in the eyes.

"But that's all right," he said, "'cause I still love you."

Joy inhaled sharply at his words.

"You... love me?" she choked.

Leaning forward, Jack briefly kissed her on the lips.

"Yep," he said with a grin.

Staring at him with wide eyes, Joy sat frozen in shock.

"I'd marry you right now, if I could," he said.

Joy remained silent for a few more moments.

"We could elope," she murmured. "Then I wouldn't have to go back to... that place."

"Elope!" Jack exclaimed.

"Shh! You'll wake your parents," Joy hissed.

"Don't worry about that," Jack said with a wave of his hand. "They left to visit my uncle and aunt a few days ago. My aunt's been ill. And Harvey sleeps like a rock."

Joy's eyes lit up.

"You see!" she cried. "It would be perfect! No one would even know we're gone until at least morning."

"Now, Joy, don't be hasty in making such decisions. Do you really want to leave your family? I know that you're angry with them right now. But after a while you'll realize that you still love them and want to be with them."

Joy shook her head firmly.

"No, Jack. I don't ever want to see them again. You said that you love me."

"Well, sure I do. And that's why I want you to make the right choice. You'll regret it later if we elope. Besides, do you even love me?" Jack gave her a critical look.

"Well…" Joy said hesitantly. "I've never been in love before so I don't suppose I know what it feels like. But I can tell you that right now I feel for you like I've never felt for anyone else. It could very well be love."

Jack rose from his chair and began pacing the kitchen floor. Joy followed him with her eyes.

"I still don't know, Joy. It would be such a risk. Besides, where would we go?"

"My plan - before I got too cold to go on - was to walk to the nearest stage coach stop and catch a stage west as far as I could go."

"Do you even have any money for a ticket?"

Joy frowned; she hadn't thought of that before.

"No, I guess I don't. Doesn't it sound like a good plan, though, Jack? You don't really want to work in that dusty old mill for the rest of your life, do you?"

Jack stopped his pacing and looked at her.

"No, I don't suppose I do. I have always wanted to go west, look for gold in California."

Joy stood up and took both of his hands in hers.

"I'd be happy to share that dream with you, Jack. I'll be right alongside of you as your wife. You did say that'd I'd make a good wife. I'll help you look for gold, and we'll become rich together."

Jack glanced down at their clasped hands. He rubbed the back of her hands with his thumbs. He lifted his eyes and gazed right into her bright blue ones.

"All right, Joy, if you're sure this is what you want."

A small smile touched her lips, and she nodded.

"Yes, Jack, I'm sure."

Jack leaned down and briefly kissed her again.

"Let me pack a small bag quick and we can be on our way. Find some food and throw it into that flour sack over there."

Jack left, and Joy poked around the kitchen looking for suitable foods to take along. She put bread, cheese, blackberry jam, and cold beef into the sack.

Jack returned ten minutes later carrying a bag in one hand and a pile of clothes tucked in his opposite arm.

"Here," he said, handing her the clothes. "You're about Harvey's size. Those are a pair of his trousers, a thick wool shirt, wool socks, and his old coat. You'll freeze to death in what you have on."

Joy accepted the clothes and waited until Jack had left to put them on. She rolled up her dress and stuck it in the bag with Jack's belongings.

"All right, you can come back in now," Joy called into the other room.

"I also found these mittens and a hat for you," Jack said as he reentered the kitchen. He grinned at the site of her. "Gee, Joy, you even look good in boys' clothes."

Joy blushed slightly as she accepted the hat and mittens and pulled them on.

"I'm ready," she announced, picking up the sack of food.

"Then let's go." Jack took up his bag and patted his pocket. He glanced at her and grinned lopsidedly. "Just making sure my money's still there."

"Don't want to forget that," agreed Joy.

Jack held the door open for her, and Joy was relieved to see that the wind had died down some.

"We'll borrow Pa's horse from the livery," Jack said as he pulled the door securely shut behind them. "Once we get to the next town, we'll let her loose. She can find her way home in the middle of a blizzard."

"That's a good idea." Joy nodded her agreement.

Taking her hand, Jack led Joy through the snow to the livery.

"I won't tack her up. That way the folks might just think she got loose, instead of thinking someone rode her," Jack informed Joy once they were inside the dusty building.

"Smart," Joy said, pleased with his cleverness.

"Come on, girl," Jack called softly to the mare as he led her out of her stall. The mare nickered quietly and obediently followed Jack outside.

"I'll get on first, and you swing up behind me," said Jack to Joy once he had closed the livery door.

Joy nodded. She was thankful for the boys' clothes she wore since they would be more practical for riding.

Jack grasped the mare's mane and easily swung onto her back. Once settled, he held out his hand for Joy.

Hesitating, Joy wondered when the last time she rode a horse was. Perhaps never.

"Come on, Joy. You can trust me," Jack spoke gently.

"I trust you," Joy whispered. She grabbed onto his hand, and, in a moment, found herself safely on the mare's back. She slipped her arms around Jack's waist and held on tight, still clutching the sack of food in her right fist.

"You ready?" Jack asked.

Joy nodded her head against his back.

"Yes," she murmured.

"Let's go, girl," Jack called to the mare. He whistled, and the horse immediately began to pick up pace, lifting her hooves high above the deep drifts.

Joy closed her eyes as they rode past her house. She never wanted to see that house - nor the people who lived inside it - ever again.

The mare continued to trot west out of town. Both Jack and Joy faced straight ahead, toward a land filled with riches, where hopes and dream came true. Neither of them once looked back.

Chapter 19
The Search Begins

~*~*~

Rose shook her husband awake before six o'clock the next morning. "Harold, Joy never came back. You must go look for her now."

Harold moaned as he stretched and rubbed his eyes open.

"Give me five minutes to get dressed and bundled up, dear. Then I'll be on my way."

"Frank woke up a little while ago. I explained the situation to him, and he's going out to round up the men just as soon as he eats his breakfast. Eva made eggs; she has some ready for you."

"Sounds good." Harold pushed back the covers and swung his feet to the cold floor. "I'll eat quick as I can."

There was a knock on the bedroom door. Frank poked his head inside.

"I'll be leaving now, Teddy's coming with me," he informed his parents.

"Thanks for telling me," Harold said. "Keep your eyes open for your sister, son. Make sure to get her home as soon as possible if you find her."

"Yes, sir," Frank nodded and left.

Rose sat in the bed and watched as her husband pulled his trousers on over his long johns.

"I feel so helpless. I wish there was something I could do," she said sorrowfully.

Harold finished buttoning his shirt. He leaned down and kissed her forehead.

"You can pray, dear. That's the best help there is. I'm sure some of the wives will be over to pray with you once they hear the news."

"I know, but sometimes it feels like prayer doesn't work. I guess I get impatient too easily."

"We all do." Harold kissed her again and left the room.

"Your eggs, Papa," Eva said, setting a plate on the table and returned to washing dishes.

"Thank you, sweetie. They look good." Harold sat and quickly devoured the eggs.

"I'm sorry about what happened with Joy," Eva spoke from her place by the wash basin. "I suppose that it is..."

Harold held up a hand and gave her a stern look.

Eva hung her head sheepishly and gave him a weak smile.

"Sorry, Papa. I suppose that it is *not* my fault. Not entirely anyway."

"Now, Eva. It's not your fault in any way. You really need to stop thinking that way."

"Yes, Papa," said Eva meekly.

Harold stood and moved to place his plate in the wash basin. He embraced Eva and planted a kiss on the top of her head.

"I love you, sweet girl. Be strong for your mama while I'm gone."

"I love you too, Papa. And I'll try my very best."

"I know you will." With that, Harold pulled on his coat and left.

~*~

Frank and Teddy trudged down the street through the deep snow. They had already stopped at two houses, and both of the men were willing to help look for Joy.

"The Kline's house is next," Frank announced.

They arrived at the Kline's front door. Teddy knocked.

Mrs. Kline opened the door a couple of minutes later.

"Good morning, boys. What are you two doing about at this hour?"

"Joy's missing," Frank explained. "She left the house late last night and never returned."

"Oh my!" Mrs. Kline gasped. A hand flew to her mouth. "I'll tell Joshua right away. I'm sure he'll help you look for her."

"Thank you, ma'am," Frank said.

"Yes, thanks, Mrs. Kline," Teddy echoed.

The boys turned and walked back to the street. They stopped at the Crews's house next. Both Adam and Thomas agreed to help look for Joy.

"The Greens are next," Frank said looking down the road. "Harvey said that his parents are visiting some relatives for a couple of days. But I'm sure that he'll help look, and maybe Jack will, too."

Harvey was just coming out the front door as Frank and Teddy turned into the fenced yard.

"Mornin', Frank, Teddy!" Harvey called. "What are you two doing? I was just going to come see you to ask if you wanted to go hunting with me."

"Sure, we'll go hunting, Harv. But it'll have to be for my sister," Frank replied as the three boys met in the middle of the pathway.

"What do you mean? Is Eva missing?" Harvey asked.

Teddy shook his head. "Nope, Joy is."

"Really?" Harvey said with a frown. "That's strange. I thought she never even left the house."

"Well, she did last night," Frank said. He gave his friend the rough details.

"Wow!" Harvey exclaimed, scratching his head. "I never would have thought that of Joy. Sure I'll help you look for her."

"You wanna see if Jack will help, too?" Frank asked.

"I would, but I don't know where he is. He was gone when I got up."

"Oh, well. I guess one less man won't make much difference," Frank decided with a shrug. "We have to ask a few more people to help, and then we can start searching ourselves."

"Sounds like a plan," Harvey said, nodding. "I'll take the other side of the street."

"Ah, actually, I think I will," Frank spoke. He rubbed the back of his neck and felt red tint his cheeks.

Teddy winked at Harvey.

"That's because the Quants live on that side of the street," he said with a snicker. "Frank's sweet on Sarah."

"*Oh*, I see how it is." Harvey chuckled. "All right, Teddy, you and me can take care of this side of the street so that lover boy here can visit his sweetheart."

Frank ignored the laughter from his friend and brother as he made his way across the street.

"I'm not gonna let them ruin my spirits," he told himself. "I'm old enough to like a girl. Let them tease me all they want."

"Frank, look out!"

Frank whipped his head up. His eyes widened as a bay horse came galloping down the road towards him. He tried to jump out of the way, but the deep snow made his effort worthless. He landed head-first into a drift, and the horse raced past him.

"Frank! Are you all right?" Teddy called, stumbling through the snow towards his brother. Harvey was right on the younger boy's heels, and they worked together to pull Frank to his feet.

"I think so," Frank muttered, brushing the snow off the front of his coat. "Boy! That horse came out of nowhere!"

"That looked like my father's horse," Harvey said. "I can't be sure though. It was running so fast."

"She went into the livery," Teddy informed them. "Let's go look."

"We're supposed to be looking for Joy, but I guess we should make sure the horse is all right," Frank agreed somewhat reluctantly.

The three boys rushed as fast as they could to the livery. A couple of the men who had gathered to make a plan to search for Joy broke from the group, also curious about the horse.

Mr. Kline managed to get hold of the mare's mane. He and Mr. Henning struggled to put the horse back into her stall.

"That *is* my father's horse!" Harvey exclaimed when the boys arrived. "I wonder how she got out."

"Maybe your brother went for an early morning ride," suggested Fred Waters, the livery owner. "He does that sometimes."

"I know," Harvey nodded. "But not usually when it's this cold. And if the horse came back without him, that means that she must have thrown him or something."

"Hear that, men?" Jacob Henning called to the group. "Now we're looking for Jack Green as well as Joy Remington."

"Let's tack up and head out!" Sheriff Jones called. Frank hadn't noticed the lawman in the group before. He was relieved to know that there would be an expert tracker along with the other men.

Frank felt a hand on his shoulder. He looked up and saw his father standing behind him.

"Why don't you and the other boys look around town and up by the river, Frank?"

"Yes, sir." Frank waved to Teddy, Harvey, Thomas and the other boys who had come to help. "Come on, fellas. We'll split up into four groups and each go in a different direction."

The men mounted their horses and rode off, half going east, and the other half headed west.

After watching their fathers leave, the boys divided themselves. Frank found himself paired with Harvey. The two friends headed north towards the river.

"You know, I was thinking," Harvey spoke up as they neared the Little Platte River. "It's kind of strange that both Jack and Joy went missing at the same time."

"Why is that strange?" Frank asked. "They didn't really. Joy left the house around nine o'clock, and Jack must have went for his morning ride around five."

Harvey looked at Frank with a raised eyebrow.

"Did he really though?"

"What do you mean?"

"Who says that Jack went for a *morning* ride?"

"What are you saying?" Frank wasn't sure what Harvey was thinking.

"Frank, have you ever noticed Jack looking at Joy?"

"Looking at her how?"

"Like he's sweet on her."

"Well... I guess so." Frank tried to remember the few occasions that Jack and Joy had been in the same room. "Yeah, I suppose I have noticed that. I still don't follow you, though."

"You don't think that they ran away together, do you?"

Frank's eyes widened.

"You mean, you think that they... eloped?"

"Just put the facts together." Harvey shrugged. "It's obvious."

Shaking his head doubtfully, Frank said, "I don't think so, Harv. Joy's pretty level-headed. She'd have to be really upset to do a crazy thing like that."

"But wasn't she upset last night?"

"She sure was. But still…"

"'But still' nothing. They eloped - plain and simple."

"When could they have possibly met - out in a blizzard - to come up with such a plan?" Frank pressed. He didn't want to believe that his sister had actually eloped, even though he was becoming more convinced by the minute.

Harvey groaned.

"Do you think that I have *all* the answers? Honestly, Frank!"

"Well, you gotta admit that the whole thing sounds rather ridiculous. Besides, from what I've heard from Joy, Jack is the most horrid boy on earth. Why would she ever elope with him?"

Harvey frowned and looked at Frank.

"She said that? About my brother? What has she said about me?"

Frank shoved his hands in his pockets and met his friend's gaze.

"Things you probably wouldn't want to know. But I never pay any mind to what she says. You're a great pal."

Grinning, Harvey slapped Frank on the back.

"Thanks, buddy. What do you say we see if we can find your father and tell him about our idea?"

Frank sighed.

"I suppose we ought to do that. I sure hate to, though. He's not gonna be happy, that's for sure."

Chapter 20

Trusting

~*~*~

Harold guided his horse carefully through the snow. He was in a group with Adam Crews and Jacob Henning. The three of them had turned south once out of town. They were stopping at every farm they came across, asking the owners if they had taken in a stray girl last night. All of the reports were negative.

"Harold, I think we should give the horses a rest," Adam suggested. He halted his gelding and ran his hand down the horse's neck. "They are getting pretty tired."

"Yes," Jacob agreed, also stopping his horse.

"We'll see if the owners of the next farm will let them stay inside their barn for a while and maybe eat some hay," Adam added.

"All right," Harold said reluctantly. He took his hat off and scratched his head. "Maybe they'll have some hot coffee for us, too. I sure could use a cup."

"I know you're feeling hopeless right now, Harold. But don't worry, we'll find her," Jacob said. "I can tell by the look on your face that you're feeling exactly how I felt when my Angelina was missing."

"Yes, I suppose I am," Harold admitted. He turned to his friend with a look of sincerity. "I'm sorry, Jacob. When I was helping you look for her, I wasn't trying very hard, I don't suppose. Now I know exactly what you were going through, and I'm afraid that I wasn't the friend you needed. Thank you for being that friend for me. And you too, Adam."

"That's what friends are for. We need to stick together in our little town," Adam said. "I'm glad that I'm able to be of help to you."

"Same here," added Jacob. "You're right, Adam. We do need to stick together. Otherwise, the mill would never run, and Smithville wouldn't even exist."

Harold swept his gaze across the vast snow-covered prairie.

"Seems never-ending. She could be anywhere. These drifts are so high. She could be buried under any of them, and we'd never know."

"The Lord will help us find her," Jacob declared. "We just have to put our trust in Him."

"That's right," nodded Adam. "For all we know, one of the other search parties could have found her by now."

"True. Maybe we should turn around and head back to town to check," Harold said, surprising himself along with his friends. "Or does that seem as though I'm giving up?"

"Not at all," Jacob disagreed.

Adam shook his head. "No, I think that it would be smart to check in with the others."

"All right, we'll turn around. I'm sure that Mrs. Potts from the last farm will give us some coffee."

"I know she will," Adam said positively. "She's good friends with my Ester. They often get together to sew and bake."

"Wonderful, I could really use some good strong coffee," announced Jacob.

"Yep, just what I need to revive my body so that I can continue searching," Harold agreed.

The three men rode into the Potts's drive a couple of minutes later.

"Back so soon?" Vila Potts asked when she answered Harold's knock. "Did you find your daughter?" Glancing among the men, she frowned. "Oh, I see that you didn't. I'm so sorry. Do come in, I'll get you some coffee."

"That's just what we were hoping you'd say," Adam said with a chuckle as he followed her inside, the other two men on his heels.

"Well, you men certainly need to keep yourselves fortified if you're going to be out searching in this bitterness all day," Vila declared as she bustled about the kitchen.

The men sat down around the table. Soon there were three cups of steaming coffee and a fresh loaf of bread before them.

"Thank you, ma'am. This was wonderful," Harold said politely once they had finished.

"My pleasure. I hope you find your daughter. I'll be praying for you."

"Thank you."

"Goodbye to you all. Adam, tell Ester to come visit me soon."

"I'll do that," Adam promised.

The men retrieved their horses and continued towards town.

Once they arrived in Smithville some twenty minutes later, Adam suggested that they go to the sheriff's office to see if any of the other men had checked in.

"Harold, there's your son and Green's boy running in our direction," Jacob called to his friend, pointing down the street.

Harold followed Jacob's finger and saw Frank and Harvey running towards them, waving their arms.

"Maybe they found Joy!" Harold shouted. He urged his horse into a gallop.

"Pa!" Frank cried as Harold pulled the gelding to a halt. "Harvey just thought of the craziest thing, and we both believe that it's true!"

"What's that?" Harold slid off his horse. Jacob and Adam had caught up with him and also dismounted.

Frank nudged his friend.

"You tell him, Harv."

Harvey shook his head.

"No way, pal. He's your father."

"Someone please tell me!" cried Harold in exasperation.

"Joy and Jack eloped," Frank blurted.

Harold was certain that his heart stopped beating as his son's words echoed in his head.

Jacob placed a comforting hand on Harold's shoulder.

"Why don't you explain how you came to this conclusion, son?" Jacob asked Frank.

The boy nodded and went on to say how Harvey had figured that the disappearance of the two young people was connected.

"I hate to say this, Harold," Adam said once Frank had finished. "But it really does look as though they eloped."

Harold blinked his eyes slowly and finally spoke, "I... I can't believe that Joy would do this to us – to her mother. We always counted so much on her, and..."

"And maybe that's why she left," Jacob interrupted. "Maybe she felt pressured."

Harold covered his face in his hands.

"You're so right, Jacob. I placed too much responsibility on her shoulders. Rose, she tried to tell me... Oh, dear! How will I ever explain this to Rose? She'll be heart-broken! I'm a failure as a husband and father!" Harold slumped against his horse, shaking with sobs.

"Don't say that, Harold!" Jacob scolded gently, squeezing Harold's shoulder. "You most certainly are not!"

"You're the best father ever," Frank agreed. He wrapped his arms around Harold. "I love you, Pa."

Harold removed his hands from his face to look at his son. He hadn't heard those words come from Frank's mouth since the boy had turned twelve. Harold pulled Frank into a tight embrace.

"I love you too, son."

"Do you want me to go with you when you tell Rose?" Jacob offered. "...For support?"

Harold shook his head.

"I'll be fine, but thank you, friend."

"I'll head to the sheriff's office to notify the others of this news," Adam said. "Then we'll see about going after those two young fools."

"I'll go with you," Jacob announced.

"Harvey," Harold spoke to the boy once he had released his son. "Jack is your brother; do you have any idea where he would go? Which direction?"

Harvey shook his head.

"Sorry, Mr. Remington. I never would have thought that Jack would elope so I never thought about where he would go if he did."

"That's all right, Harvey. Don't worry yourself over it."

"I do wonder where they came up with the idea to elope," Adam said.

"Me too," Harold agreed. "I know that Joy would never think of such a thing. And I believe you, Harvey, when you say that Jack wouldn't either. But I guess - since they most likely *did* elope - that that is better than them both being lost. Unless, of course, they did get lost. Oh, this is so hopeless!"

"Just remember to trust, Harold," Jacob said. "Trust in the Lord. This will turn out fine. Just wait and see."

Adam and Jacob left for the sheriff's office with Harvey trailing along behind. Frank followed his father back to their house to break the news to the rest of the family.

Chapter 21

Breaking the News

~*~*~

Eva sat next to her mother on the sofa, holding hands as they each silently prayed for Joy's safety. Rose had insisted that she sit in the parlor so that she could see out the front window, Eva had reluctantly agreed after making her mama promise only to stay for an hour.

"That's all I will need," Rose had said. "The good Lord will have my Joy home by then."

Now, however, as the hour was drawing near its end, Eva wasn't sure that Joy would be home any time soon.

There was the sound of footsteps crunching in the snow.

"See!" Rose exclaimed. "Here is your papa now!"

Eva knew that from the angle her mother was sitting, she could not see who was coming - unless she had seen the person before he turned into the gate.

The front door opened, and sure enough, it was her papa. Frank and Teddy also followed. Teddy appeared quite confused, while Frank's face was solemn like their father's.

Joy was not among them.

"Where's Joy?" Rose asked, rising from the sofa. Eva saw tears in her mother's eyes. She felt one spill onto her own cheek.

Harold grasped his wife's arm and helped her back down.

"I think that we should all sit," he said.

Rose let out a wail as she collapsed onto the sofa.

"Oh, she's dead! My baby girl is dead!"

"Be calm, Rose darling. She's not dead... that we know of anyway. But the news I have for you is almost as bad." Harold took both of his wife's hands in his own.

"What could be as bad as her dying?" asked Rose tearfully.

Harold took a shaky breath.

Eva stared at her father, waiting for him to speak. She also wondered what could be as bad as death.

"Earlier - before we even headed out to search - we discovered that Jack Green was also missing."

"Yes, I know that. Mrs. Lewis informed me when she stopped by," Rose interrupted with a nod. "I don't see where you're going with this."

"Well, while Frank and Harvey were searching up by the river, they put two and two together and realized that Joy and Jack..."

Eva sucked in her breath as her father choked on his next word.

"...Eloped."

Rose's hand flew to her mouth, covering a cry.

"Oh, no! No, no, no!" she exclaimed. "This can't be true! Tell me it's a lie!"

Feeling completely helpless to comfort her mother, Eva broke into tears.

Harold tried to calm Rose.

"Sweetheart, you need to settle down. You'll make yourself weak again."

"I don't care!" Rose shouted, surprising everyone. "Harold, you go back out there and bring that crazy girl back!"

Eva and her brothers stared at their mother with wide eyes. They had never seen her act like this before.

Harold grasped his wife's upper arms and tried to get her to sit still.

"Jacob Henning and Adam Crews went to tell the sheriff, Rose. We're all going to go back out and look for them. Just calm yourself. We'll find them."

Rose took a trembling breath. She looked over to her shocked children.

"Oh, dear," she murmured. "I'm sorry, children. I shouldn't have let myself get all worked up like that."

Eva smiled slightly and patted her mother's arm.

"That's all right, Mama. We know that you're just worried about Joy. We all are."

"That's right, Mama. We understand," Frank added.

Teddy simply nodded since he was still in shock himself.

"I'll be leaving now," Harold announced. "Take care of your mother, children. Especially you, Eva."

Eva nodded. As she watched her father leave, the full meaning of his words sunk in. If Joy wasn't found, it would be her who would have to take her sister's place.

Chapter 22

Continuing the Search

~*~*~

"Harold, we were just going to get you," Sheriff Jones said when Harold walked into his office.

"Did you come up with a plan?" Harold asked.

"Yes," the sheriff nodded. "We decided that since Mr. Green's horse came from the west, that Jack and Joy must have gone in that direction. Assuming, of course, that they were riding the mare, which I'm sure they were."

"But the horse wasn't tacked."

"No," Jacob spoke. "We figured that they purposefully didn't saddle her so that we might simply think she'd gotten out - on her own."

"Makes sense," agreed Harold with a nod.

"Our horses should have had plenty of time to rest now," said Sheriff Jones. "Let's tack them back up and head west."

"I'll stay behind to inform the women," Adam suggested.

"That will be fine," the sheriff agreed. "We only need about four of us anyway. No need for you all to spend the rest of the day out in this weather. Do I have any volunteers to go? The rest of you men go home to your wives."

"I'll go," Jacob immediately offered.

"No, Jacob," Harold said. "You've been so helpful already. Go on home to Beth and the girls."

"If you're sure," Jacob hesitated.

"I am. Thank you for staying by my side today. I really appreciate it. You're a true friend."

Jacob shook Harold's hand firmly.

"You're most welcome, Harold. I'll be praying that you find them quickly."

"Thank you."

Jacob followed Adam out the door.

"I'll go," Joshua Kline piped up.

"And I," Michael Baker added.

Harold hadn't noticed Violet's father in the group before.

"Michael, how long have you been here?" he asked.

"Just walked through the door a minute ago. One of the search parties stopped by my house earlier. When Violet heard the news, she wanted to be with Eva - such good friends are those girls. So I just dropped her off at your house. I came by to see if you had found Joy yet, and passed Jacob Henning and Adam Crews on my way over. They told me what you are about to do, and I think that it's my turn to lend a hand."

"I would be most grateful to you, Michael. Thank you for coming."

"Ready when you are," Sheriff Jones broke into the conversation.

"My horse is waiting outside," said Michael.

"Then let's head out, men."

~*~

It was about two hours later when the four men arrived in Platte City.

"Where should we look first?" Harold asked as they guided their horses down the main street.

"Well, since they were eloping, I'd guess we should find the preacher and see if they got themselves married yet," Sheriff Jones suggested.

"Good thinking."

"And we could also check the stage depot," Joshua suggested. "I'd imagine that they'd want to get as far away as possible."

Harold nodded silently, wondering how far his daughter could have gotten if they had indeed caught a stage.

"Pardon me, ma'am," the sheriff called to a lady walking along the street. "Can you tell me where the preacher lives?"

"Why, next to the church," replied the lady.

"And that would be...?"

Smiling, the lady pointed north.

"You just go on until you get to the crossroad, then turn right onto Church Street. You'll see it. The reverend's house is the whitewashed one on the left of the church building."

"Thank you, ma'am," said Sheriff Jones with a nod.

Harold tipped his hat to the lady as he rode past her.

"Joshua, Michael, why don't you wait outside? No sense in crowding up the preacher's house," the sheriff said once they had arrived.

The four men dismounted and tied their horses to the hitching post. Harold followed Sheriff Jones up the steps to the little white house. His hands were sweaty as he thought about what he might learn from the man inside.

The sheriff's knock was answered by a pretty lady with dark brown hair and hazel eyes.

"Hello," she greeted them. "I don't think I've seen you before. New to town? Do you wish to see the reverend?"

"Yes, ma'am. Is he in?"

"Yes, he's working on his sermon for tomorrow in his study. I'm Agatha Little, the reverend's wife. Do come in."

"Thank you. Oh, I suppose we should introduce ourselves. I'm Roger Jones - sheriff of Smithville, and this is Harold Remington."

Harold held his breath, waiting for the preacher's wife to show recognition of his name, but she didn't act as though it was familiar.

"Nice to meet you both, follow me if you please," Mrs. Little motioned to them. "Nicholas dear, sorry to interrupt, but there are some men here to see you."

The reverend looked up from his papers and smiled at the sheriff and Harold.

"Welcome, please, sit down."

"Thank you, Reverend Little. I'm Sheriff Roger Jones, and this is Harold Remington. We've come from Smithville, a small mill town east of here."

Reverend Little nodded.

"Yes, I am familiar with Smithville. I have a second cousin who lives there. Paul Lewis. You know him?"

Harold grinned. "Yes, of course. Everyone knows Reverend Lewis."

"What can I do for you gentlemen?" Revered Little asked. He set down his pen and turned full attention to his guests.

Harold wrung his hands together.

"Well, you see, Reverend. My daughter… Oh, this is such a long story, I don't even know where to start."

"Would you care for some coffee or perhaps tea?" Mrs. Little politely interrupted.

"Coffee would be wonderful, if you don't mind, ma'am," said the sheriff.

"Same for me please," Harold added.

Mrs. Little left.

Reverend Little folded his hands and placed them on his desk.

"You were saying about your daughter?" he gently pressed.

"Yes, my daughter - Joy - she… We have reason to believe. Oh, I'm just going to blurt this out. She eloped last night, with a boy we all thought she hated. She's only fifteen."

"And you thought that perhaps she came here to get married?" Reverend Little asked.

Harold nodded. "Yes, she obviously couldn't go to our own preacher - who is apparently your cousin."

"Well, I'm sorry to say that I haven't married anyone since last spring when Ruthie Albertson married Hugh Alcott. Maybe, though, that is a good thing. Perhaps she hasn't gotten married yet, and you can catch her before she does."

"Or it could mean that she and Jack got lost in the storm and froze to death," Harold said, rubbing his forehead with the palm of his hand.

"Well, Reverend, thank you for your time just the same," Sheriff Jones said, rising from his chair.

"Here's the coffee," Mrs. Little announced as she returned to the study. "Oh, you're leaving already?"

Sheriff Jones glanced at the coffee.

"I suppose we can stay to have a cup. I sure could use some."

"Please do," invited the reverend. "I'm sure that you've been out in the cold all day. If you want to, you could explain about your daughter in more detail."

"That may be more relieving than the coffee, Reverend," Harold decided.

"I invited your two friends inside," Mrs. Little said. "They are having coffee in the parlor."

"Oh, thank you, ma'am. I nearly forgot about Joshua and Michael." Harold was grateful for the woman's thoughtfulness.

Mrs. Little served the coffee and turned to leave.

"You can stay if you wish to, Mrs. Little," Harold invited.

Smiling, Mrs. Little said, "If you don't mind."

Harold shook his head.

Agatha Little made herself comfortable in a chair in the far corner of the study.

The next hour was spent with Harold freely telling the Littles about his family. He could see the concern on their faces - and knew by that that - they were truly related to Reverend Paul Lewis of Smithville. By the time Harold was finished - with the sheriff adding a few things here and there - he felt more at peace than he had in a long time.

"That is quite a story you have there, Mr. Remington," the reverend spoke once Harold was finished.

"Yes, indeed it is," agreed Mrs. Little. "It is a shame how your daughter left you. Why, there is a family much like yours here in Platte City. The eldest daughter cared for the sickly mother, same as yours does, and she grew up to be a very responsible woman who now has five children of her own. Her mother passed on shortly before the girl married."

Harold sighed.

"I had hoped that Joy would turn out the same way," he said. "Responsible and caring. For a while it seemed as if that was the direction she was headed. But when the stress of it all began to pile up, I'm not sure she could handle it. As I said before, she turned into an old woman - so to speak."

Reverend Little nodded thoughtfully.

"Yes, I suppose such great responsibility can make a person age faster. How old did you say she was when she began the task of caring for the household?"

"Nine."

The reverend rubbed his chin.

"Yes, quite young indeed. Don't blame yourself or your wife, Mr. Remington."

With a dry chuckle, Harold said, "As I told you, we've been down that road before, and look where it got us. No, I don't blame myself... Well, maybe I do. After all, I was the one who sent her out of the house."

"God has a plan for everything that happens. You must believe that this will all work out for good."

"I want to, Reverend. It's just hard right now."

"I understand. Never give up hope, though, dear brother. Proverbs three, five says 'Trust in the Lord with all thine heart; and lean not unto thine own understanding.'"

"A very powerful verse for sure. I'll keep it with me."

"Very good. Now, I'm sure you want to continue your search for Joy," said Reverend Little, rising from his chair.

"Yes, we would. Thank you so much for giving us your time and advice, Reverend Little. It was very nice meeting you." Harold turned to Agatha. "And you, Mrs. Little. Thank you again for the refreshments."

"My pleasure. Do stop by again if you ever come this way."

"We will," promised the sheriff.

Harold and Sheriff Jones each shook the reverend's hand, then followed Mrs. Little into the parlor.

Michael and Joshua stopped their conversation when they saw the others enter.

"Well?" Joshua asked.

Sheriff Jones shook his head.

"Reverend Little didn't marry them."

Harold glanced at Mrs. Little.

"Is there any other preachers in town? Or a judge perhaps?"

Mrs. Little frowned.

"No. Well, we have a circuit judge, but he came by last month and won't come back again until spring."

"We'd best get going," Sheriff Jones said, placing his hat upon his head.

The four men bid goodbye to Mrs. Little, and headed out the door.

"To the stage depot?" Michael asked.

"Yep," said the lawman. "I know where it is so we won't need to ask directions."

Chapter 23

No more Hope

~*~*~

In ten minutes they arrived at the depot.

"Hello!" Sheriff Jones called to the clerk from the back of his horse.

The clerk looked out his window at the four riders.

"What can I do for you, men? I see you're a sheriff. Has there been a stage robbery I haven't heard about?"

The men dismounted and tied up their horses. Harold and Sheriff Jones walked up to the window.

"If there has been, I haven't heard about it either," said the lawman. "We're looking for two young people whom we have reason to believe eloped."

"Hmmm," murmured the clerk, rubbing his chin thoughtfully.

"My daughter," spoke up Harold. "She's fifteen, and the young fellow she was with is about..." Harold looked to the other men, unsure of Jack's age.

"Nearly seventeen, I would say," supplied Joshua.

"Nearly seventeen," repeated Harold.

"I can't say that I recall any youngsters getting on a coach recently. What time would you guess they would have gotten here?" the clerk asked.

"I don't really know... maybe about four...five o'clock this morning," Harold guessed.

The clerk let out a snort and quickly covered his mouth.

"Sorry, sir, I didn't mean to be rude. You see, I got in about seven this morning. You'd have to speak with the night clerk to find out if your daughter got on the six o'clock stage."

"Oh, when will he be back?"

"Should be in to take over for me at seven tonight," said the clerk.

"That's only a couple of hours away," Sheriff Jones announced, looking at his pocket watch. "We'll wait."

"Yes," agreed Harold. "I must know where my daughter went."

"You could stable your mounts in the livery next door, then come in here where it's warm," suggested the clerk. "There's a nice café down the road a little ways if you want to eat some supper."

"We'll do that. And we'll back before seven," promised Harold.

"I'll be waiting for you," the clerk called after them.

The four men untied their horses and led them to the livery. Harold gave the groomsman a dollar to feed and care for the horses.

Stepping outside of the livery, Michael sniffed the air.

"Mmm, I think I'll be able to find the café without any trouble. I'll just follow my nose."

The other men inhaled deeply.

"That way," Joshua said, pointing.

"Right," Michael agreed with a chuckle. "Come on, Harold, you paid for the horses' meal; now I'll pay for yours."

"Thanks, Michael. I am starving. Although I must say that those cookies Mrs. Little gave us were quite delicious."

"Very true," Joshua agreed, rubbing his stomach. "I must have eaten a dozen."

Harold laughed along with the other men, but then he felt a solemnness come over him as his worry about Joy returned.

The others noticed Harold sudden state of silence. Their laughter quickly subsided, and the rest of the walk to the café was quiet.

Inside, a waitress introduced herself as Jane and seated them, informing the men of that day's menu.

"I'll take the steak and potatoes," Joshua spoke up first.

"Sounds good to me," agreed the sheriff.

"Me too," Michael added.

"And for you, sir?" Jane asked Harold.

Harold didn't speak. He remained staring at the glass of water before him.

The waitress looked at Harold for a minute than glanced at the other men, perhaps wondering if he was deaf or mute.

"Sir?"

Harold slowly looked up at her.

The young girl's eyes grew wide at the blank look on Harold's face.

~ 130 ~

"Yes, I'll have the same," he finally spoke.

"Y-yes, s-s-sir," Jane stuttered and practically ran back to the kitchen.

"Do you even know what you ordered, Harold?" Michael asked.

"Does it even matter?" Harold replied dully.

Joshua was sitting next to Harold. He leaned over and shook his friend's shoulders.

"Snap out of it, Remington. You nearly frightened that poor girl to death. You should see how you look right now."

"Yes, Harold," agreed the lawman. "You're no good to look for Joy if you go into a state of depression and hopelessness. I think you should apologize to our lovely waitress when she returns."

Harold rubbed his face and nodded.

"You're right. All of you."

Jane returned a short while later, eyeing Harold warily.

Doing his best to make his face appear more alive, Harold turned to the girl.

"I'm sorry for frightening you the way I did," he began as Jane set the plates of food before the men. "You see, I'm feeling rather lost right now. My daughter eloped last night, and we've been looking for her all day with no results."

Sympathy showed on the girl's face.

"I'm sorry for you, mister. Now I understand why you looked that way before, but you certainly did give me a fright. What does your daughter look like?"

"She has dark hair, blue eyes, and is about your height. She would have been wearing a green... no blue dress, and a black cloak."

Jane frowned thoughtfully.

"You know, there was a girl with that description who came in earlier today with a young man. Said they were brother and sister. There was something strange about them though, but I can't place my finger on it. Hmmm."

Harold's eyes lit up with hope.

"Did it seem as though they were running away?"

"No, I don't think that was it... Oh, I know! The girl, she was wearing boys' clothes."

"Boys' clothes?" Harold repeated.

Jane nodded.

"That makes sense," said the sheriff. "It would be easier - and warmer - for her in boys' clothing. What time were they here? Did they say where they were going?" he asked the waitress.

"I would say about eight. I remember getting them breakfast, but the sun was only just rising. As for where they were going next, I can't say."

"That is the most information we've had all day," Harold said. "Thank you, Jane."

Smiling, Jane nodded and left them to eat.

"So..." Joshua spoke after a couple of bites of the steak. "If they were still in town at eight to eat, that means that they didn't leave on the six o'clock stage, and they didn't get on any other stage since the clerk hasn't seen them."

"That's right," Harold agreed. "I was so grateful for the news she gave us, that I didn't stop to think about that."

"Which means..." Michael said, catching on to what Joshua was thinking.

"That they're still in town," finished Sheriff Jones.

"Right," said Joshua.

"Then they couldn't have gotten married yet!" Harold exclaimed in delight. "Let's eat quickly, divide ourselves, and search for them."

"Good plan," the lawman agreed.

The men finished their meal in haste. Michael paid the bill, and they headed back outside.

"You and Michael go right and then split up at the intersection, Harold. Joshua and I will go left," instructed Sheriff Jones.

"All right," Harold nodded.

"Sheriff! Sheriff!"

The men looked up and saw the depot clerk running down the street. Out of breath by the time he reached them, the clerk placed his hands on his knees, panting for air.

"What's the matter?" Sheriff Jones asked the man. "Has there been a stage robbery now?"

Unable to speak, the clerk shook his head.

Sheriff Jones and the others waited for the man to catch his breath.

"I just remembered something," he finally spoke, though still breathing heavily. "This afternoon - oh, my, I really am out of shape - this afternoon, about the time that the one o'clock stage was to come in, my little girl came running to tell me her big brother fell off the roof and broke his leg."

"What was he doing on the roof?" asked Joshua.

"He likes to climb up there to get away from his sisters. I've told him a dozen times not to, but he's such a little trouble maker. Anyway, I went straight home to check on him and see if the doctor had set the leg. I was only gone for about twenty minutes, but the one o'clock stage had already come and gone when I returned."

"Why didn't you tell us that before?" Harold questioned, feeling the hope leave his body as quickly as it had entered.

"I guess I didn't think it was important."

Harold raised an eyebrow.

"Not important?" The sheriff exclaimed. "I would most certainly say that it is. So, it appears that those two young fools got on the stage without paying?"

The clerk squirmed under the lawman's gaze.

"Old Will, the driver, wouldn't let anyone board without knowing that they had paid. I uh, found payment for two tickets on my desk."

Sheriff Jones removed his hat and slapped it against his legs.

"Some stage depot clerk you are!" he cried.

"Now, Roger, don't get angry with him," Michael said, grabbing the sheriff's arm. "He was just being a good father."

"I apologize," Sheriff Jones mumbled, shoving his hat back on.

"Where were they going?" Harold asked the clerk. "How far did they pay to go?"

"Yes, where?" asked Joshua. "If we ride fast enough, we might be able to catch them before the stage gets there."

"You won't have to ride very fast to catch up with them," the clerk muttered.

"What do you mean?" Harold demanded, grasping the clerk's skinny arms.

"Just before I came to find you, a rancher who lives west of here rode in with some bad news."

Harold felt his mouth grow dry.

"About fifty miles out of town, there's a steep ravine. Horses must have spooked, or a wheel slipped or something. The coach rolled down into the ravine..."

Harold's knees grew weak. He felt Michael's hand on his shoulder, steadying him as the clerk's words rang in his ears.

"...There were no survivors."

Chapter 24

The Joy is Gone

~*~*~

A month passed.

Eva bustled about the kitchen, preparing stew and cornbread for supper. Although on the outside she looked energetic and alert, on the inside she was tired and sorrowful.

Ever since Harold had returned bringing the news of the stage coach disaster, the Remington household had become quite depressed. Rose remained in bed, too weak in her mourning to get up. Harold went about his regular routine rather listlessly. At ten, Peter firmly declared that he was too old to cry, but Eva heard him each night after she sent him up to bed. Teddy had always been the most sensitive of the boys and wasn't ashamed to shed tears once in a while, often in the evening when the family sat quietly in the parlor. As the oldest, Frank tried to be strong for the rest of the family, but Eva knew that he was also struggling to keep his emotions in check.

Eva poured the cornbread mixture into a pan and carefully slid it into the oven. Then she stirred the stew, adding a few seasonings. Her mind flashed back to the conversation she had had with her parents the day after they had found out about Joy.

"Now that Joy is gone, Eva, you understand that you will have to take her place, don't you?" her father had asked.

"Yes, Papa," Eva had replied sadly. "I shall miss school terribly, though."

"I know, but that's the way it has to be."

"Oh, Harold, don't you think it would be possible for her to stay in school?" Rose entered the conversation. "She's so smart ,and I would really hate to see her loose that privilege."

Harold hesitated.

"Please, dear. I truly believe that's where we went wrong with Joy. We should have never taken her out of school. I would be devastated if Eva turned out the same way."

"I won't, Mama," Eva promised.

"I suppose we can give it a trial run. But if you can't keep up with both you school and the housework, you'll have to drop out. Is that clear, Eva?"

"Yes, Papa."

"You'll have to go back to the sixth grade, though. It hasn't been very long since you advanced to grade seven, and I highly doubt you'll manage to keep good marks when you'll have such little time to study. I'll go speak with Mr. Wessington tomorrow."

"Yes, Papa."

Back in the present, Eva remembered how disappointed she had felt at the time. She still was but now understood that her father had been right in doing what he had. She was grateful to still be going to school.

Peeking into the oven, Eva guessed that the cornbread needed about ten more minutes. She stirred the stew again.

"I trust you, Eva."

Joy's words from long ago flashed into Eva's mind.

"I trusted you too, Joy. And you ran away," Eva said aloud.

Eva often said this to herself. Ever since Joy had left, she had difficulty trusting people. Except Violet. Eva completely trusted Violet.

"Violet would never leave me."

Checking the cornbread again, Eva decided that it was done. Carefully, with a folded up towel in each hand, she removed the pan from the oven.

"I'll set the table," Teddy offered, entering the kitchen.

"Thank you, Teddy. Supper is just about ready."

Teddy retrieved the proper dishes and began to set them about the table.

"Oops," he muttered.

Eva looked up. It only took her a minute to realize the mistake her brother had made.

He had set a place for Joy. Again.

~ 136 ~

Teddy quickly removed the extra dishes.

"Supper ready?" Frank asked, wandering into the kitchen. "I'm starved."

"You always are," Eva replied with a chuckle. "And, yes, it is."

"Did I hear someone say supper's ready?" Harold questioned as he came in behind Frank.

"Sure did," said Frank.

"Then let's all sit down and bless this delicious food so that we can eat."

"Where's Peter?" Eva asked.

"He's in the room with your mama."

Eva nodded silently. Joy had been the main mother-figure in Peter's life. Now that she was gone, he spent nearly every minute he wasn't in school with Rose.

"He can come when he's ready," Eva said. "I know how much he enjoys his time alone with Mama."

So the family sat down and prayed.

Harold helped himself to a large bowl of stew and thick slice of cornbread, saying, "Looks goods, Eva."

"Sure does," Teddy added.

Frank just nodded and smiled, as his mouth was already full.

They were about halfway through when Peter entered.

"Sorry I'm late," he said.

"That's all right, son," Harold replied. "You spend all the time with your mother you want. I know how much she enjoys your company."

Peter gave them all a melancholy smile and sat down at his usual place.

"Here you go, little brother," Eva said softly. She passed Peter the stew and cornbread.

"Thank you, Eva."

The rest of the meal was quiet, as each was lost in his or her own thoughts.

"Sorry that there's no dessert," Eva spoke as she began clearing off the table. "I barely had time to prepare what I did."

"That's all right. I don't think I can eat anymore, anyway," Harold said, leaning back and patting his stomach.

"Me neither," Frank agreed.

"Me neither," echoed Teddy.

"I could," said Peter, making them all laugh.

"Well, I might be able to find a little something for you," Eva said with a smile. She was pleased that they were still able to laugh, for it seemed as if all the joy had gone out of the house.

Joy took the joy, Eva thought as she looked about the kitchen for a treat for Peter. *Was Joy our joy?* Eva pondered the question. *Not really,* she decided. Not lately anyway. *She was always so angry or depressed. Then why are we all so sad that she's gone?*

Because, silly, she's your sister, and you love her. Loved her, Eva corrected herself. *No, love her. You'll always love her, even though she's not alive anymore.*

"How about some cookie crumbs?" Eva asked, breaking herself away from her thoughts. She held out a jar that had held cookies the day before, but the contents had mysteriously disappeared overnight.

"Sure!" Peter cried, excited to get any little bit of sugar.

Everyone chuckled as Peter eagerly began shoveling the crumbs into his mouth.

Eva smiled again.

Maybe not quite all of the joy is gone, she thought.

Chapter 25

No other Options

~*~*~

Time passed. Life went on.

It was Saturday, September second, eighteen forty-eight. Eva had turned twelve exactly a month earlier. She had started the seventh grade - for the second time - that week. Now it was only her and Peter in school, as Teddy had finished the past spring.

That particular day, Eva had sent Frank to Luke's Mercantile to pick up some groceries. She was planning on making a chocolate cake for dessert and was out of sugar. Besides that, the only flour she had left was needed for the bread she was making to go with the beef and potatoes. Eva felt as though she was always planning meals. She was worried that her family was becoming bored eating the same foods over and over again.

How did Joy ever manage? No wonder she left. But I won't leave. No, Eva, you are strong. You won't give up on yourself and your family. You'll stay here until Mama is well again.

Eva told herself that nearly every day, but she knew - deep down inside - that her mother was never going to be completely well. Not on this earth, anyway.

Well, I certainly won't just up and leave like Joy did. When I get married, I'll take Mama into my home, Eva decided. *...If I ever get married. Who would want to live with his mother-in-law? No, I don't suppose I'll ever marry.*

Eva wiped an unshed tear from her bright green eyes as she thought of that possibility.

"Oh, Frank, where are you with that sugar?" she said in annoyance, trying to push her thoughts aside.

Taking a bowl from the cupboard, Eva began adding the ingredients that she already had.

"Hey, sis, look who I found in town!" Frank called as he came in through the back door. He dropped a paper sack on the counter and then peeked into the pot that the beef was cooking in. "Mmm, smells good."

Eva looked up from her bowl to see Violet, Joe, and Daniel Baker enter the kitchen.

"Violet!" she exclaimed, hurrying to embrace her friend. "I'm so glad to see you!"

Violet squeezed her tightly. "Me too. You do remember that we saw each other yesterday in school, don't you?"

Eva laughed.

"Of course, but that was ages ago. Joe, Daniel, nice to see you, as well."

Joe grinned and gave her a brief hug.

"Good to see you, Eva," Daniel said, smiling at her. "Don't hardly ever see you anymore, now that I'm done with school."

"That is true. Won't you all stay for supper? It will be ready in about a half an hour. I'm making chocolate cake for dessert."

"Yes, Frank told us that when we ran into him at Luke's," Joe said with a chuckle. "That's why we followed him home."

Violet nudged her brother.

"*Some* of us came for the cake; *I* came to see my best friend."

"Come on, Daniel. I know you came for the cake," Joe turned to his brother for support.

"Aw, well, Joe. I came just as much to visit with Eva… and Teddy, too," Daniel replied, rubbing the back of his neck.

"I thought we brothers stuck together," Joe said with a scowl. "Come on, Frank. Let's go outside and whittle."

"Don't plan on being around too long, Joe. Mama wanted us home for supper," Violet called after the boys. "Sorry, Eva, we can't stay."

"That's all right, Violet. I understand. Next time we'll plan ahead. We really do need to spend more time together."

"We really do," Violet agreed.

Eva noticed that Daniel hadn't followed the older boys outside.

"Did you want something, Daniel?" she asked.

"Huh?" Daniel had been resting his hand on the door frame, watching her. When she spoke, he startled, hand slipping and banged his head on the door frame.

"Are you all right?" Eva asked with concern, although she was biting back a giggle.

"Oh, yeah. I'm fine," Daniel assured her, rubbing his head. "Ah, where's Teddy?"

"Playing checkers in the parlor with Peter."

"Oh, I'll go join them and play the winner." Daniel headed towards the parlor, still massaging his head.

"It'll be Peter!" Eva yelled after him. "It always is!" She turned to Violet, saying, "I really don't know how he does it. He has amazing strategic planning."

Violet dug the sugar out from the paper sack. She handed it to her friend. "I believe this is what you're waiting for."

"Yes, it is. Thank you."

Eva took the sugar and added the correct amount. Then she mixed in the remaining ingredients and poured the batter into a pan.

"I'll wait until the bread is done to put this in," she said.

Violet touched Eva's arm gently.

Eva raised her head to meet her friend's soft gaze.

"Eva, you were crying when we came in. Is there something wrong? I wanted to wait until everyone else had left to ask."

"That was thoughtful," Eva said with a slight smile.

"Well?" Violet gently pressed. "What's the matter?"

"Oh, it's nothing really. I was just thinking about my future."

"What about it?"

"That - like Joy - I'm forever stuck taking care of Mama. Don't get me wrong, Violet, I love caring for my family. It's given me a wonderful sense of responsibility. And I'm ever so grateful that I'm still in school, but..."

"But what?"

"I'm just afraid - I know it's a long way off - but I'm afraid that I'll never..."

"Aha! Ha, ha, ha! I finally did it!"

Eva was interrupted abruptly by excited shouts coming from the parlor.

Both girls rushed into the adjoining room.

Teddy was dancing about in excitement, repeating his shouts over and over. He halted his dancing when he saw the girls. A deep shade of red colored his cheeks.

"Just what did you do, Teddy Remington?" Eva demanded, hands planted on her hips.

Daniel chuckled as he watched the scene. Peter sat on the chair next to the checker table, arms crossed over his chest and a scowl on his face.

"Oh, I ah..." Teddy's blush deepened when Violet giggled. He tugged at the collar of his shirt and plopped back into his chair. "Never mind."

A wide grin spread over Daniel's face.

"He beat Peter at checkers," he explained.

"Is that all?" Eva crossed her arms, not terribly impressed.

"Is that all!" Teddy exclaimed indignantly. "That's the first time he's been beat since Frank showed him how to play when he was eight years old!"

"He cheated," Peter grumbled.

"You boys are ridiculous," Eva muttered, shaking her head. "Now my bread is probably burnt. And if it is, you'd better not complain."

Eva returned to the kitchen with Violet on her heels.

"Teddy is so silly," Violet giggled as Eva pulled the bread out of the cook stove.

"He sure is," Eva agreed. "Hmm, it's a little dark, but it should be fine." She set the bread aside and set the cake pan in its place.

"We really ought to be leaving," Violet said, glancing at the clock. "I'll go round up the boys. Hopefully, Joe didn't stray too far."

"He shouldn't have. Frank usually whittles on the back steps."

And that was where Violet found her eldest brother.

"Come on, Joe, it's time to go," Violet called out the back door.

"Hey, that rhymed," Frank said with a chuckle.

"Yeah, she likes to do that to me," Joe replied. "And only me."

"That's because it's too hard to think up something to rhyme with Daniel," Daniel said as he entered the kitchen. "If it's all right with you,

Eva, I'll come over after church tomorrow and play that game of checkers I owe Teddy."

"That would be fine. All of you can come and join us for dinner. Invite your parents and Mary, too."

"Are you sure you can handle that, Eva?" Violet asked with concern. "That's a lot of extra people to cook for."

"It won't be any trouble at all."

"I'll be sure to help you then - and so will Mama and Mary," Violet promised.

"I'll hold you to that," Eva replied with a smile.

"We'd best be going. Goodbye, Eva." Violet embraced her friend, whispering, "And tomorrow we can talk more about your problem."

Eva nodded.

"Oh, Joe, before you leave, I have something I was going to give you." Frank dug in his pockets. "Nearly forgot." There was a crumpling sound, and Frank pulled out a piece of paper. He glanced briefly at it, "No, not that. Oh! Eva this is for you!"

Eva took the paper and saw it was an envelope.

"Where did you get this from?"

"Luke gave it to me. I think it's a letter or something." Frank continued digging around in his pockets. "Ah, here it is! A real Indian arrowhead."

"Hey, that's neat!" Joe said, taking the arrowhead. "For me?"

Frank nodded. "Yeah, I found it out by the river."

"Does that mean there's Indians around here?" Violet asked in worry.

"Not too close, I don't think. It probably washed downstream or something."

Eva wasn't paying much attention to the conversation as she stared at the envelope. Her first thought was, *Could it possibly be from Joy? But, no, she's dead.*

"I've never gotten a letter before," she said aloud.

"Who's it from?" Teddy asked.

"The return address says Georgia Female College," Frank informed them.

Eva caught her breath.

"That's the school Mr. Wessington was going to try and get me into. I had forgotten all about it."

"Aren't you going to open it?" Frank asked.

Eva looked up from the envelope and saw that everyone was watching her.

"I'm scared to," she admitted.

"Why?" asked Teddy.

"Because, wouldn't they only write me if I got in?"

Frank shrugged. "I guess so. Maybe."

"That's why I'm worried."

Everyone looked at her in confusion.

"Go on and open it," Frank prompted.

With trembling fingers, Eva ripped open the seal. She slowly extracted the single sheet of paper and unfolded it. Holding the letter with both hands in order to keep it still, Eva read it aloud.

"Dear Miss Eva Remington, We at the Georgia Female Collage are pleased to inform you that you have been accepted..." Eva trailed off as tears filled her eyes.

"Hey, that's wonderful! Congratulations!" Joe exclaimed.

"Yeah, sis, that's great," added Frank. "I knew you'd get in."

"What's wrong, Eva? Aren't you glad you're accepted?" Violet asked, placing a hand on Eva's arm.

"Those are tears of joy. Right, sis?' Frank asked.

"I don't think so," Daniel spoke. "Eva, are you all right?"

Eva took a shuttering breath. "No. Don't you understand? I can't accept this. Look, I even got the scholarship." Eva handed the letter to Daniel. "I wish I could go; I really do. But I have to stay here and..."

"Take care of your mother," Daniel finished for her.

Eva nodded, leaning into Violet's comforting arms.

Frank, Teddy, Peter, and Joe all stared at Eva as they finally understood.

"I just can't up and leave," Eva said between sniffles. "Everyone is depending on me. I want to go further with my education, but it just isn't possible. I'm grateful enough to still be in school here. It would have been different if Joy was still here, but she's not. There are no other options."

"I know this probably isn't what you want to hear right now, Eva. But back when you first learned about the possibility of going away to school, I was devastated thinking of how far away you would be going. I would have missed you terribly," Violet said. "I didn't want to say anything before because I knew how much you wanted to go."

Eva squeezed Violet tighter.

"I really appreciate you saying that, Violet. Of course I would have missed you, too." Eva gazed at the others with teary eyes. "I would have missed all of you."

"I wasn't exactly looking forward to you leaving either, when you said you might be," Teddy said.

"Me neither," added Frank.

"I would have missed you, as well," Daniel spoke up.

Eva smiled slightly.

"Well, we won't have to worry about that anymore. But it sure is nice to know that I would have been missed." Eva stuffed the letter back into the envelope. "I'm going to burn this." She headed towards the stove.

Daniel's hand shot out, grabbing her arm.

"Don't!" he cried.

"Why not? I won't be needing it."

"You never know. Your situation might change. Save it - just in case."

"All right," Eva agreed. "But I don't want Mama to know that I won the scholarship. I don't want her to feel as though she was holding me back." Eva swung her eyes over the others, satisfied when they all nodded in agreement. "Good. And don't tell Papa, either. Thank you for keeping this a secret."

"I'm starved. We should be halfway home by now," Joe announced. "I'm really sorry, Eva."

Eva smiled more sincerely this time.

"Thanks, Joe."

Violet hugged Eva one more time.

"I'll see you tomorrow. We will bring something to add to the meal."

"Goodbye, Violet. See you tomorrow."

"Bye, Frank. Goodbye, Teddy, See ya, Peter," Joe called as he headed down the back steps.

Violet said much the same thing and followed her brother.

"I'm looking forward to beating you at checkers tomorrow," Daniel teased Teddy. "And if I win, I'm going to play against Eva. She's so smart that she might beat me." He grinned at Eva.

Eva returned the grin, saying, "I might just do that."

"You can warm up playing with me tonight," Peter suggested. "Teddy isn't a very good winner." He frowned at his brother.

"We can do that if you help me clean up after supper," Eva promised.

"I will."

"Well, I'd best get going, Joe and Violet are probably out of town by now. Goodbye to you all," Daniel said with a little wave as he stepped out the door.

"Goodbye, Daniel!" the four Remingtons called in unison.

Frank shut the door behind Daniel.

"Smells like your cake is about done, sis," he said, sniffing the air.

"Oh, my! I nearly forgot!" Eva exclaimed. She wiped her eyes and grabbed a towel to keep her hands from burning.

"I'll get it out," Frank offered. He took the towel and removed the cake from the cook stove.

"It's perfect," Eva announced after testing it. "Papa should be home any minute now. Oh, I need to go hide this letter! Teddy, Peter, would you please set the table?"

"Sure," Teddy instantly replied. "You get the plates and silver, Pete."

Eva dashed out of the kitchen, colliding with her father.

"Whoa, where's the fire?" Harold asked, steadying her.

"Papa! I didn't hear you come in. I just have to put something in my room. Supper is nearly ready." Eva pulled away from him and hurried the rest of the way to her room.

Now that Joy was gone, Eva had the bedroom all to herself. It was where she missed her sister the most, but it was also where she could go if she wanted to be alone.

~ 146 ~

"Where should I put it?" Eva wondered aloud, tapping the envelope on her cheek. "I suppose it doesn't really matter since no one ever comes in here, except Violet when she visits me."

Eva decided that the bottom of her hope chest was the perfect place.

"Quite suitable really," she muttered. "I'll probably never go to college, just as I'll probably never get married. I should call this my 'hope*less* chest' or 'the chest of lost hopes'. It's filled with dreams that will never come true."

Chapter 26

In God we Trust

~*~*~

The next morning Eva was up bright and early. She donned her green Sunday dress and braided her hair, tying it with a ribbon to match. She had breakfast made by the time the boys were ready.

Harold wanted to stay with Rose that morning so the four Remington children headed off to church on their own. Eva and Peter led the way, Frank and Teddy lagged behind.

It was a dry and hot September. The sun was just starting to peek up over the prairie grasses. Eva was glad that she had decided not to bring her shawl, as she didn't want to be sweaty when they arrived at the church building. The boys had all rolled up their shirt sleeves, agreeing that it was a very warm morning.

Reverend Lewis was greeting people in his usual place at the top of the church steps. Eva and her brothers stepped into line behind the others entering the building and waited patiently as those in front of them greeted the reverend.

"Good morning, children," said Paul Lewis when the Remingtons reached the top step. "I see that your father decided to stay home today."

"Yes, sir," replied Eva. "Mama doesn't do very well in this warm weather."

"We are having an Indian summer, aren't we?"

"Yes, sir."

"I'm sorry to hear that your mother isn't well. If it makes you feel better, my wife and I pray for your mother every day."

"Thank you, Reverend Lewis. We do appreciate that," Frank said.

The Remingtons moved inside to let the others behind them enter.

Once everyone was seated, Reverend Lewis went up to the pulpit to begin the service. After singing a hymn, the reverend opened his Bible.

"Trust in the Lord, and do good; so shalt thou dwell in the land, and verily thou shalt be fed. Psalm thirty-seven, three.

"There is one line, one word, more specifically I want you to concentrate on today. Trust in the Lord. *Trust.* Today I will be reading several different verses from the Bible about trust. Please listen carefully and take these verses to heart. Speaking of hearts, that makes me think of my favorite verse about trust - which I know by heart. 'Trust in the Lord with all thine heart; and lean not unto thine own understanding'. Proverbs three, five.

"Trust. What does that word mean? I read this out of the dictionary. Trust is the firm belief in the reliability, truth, ability, or strength of someone or something. Now, don't you believe that God is reliable? Truthful? Has the ability and strength to do all things? Therefore, is He not worthy of our trust? We can trust God.

"As for people. Yes, we do put our trust in people but are often let down. People *can be* reliable, truthful. But people are sinful. God is holy. People can try to do what they promise, but because of sin, are often unable to keep their promises. Haven't we all broken a promise? Doesn't it make you feel terrible when you break a promise? Or even worse, when someone breaks a promise they made to you? But, doesn't it feel good to know that God will never *ever* break a promise He made? Psalms one eighteen, eight says, 'It is better to trust the Lord than to put confidence in man. We can trust God.

"I'm not trying to make you feel guilty for past times when you may have let someone down. If I have made you feel that way, I am truly sorry. I'm just trying to make a point that while we can't fully put our trust in humans, we *can* put it in our great God - just like the verse in Psalms says. I hope you understand."

The congregation nodded.

Smiling, Reverend Lewis continued.

"When can we trust God? Well, we can and should always trust Him, of course. But I especially like this verse from Psalms, 'What time I am afraid, I will trust in Thee.' When we are afraid is a very good time to place our trust in God. But we need to remember to trust God all the time, not just when we are afraid. Just as we ought to pray on the good days as well as the bad ones - if you remember that from last week."

The congregation nodded again.

Reverend Lewis flipped through his Bible.

"Ah, here's another good verse from Psalms. I just love the Psalms, don't you? 'In God I will praise His word, In God I have put my trust; I will not fear what flesh can do unto me.' See, if we place our trust in God, we have no reason to be afraid.

"Here's a verse I found in Nahum the other day. Now there's a book we don't visit very often. 'The Lord is good, a strong hold in the day of trouble, and He knoweth them that trust in Him.' What do you think of that verse? The Lord knows who trusts in Him. And those who don't. Here's another one from Psalms, 'And they that know thy name will put their trust in thee; for thou, Lord, hast not forsaken them that seek thee.' And another one, 'But I have trusted in thy mercy; my heart shall rejoice in thy salvation. I will sing unto the Lord, because He hath dealt bountifully with me.

"You see? If we place our trust in the Lord, He will not forsake us. He will give us great blessings.

"Now I hope that this sermon hasn't caused you to completely loose all faith in mankind. We can place our trust in humans - just not ultimately. Remember, we *can* trust God.

"I was trying to think of the perfect verse to end this sermon with. I'm sure that there might be one more suitable, but I do like this one. 'He that handleth a matter wisely shall find good; and whoso trusteth in the Lord, *happy* is he. Amen."

Chapter 27

Sunday Visitors

~*~*~

After the service, the Bakers left their wagon in the church yard and walked home with the Remingtons. Eva remained silent on the ten minute walk, contemplating the reverend's sermon. Two verses stuck in the mind. The one that said to trust in the Lord with all thine heart, and the one that said it was better to trust the Lord than put our confidence in man.

Eva had learned from Joy that the latter verse was certainly accurate.

Violet noticed Eva's silence but didn't mention it.

Harold was waiting by the gate of the Remington house.

"Good morning, Michael and Ellen," he called. "Come right on into the parlor. I have coffee ready."

"Thank you, Harold," Mrs. Baker said, giving him a quick hug. "How is Rose this morning?"

"Not very well, I'm afraid. She doesn't do well in the heat."

"That's too bad. Is it all right if I go say hello to her?"

"I'm sure that she would enjoy that very much. Go right on in."

"I'll be in the kitchen in a couple of minutes to help you with dinner, girls," Mrs. Baker said to Eva, Violet, and Mary.

Eva nodded and led Violet and Mary into the kitchen.

"Come on, Teddy. Let's play that game of checkers," Daniel said as the boys followed the girls inside the house.

"The board is ready and waiting," replied Teddy.

"Are you feeling well?" Violet asked Eva once they were out of earshot. "You were awfully quiet on the way home."

Mary looked at Eva with concern but didn't speak.

"I'm fine. I was just thinking about Reverend Lewis's sermon."

"Oh, yes. I was very interested myself. I suppose that we do often put our trust in people we shouldn't. I hope that I don't ever let you down in any way."

Eva smiled at her friend.

"You haven't so far."

"And we've been friends for a very long time," Violet replied.

"And we will be best friends until we die," Eva declared.

"Now there's a promise you'd better not break," Violet responded with a sly grin.

~*~

"Knock, knock."

Rose smiled as she saw Ellen Baker standing in the doorway of her bedroom.

"Ellen, how wonderful to see you. Please, come in."

"Hello, Rose. Harold tells me that you aren't feeling too well today." Ellen sat in the chair next to the bed.

"I feel better just seeing your pleasant face. But he is right; I don't feel very well."

"I'm honored by your compliment. Is it the weather that makes you ill? Do you know why?"

Rose shook her head.

"No. Midwife Stevens suggested that perhaps the heat in the air makes me feel feverish, and that may be partly true. But I think there's more to it."

"Such as?"

"I don't know for sure. I think it's the dry air." Rose waved her hand about. "The dust. It makes my throat dry, and then I cough a lot." As if on cue, Rose felt her throat choke up. She buried her face in the crook of her arm to cover the coughing fit.

Ellen leaned forward and rubbed Rose's back.

"Are you all right, dear?"

Rose nodded from behind her arm.

"I'm fine."

"So, if you feel this bad when the air is dry, are you better when it's raining?" Ellen asked.

"Yes. Funny how that works, isn't it?"

"It's too bad there isn't a place where it rains all the time or has cool, damp air, I mean. Then you could move…"

"No," Rose said, shaking her head determinedly. "Even if there was a place I knew of, I couldn't ask Harold to move. Not just for my sake."

"But you are the most important person in Harold's life. Don't you think he would do it for you?"

Rose smiled softly.

"Yes, he would. But I can't ask him to leave his job. I know how much he enjoys the mill work. And the people here, I would miss all of you terribly. Although I suppose that I don't see anyone very often. It's the children I'm most worried about. I certainly can't uproot them from the only home they remember. All of their friends. Can you imagine if we separated Eva and Violet?"

Ellen chuckled.

"That would be tragic, wouldn't it? I know that it would be hard for your family - and mine as well - but don't you think that you regaining your heath would be worth it?"

"No," Rose said softly. "My family means the world to me. God has led me and Harold here. To a place where we could be happy - despite the hardships…" Rose trailed off for a moment as she thought of her two lost children. "…And surrounded by wonderful friends." Rose smiled at Ellen. "Every cough, every hour I lie here in weakness, is worth it. Worth the knowledge that Eva is filled with joy each time she sees your Violet. Seeing the strong bond my older two boys have formed with yours. Even Peter is close to them, despite their age difference. And Frank, he's falling in love with Sarah Quant from what Teddy tells me. And I do believe that Teddy is falling in love himself. I can't take them away from the ones they're meant to be with. And I believe that there is a young man out there waiting for Eva to get a little older."

Ellen chuckled. "No doubt there is."

"So you see why I can't ask Harold to leave?"

Ellen nodded. She rose from her chair and bent over to give Rose a kiss on her pale cheek.

"I do understand, dear. And I think that you are the most wonderful wife and mother that anyone could ask for."

Chapter 28

Time for Fun

~*~*~

The three girls had most of the meal prepared by the time Mrs. Baker entered the kitchen.

"Sorry I was gone longer than I had said I would be. I was having a lovely conversation with your mother."

"That's all right, Mrs. Baker. We have everything under control. I know how much Mama enjoys your company. She always says once you leave that she hopes you'll come again soon."

"How nice of her," Mrs. Baker said, smiling.

Mary and Violet began carrying dishes to the table. Eva removed three loaves of bread from their pans, and Mrs. Baker began slicing them.

Teddy and Daniel entered the kitchen.

"Game over already?" Mrs. Baker asked.

"Yep," responded Teddy glumly.

Daniel was grinning.

"That was fast. Who won?" Eva asked, although she had a good guess.

"I did!" Teddy said brightly.

"Huh?" Eva was confused.

Daniel and Teddy both laughed.

"We knew that would work!" Teddy exclaimed through his laughter. "We purposefully acted that way so that you would think Daniel had won."

Mrs. Baker chuckled. "You had me fooled."

"You boys are so silly," Violet said with a giggle.

"Childish is a better word," said Eva, although she was grinning at the boys attempt at humor.

Mary just smiled.

"Well, I must say, Daniel, you're not a sore loser," Eva told him as she began scooping potatoes into a bowl.

Daniel smiled lopsidedly at her.

"I hope you're not either, Eva Remington. You didn't forget our game after dinner, did you?"

"No, and you certainly are confident of yourself, Daniel Baker," Eva replied, waving her spoon at him.

"Everything is ready, Eva," Violet announced.

"Good. Will you call the others in here for me?"

Violet nodded and went to the doorway of the parlor.

"Dinner is ready!"

Joe, Peter, Frank, Samuel - the youngest Baker son - and Michael came into the kitchen, with Harold bringing up the rear. All of the men were saying how wonderful the food smelt and how hungry they were.

After a pleasant meal - which the younger children enjoyed on the back porch due to lack of chairs - the women cleaned up the kitchen while Harold brewed a pot of coffee.

"Ready for our game, Eva?" Daniel asked her as they followed the other young people into the parlor. The adults were drinking their coffee in the kitchen. Mary had stayed with them.

"As ready as you are," responded Eva. "You should know that I beat Peter last night."

Daniel chuckled and turned to Peter who was sitting cross-legged on the floor with Samuel. "Looks like your winning streak is over, huh, pal?"

"Just temporarily," Peter replied, glaring at Eva.

Everyone else in the room laughed.

Eva sat down at the checker table, and Daniel sat across from her.

"Ladies first," he said gallantly.

Eva smiled at him.

"That's not what Peter said last night when we started. Aren't you a gentleman?" She moved one of her pieces.

"I try," Daniel said jokingly.

"Joe and I are going out," Frank spoke.

"Can I come?" Teddy immediately asked.

"No," said Frank firmly.

"Where's 'out'?" Eva questioned. Frank usually told her exactly where he was going.

"Just out," Frank replied, his cheeks turning slightly red.

"Out to see Sarah Quant," Teddy said teasingly.

"Am not!" Frank's blush deepened.

"Are too! Otherwise you wouldn't be so insistent on me not going."

"Teddy, enough!" Eva exclaimed. "If Frank wants to go without you, let him and be a good sport about it. You wouldn't want him tagging along if you were going to see your girl, would you?"

"Don't gotta girl," Teddy muttered, but Eva didn't miss him dart a glance in Violet's direction. "But you're right, Eva. Sorry, Frank. I won't bother you anymore."

"Thanks, Ted. And Sarah Quant is *not* my girl."

"Not yet," Teddy muttered as Frank closed the door behind him.

Eva shook her head and groaned, but there was a smile on her face.

"Your turn."

Eva turned her attention back to the board.

"Sorry, Daniel."

"That's all right. I thought you handled the matter quite well."

"Why, thank you," Eva said, slightly embarrassed.

Teddy walked over and stared down at the checkerboard.

"Well, Eva I would give you some advice, but I'm not sure if you want any or not. So I'll just watch if you don't mind."

"Not at all. What advice were you going to give me?"

"That one there," Teddy said, pointing.

"This one?" Eva asked, moving the piece.

Teddy nodded.

Daniel raised an eyebrow at her.

"Are you sure you want to do that?"

His look caused Eva to hesitate.

"Just ignore him," Teddy told her, waving his hand at Daniel. "He keeps trying to fool me with that same look. Making me second guess every perfectly good move."

"Your turn, Daniel."

Daniel shrugged. "Don't say I didn't warn you." He made his move, capturing two of Eva's men.

Eva turned to glare at Teddy.

Teddy held his hands, palms out, in defense.

"Sorry, I told you not to take my advice. From now on, I'll just watch." Teddy retrieved a stool and placed it next to the table.

Eva took her next turn and glanced at Violet sitting alone on the sofa.

"Are you terribly bored over there by yourself?" Eva asked.

Violet smiled.

"No, I watching. It's quite amusing really."

Teddy jerked his thumb over his shoulder at Violet.

"She thinks I'm amusing. How 'bout that?"

Eva smiled and shook her head.

"Unbelievable," she said sarcastically.

Daniel snickered.

"Actually, I meant Sam and Peter," Violet teased.

Everyone looked at the ten year old boys, playing with wooden soldiers.

"Very interesting," Teddy said, rubbing his chin. "That pretend war doesn't even look very exciting."

"We're on a scouting mission," Samuel hissed.

"Oh." Teddy shrugged and returned his attention to the checker game. By that time Daniel had seven pieces left and Eva had six.

"You're a lot better than I thought you'd be," Daniel admitted. "Oh, I hope I didn't hurt your feelings by saying that. It's not because you're a girl."

Eva smiled.

"No offense taken. You probably think I don't have much time for fun, and you're right. But I believe that - even with all of my responsibilities - I should spend quality time with my family. Playing games with my brothers is just as important as making dinner."

"Not quite," Teddy protested.

"Maybe that was a bad example," Eva said with a chuckle. "But I think you understand what I mean."

"Yes, I do," replied Daniel. "It's good that you make time for fun. It's your turn again."

Eva glanced at the board.

"Daniel! You jumped me again! I think that you are purposely distracting me by making conversation."

"Sorry, I didn't mean to. I'll stop taking now, I promise."

"Thank you."

"I'll just smile at you instead." Daniel placed his elbows on the edge of the table and rested his chin on his hands, a slow grin spreading across his face.

Eva giggled.

"Oh, Daniel, you are quite impossible sometimes."

"Why thank you. That is the nicest compliment I've received all day. It's still your turn."

"And you're still talking,"

Eva was about to move one piece - which would have been that piece's last move - when she saw a better option. She took one of her two kings and jumped not one, not two, but three of Daniel's men.

"Hey!" Daniel exclaimed. "When did you get so sneaky?"

"I learned from you," Eva said, laughing.

Daniel studied the board. He now only had four men to fight against Eva's five. His were clustered in one corner. Every move he could make would end up with him losing at least one checker.

"I think you've got me trapped," he admitted.

"Do you give up?" Eva asked.

"No, you still have a good game," Teddy insisted.

"I surrender," Daniel said. He removed a hankie from his pocket and waved it in the air.

Eva giggled, as did Violet from the sofa.

"Do you want to play, Violet?" Teddy asked.

"No, I was never very good."

"Yes, you boys can play again. I want to talk to Violet for a while," Eva said.

"I've had enough checkers for now," Daniel declared. "How 'bout you and me go get some fresh air, Ted?"

"Sure. You little fellows want to tag along?"

"Yes!" Peter and Samuel both exclaimed. They leapt up, instantly forgetting about their soldiers and raced out the front door.

"Do you want to go into your room to talk?" Violet asked once the boys had left.

"Sure." Eva led the way, closing the door once Violet was inside.

"So what was that you were going to tell me yesterday?" Violet immediately questioned.

"You sure do get right to the point, don't you?" Eva said, grinning.

"Sorry. It's just that my parents want to leave by four so that only gives us about a half an hour to talk."

"All right, then. I'll try to be brief." Eva poured out her fears of never getting married and her newly added disappointment of not being able to go off to college.

Violet sat next to Eva on the bed, patiently listening.

"I think," she began once Eva had finished, "that it is needless for us to worry. God has everything planned out for our lives. One day, when the right time comes, He'll make a way so that you can become married and, possibly, even go to school."

"But what if God doesn't have it in His plans for me to marry? Don't you think that's why Joy eloped? She probably felt the same way I do."

"But look at what happened to Joy because she tried to take matters into her own hands. I certainly wouldn't want that to happen to you."

"Don't worry, Violet. I'd never elope."

"I'm sure Joy would have said the same thing. But I won't worry if you won't."

Eva smiled at her friend.

"Oh, Violet. That sounds exactly like something you'd say."

Violet laughed. "It should. I do believe it is me talking."

Eva joined in her laughter.

Once the girls had calmed down, Violet gently touched Eva's arm.

"You just need to have faith and be patient. Trust in God, just like Reverend Lewis said in his sermon today."

Eva nodded. "I know. I was thinking about that on the way home. Oh, that reminds me, I was going to write down that one verse and put it in a place where I can see it often. That way it will be a reminder to me."

"That is a wonderful idea!" Violet exclaimed, beaming. "Which verse?"

"Proverbs three, five."

"Trust in the Lord with all thine heart..?"

Eva nodded.

"I like that one, too. I shall also write it down when I get home, along with those verses from first Corinthians thirteen that I like."

Eva rose from the bed and went to her dresser to see if she had any paper. After briefly riffling through the contents of the top drawer, she remembered that she had recently used the last piece she had had in her room.

"There's some in the kitchen. I'll be right back," Eva told Violet.

Violet nodded, fingering the quilt on Eva's bed.

The adults were now talking in the parlor. Mary smiled at Eva as she walked through the room. The others didn't notice her.

Eva found the last piece of paper in the house along with a pen and ink. She sat down at the table and began carefully writing out the passage, using her best penmanship.

"Whatcha doin'?"

Eva startled, not having heard anyone enter. The pen slipped from her fingers. Ink spilled out of the pen, causing the words to run together.

"Oh, man. I'm sorry, Eva. I didn't mean to scare you," Daniel said. He grabbed a rag from a pile on the floor and helped her clean up the ink. "I'm real sorry."

"I thought you had gone out with Teddy, Peter, and Samuel," Eva said as she held the paper up so Daniel could wipe up the ink from underneath it.

"I came back to see if my parents were ready to leave. It's about that time. So what were you writing down? I'm sorry I spoiled it."

"It wasn't your fault. Not directly anyway. I was writing one of the verses Reverend Lewis used in his sermon today as a reminder for me."

"That's a clever idea. Which one?"

"Trust in the Lord with all thine heart, and lean not unto thine own understanding."

"Looks like you have it memorized already," Daniel said with a grin. "That's the one from Proverbs, right?"

"Yes. Three, five," Eva said with a nod.

"Children, time to go!" Mr. Baker called from the parlor.

"Looks like I'm leaving," Daniel said, almost reluctantly. "See ya later, Eva. I'm sorry again."

"Goodbye, Daniel. And don't worry about it."

Giving her a little wave, Daniel walked into the parlor. Eva was almost certain she heard him mumble, "Proverbs three, five."

Chapter 29

Holidays

~*~*~

The Indian summer ended abruptly when a blizzard hit in the middle of October. Rose's health improved, and Eva began to wonder if it was indeed the weather that caused her mother's illness to improve or decline. Eva wished that there was something she could do about it.

~*~

There was a good three feet of fresh snow on the ground when Eva woke up Thanksgiving morning. The Remingtons had been invited to the Baker's house for dinner. But with the new snow added to the two feet previously on the ground - not to mention the drifts - Eva figured that the trip wasn't going to happen.

Sure enough, when Harold came out of his bedroom shortly after Eva began breakfast, he announced with great disappointment that they would be eating Thanksgiving dinner at home.

"You mother isn't doing very well this morning, anyway. I wouldn't want to risk her catching a cold or fever."

Eva silently nodded as she cracked eggs into a bowl. Even though she was saddened that she couldn't be with her friend that day, she knew that even something as simple as a cold could possibly kill her mother.

"We still have plenty of things to be thankful for," Harold said in an effort to cheer her up. "Such as wood for the fire and lots of food."

"I know, Papa," Eva murmured. She beat the egg yolks with a fork and poured them into a pan to scramble. The eggs were ones they had bought from the Bakers. Either Violet or one of her brothers brought some into town to sell every so many days. The Bakers always sold eggs directly to the Remingtons so that they wouldn't have to pay the extra pennies Luke added to the price once they were in his store.

"Happy Thanksgiving!" Peter called loudly, entering the kitchen. "I can't wait to go to the Baker's today so that I can play with Sam."

"Sorry, son. We won't be able to go. Have you looked outside?" Harold asked.

Peter's eyes lost their sparkle when his father said that they wouldn't be going, but they lit back up when he heard the question.

"I sure did! I can't wait to go and play in all of that snow!"

Both Harold and Eva chuckled.

"Sorry, little brother," Eva said. "The snow is the reason we won't be going. We don't want Mama to get sick."

"Can't we ask God to take it back?" Peter asked with a frown. "He can return it tomorrow if there's too much up in heaven."

"I don't know if there's any snow in heaven," Eva told him with a laugh. "And God can't take the snow back. Well, I guess He could if He wanted to, but I don't think that's ever happened before."

By that time Frank and Teddy had arrived and were standing in the doorway, snickering.

"Breakfast ready, sis?" Frank asked. "Or are we going to find a way to melt all of this snow?"

"Ha, ha," Eva said sarcastically. "Wash up and set yourselves down." She scooped the eggs out of the pan and into a dish. She had also made sausage, and there were biscuits leftover from dinner the previous day.

The boys were washed and waiting in their seats by the time she was finished setting the table.

"I know we usually do this at dinner time," Harold began once they had blessed the food. "But I'm going to see if any of our neighbors need help after we eat, and I might not be back in time. So I want us all to say what we're thankful for right now."

"All right, Papa. That's a good idea," Eva said. "But this year, since we're changing one thing already, could we do it in your bedroom so that Mama can be there also?"

Harold smiled at her.

"Of course we can. We certainly don't want your mama to be left out of holiday traditions, do we?"

The children all shook their heads.

So once the family was through eating, they filed into the bedroom.

"Well, well," Rose said with a smile. "Isn't this a pleasant surprise? What are you all up to?"

"Papa suggested that we say what we are thankful for at breakfast instead of dinner in case he wasn't back from helping people yet. And it was Eva's idea to come in here so we can share them with you," explained Peter.

"How thoughtful," Rose said. "Peter, why don't you go first?"

"Hmm, let's see. I'm thankful for my friends, and all of you, and new wooden horse Frank made me for my birthday."

"That's all very nice. How about you, Frank?" Rose looked at her oldest son.

"My family, of course, and my friends... just like Pete said. And..." Frank's cheeks tinted red.

"Sarah Quant?" Teddy pressed. He never seemed to tire of teasing about his older brother's crush.

"...Her too," Frank admitted. "But I was going to say... oh, never mind."

"I'll go next," Teddy volunteered. "I'm thankful for the friendship that I have with Daniel and the other Bakers. I'm thankful for the snow, even though it means we can't go visit the Bakers, because Mama is usually better when it snows."

"Aw, Teddy, that's very sweet," Rose said, touching her heart.

"You already know what I'm thankful for," Harold spoke up. "All of you. And also my good job at the mill and a safe place for us to live."

"How about you, Eva?" Rose turned to her daughter.

"I'm thankful for..." Eva began. Suddenly what she had said several years ago flashed into her mind. *"I'm thankful for all of my family, but I'm especially thankful for Joy. You're always there when I need you, Joy. You're someone I completely trust."*

~*~

Christmas arrived before Eva knew it. She had a hard time getting into the holiday spirit, however. This was their first Christmas without Joy.

Since there weren't many trees growing on the prairie - let alone pines - the townsfolk decided to share a tree that year. A group of teenage boys found a good sized tree about a mile up river and hauled it back to town in Mr. Baker's wagon. Once there, the tree was placed in the schoolyard. It was to be decorated on Christmas Eve.

Eva was greatly disappointed that she couldn't be in the Christmas program that year. Not that anyone had told her she couldn't. But it was enough for her to keep up with her lessons, and she didn't need anything extra to learn. She had, however, volunteered to bake three cakes for the tree decorating party. It wasn't much, but at least she was involved in some way.

The big day finally arrived. Eva was up early that morning. First she made sure that all of her gifts were wrapped properly. Satisfied that they were after several minutes of careful examination, she slipped into the kitchen to start on breakfast. She decided that oatmeal would have to do since she wanted to have plenty of time to make her cakes. They were to be perfect.

Teddy was the first one to enter the kitchen.

"Oh, boy! You're making the cakes! Can I help?"

Eva was slightly surprised by the offer, although she knew that Teddy did enjoy helping in the kitchen.

"Sure. Just eat some oatmeal first. It's on the stove."

Teddy helped himself, adding some molasses for sweetening. He made quick work of the hot cereal.

"All righty, Eva. I'm ready to help," he said, placing his bowl in the wash basin.

"Wonderful. I'm mixing the batter for each cake separately because they're all different kinds, but I want to bake them all at once. It will save time that way. Could you start mixing the ingredients for the next cake? I already have the first one done."

Teddy nodded. He asked how much of each ingredient he needed, and Eva showed him where she had written down the recipe.

Frank and Peter entered the kitchen. Eva and Teddy called good morning to them.

"Where's Papa?" Eva asked.

"In his room, talking to Mama," Frank informed her. "He said he'll be out in a couple of minutes."

Eva nodded and turned back to her cake batter.

Frank and Peter both scooped some oatmeal and sat down to eat.

"I'm going to put cherries on the one that you're making, Teddy, because I thought that that would look quite festive," Eva said as they both stirred their mixtures. "But I can't think of anything green I could use."

"Hmm…" Teddy rubbed his chin thoughtfully.

"Um, Teddy. There's flour on your chin," Eva giggled.

Teddy laughed and wiped it off.

"That batter looks perfect if you want to pour it into this pan," Eva said, pushing the pan in his direction.

Teddy carefully poured the batter out of the bowl. Eva was also done with hers. Soon all three cakes were in the oven.

"I'll check on them in about half an hour," Eva told her brother. "Thank you so much for helping."

"You're welcome. I enjoyed it. I can help decorate them, right?"

"Sure thing."

"Good morning, children! Merry Christmas Eve!" Harold greeted them cheerfully.

"Good morning, Papa," came the unanimous response.

"Merry Christmas, *Eva*," Frank teased, nudging Eva as he passed her on his way to take care of his dirty dishes.

Eva rolled her eyes. Frank said that every year. Apparently, it never got old.

The day flew by. Before Eva knew it, the Remington family was bundled up and walking down to the school house. Eva, Teddy, and Rose each carried a cake. Eva was pleased that her mother was well enough to come. Christmas seemed to be the one occasion that she insisted on going out and joining in on the festivities. Harold had been somewhat reluctant in letting her go. But after Rose had promised that she would only stay for the children's program, he relented.

The weather was surprisingly pleasant. The air wasn't very chilly, and it hadn't snowed in a couple of days.

Once they arrived at the school, the three cakes were placed on one of the table that had been set up in the school yard. Eva was quite pleased of how they had turned out, as was Teddy. He had found some wintergreen berries growing along the Platte River. The bright red berries and green leaves were arranged skillfully on top of the chocolate flavored cake. Eva was amazed by her brother's decorating abilities.

"Merry Christmas, Eva!" Violet waved.

Eva waved back and hurried over to her friend.

"Oh, Eva. I'm so nervous. I'm afraid that I'll mess up my recitation," Violet cried, grasping Eva's hands.

"You'll do just fine, Violet. You've never messed up before."

"But I always had you right next to me before."

"I'll be sitting right behind you so you can see me when you're standing up front. Just look right at me, and ignore all the others."

Violet nodded, but Eva could see that there was still fear in her friend's eyes.

"Hello, Eva. My, isn't that a pretty dress? Did you make it yourself?" Mrs. Baker asked.

"Yes. Well, this is actually a dress I've had for a while. I just added this black trim to make it look new."

"Very thrifty of you, Eva," complimented Mrs. Baker.

"Thank you, Mrs. Baker," Eva said with a smile.

Mr. Wessington announced that the program was about to begin. Everyone began to file inside the school house.

The program went very well. Violet recited her piece perfectly. Peter spoke with his usual enthusiasm. Eva was proud of both her friend and brother.

Once the program was over, Harold left to take Rose home. The other Remingtons went outside for the tree decorating party with the rest of the town.

All of the school children had made decorations with the help of Fred Walters and Joshua Kline. There were wooden cutouts of trees, stars and crosses - all colorfully painted, strings of popcorn, and dried cranberries. Some of the women had made candles to place on the branches. And for the top of the tree was a giant golden star donated by Mr. Humphrey Smith himself, founder of Smithville. The decorating was to begin after a potluck supper.

Eva was quite excited. She was finally beginning to feel the Christmas spirit.

~*~

"Thank you for bringing me home, Harold. Now you go on back and enjoy the fun."

"Now, Rose, I can't leave you here alone on Christmas Eve," protested Harold as he helped his wife get comfortable in bed.

"I insist. I can't be the reason you miss out on the festivities."

"You're a very good reason."

Rose smiled. "Still, I want you to go. I'll be just fine here. We'll have all day tomorrow to be together."

"If you're sure," Harold said hesitantly.

"I'm *positive*," Rose replied firmly.

"Well..."

"Oh, go on with you!" Rose exclaimed with a laugh. "Just make sure you have twice as much fun to make up for me."

Harold chuckled. He leaned down to kiss her.

"You sure are a wonderful wife, Rose Remington. I'm blessed to have you."

"And I'm blessed to have you, you wonderful, thoughtful husband," Rose said, kissing him back.

Harold squeezed her hand and left to return to the party.

Rose smiled as she watched him go.

"Thank you, Lord, for my amazing family," she whispered. She closed her eyes and settled back into the pillows to get some sleep. She was almost asleep when she heard footsteps in the kitchen.

Rose's eyes popped open, and she pushed herself into a sitting position.

"Harold, is that you?" she called, although she was certain that she had heard the front door close. Perhaps he had come back for something.

As if whoever was in the kitchen had been startled by her shout, there was the sound of a stumble and something - perhaps a chair - falling over.

"Hello?" Rose called. "Who's there?"

Fear gripped her when no one answered.

Holding her breath, Rose listened, but heard no more sounds. It was as if the other person was also holding their breath, waiting for her to forget about them.

When all was quiet for a couple of minutes, Rose uneasily lay back down.

Suddenly there were two sharp bangs.

Rose flipped the covers back, preparing to leap out of bed. Then she heard retreating footsteps. Whoever had been there was gone.

Rose sat on the edge of the bed for a few minutes, contemplating going to the kitchen to see if anything was amiss. She decided not to. There wasn't anyone in Smithville she didn't trust. Whoever it was probably meant no harm. It was Christmas after all. A time of secrets. It may have even been one of her own children.

Still somewhat uneasy, despite her self-assurance that nothing was wrong, Rose settled back into bed and closed her eyes, ready for a good night's sleep.

Chapter 30

Christmas Morning Surprise

~*~*~

It was quite late when the Remingtons returned home. Everyone went straight to bed, tired from the long day and eager to wake up Christmas morning.

There was six inches of fresh snow on the ground when Eva woke up. She quickly gathered her gifts from under her bed - since there was no tree to put them under - and went out to the parlor. She was surprised to find her entire family already there.

"We've been waiting hours for you," teased Frank.

"You have not."

"You're right, we all just got up," Frank admitted. "Are all of those gifts for me? Eva, you really shouldn't have."

"Yes, they are, Frank," Eva decided to play along. "Unfortunately, they are all the same thing. I hope you need a dozen handkerchiefs." That wasn't really what was in the packages, but the small fib was worth the sour look Frank gave her.

Eva chuckled and handed him the one gift that really was for him. "Merry Christmas, Frank."

"Merry Christmas, sis," Frank replied, grinning crookedly at her.

Eva handed out the rest of her gifts and accepted the ones given to her.

Once all of the presents were opened, Eva announced that she was going to get dressed and then make breakfast.

"Good. I'm starved," Peter exclaimed.

"I'll help you with the meal," Rose offered.

"Are you sure, Mama?" Eva asked.

"Of course, I'm sure. It's been much too long since I've been in the kitchen."

"All right, then. I'll be ready in five minutes."

Harold helped Rose back to their room so that she could also dress. In a short while, mother and daughter were in the kitchen.

"I was going to make scones," Eva informed Rose.

"Good idea. I love those," Rose said, grinning at her daughter. In a short while, Rose was shifting flour into a bowl. "You know, Eva, I wish it could be like this all of the time. I missed so much. I always longed for a daughter I could teach how to bake and sew and such. Now here I'm ill most all of the time and you had to learn everything on your own - except for what Joy taught you. And she had to learn all of those things on her own."

"We can't change our situation, Mama. I'm just glad that I *am* able to help our family in the way that I do, although this *is* nice working with you. It just makes this moment even more precious since we don't have many like it."

Rose beamed at Eva and gave her a hug.

"What a sweet way of looking at it, darling. This is a very precious moment for me." Rose covered a cough before returning to her flour.

"Are you all right, Mama?" Eva asked with concern.

Rose could only nod as a round of fitful coughing began.

"Maybe you should sit down for a while," Eva suggested.

"No, I'll be fine. Some water would be good," Rose said once the coughing had subsided.

Eva rushed to fill a glass for her mother. As she handed it to Rose, something caught Eva's attention out of the corner of her eye. She turned to get a better look. There was something hanging on the wall to the left of the back door. A wooden rectangle with letters carved into it.

"Now where did that come from?" Eva mused, moving closer to get a better look. Her eyes widened when she saw what the plaque read.

"What's that?" Rose asked from the table.

Eva ran her fingers along the smooth edge of the piece. "It's beautiful," she muttered.

Rose came up behind her and peered over Eva's shoulder.

"Proverbs three, five," Rose said, reading the verse. "That's always been one of my favorites. How long has this been here?"

Eva shrugged.

"I don't know. It's the first time I've noticed it."

"I bet whoever was here last night put it up," Rose said. "Oh, it all makes sense now."

Eva looked at her mother in surprise.

"Someone was here last night? You know that I don't believe in St. Nicholas anymore, right, Mama?"

Rose laughed.

"No, that's not what I meant." Rose explained about the noises she had heard. "The two bangs I heard must have been the person pounding in the nail to hold this up."

"Makes sense," Eva agreed with a nod.

"But I can't tell you who it was," Rose admitted. "One of your brothers perhaps?"

Eva smiled.

"I think I know who it was, Mama."

~*~

Eva walked briskly down the road west out of town. The Remington family had just finished their Christmas dinner, and Eva decided that it was the perfect time to go visit the Bakers.

There was the sound of a buggy behind her. Eva glanced over her shoulder and saw that it was Paul and Katie Lewis.

"Well, if it isn't Miss Eva Remington," the reverend called, halting his horse. "Merry Christmas! Would you like a ride?"

"Merry Christmas, Reverend Lewis, Mrs. Lewis. I would enjoy a ride very much."

"Hop on in, then. Going to the Baker's house?"

Eva laughed as she climbed into the buggy.

"I'm quite predictable, aren't I? Yes, that's where I'm going."

"We were going to stop there ourselves. Making our Christmas visiting rounds," Mrs. Lewis explained.

It was only ten more minutes to the Baker's farm. Eva thanked the Lewises and rushed to the barn where she knew she could find who she was looking for.

"Daniel!" Eva shouted.

Daniel was at the top of the haystack in the mow, gripping the rope in his hand. Even though he was going on fifteen, he still enjoyed swinging from time to time.

"Hello, Eva! Merry Christmas!" Daniel waved to her with his free hand. He pushed off, clinging to the rope as it flew across the expanse of the barn. Once the swinging slowed, he dropped to the ground and walked over to her.

"To what do I own this pleasant surprise?" he asked, grinning at her. "Aren't you here to see Violet?"

"I'm going to say hello to her in a while, but I actually came to thank you."

"For what?" Daniel asked as though he was confused, but Eva could see the glitter in his eyes.

"The plaque - with the Bible verse on it. It's lovely."

"Aww, shucks. I figured it was the least I could do since I ruined the one you were making."

"You didn't ruin it. And you could have simply bought me a new piece of paper. It is a truly thoughtful gift. I shall treasure it always."

"Aww, shucks," Daniel said again. "It was nothing."

"It certainly is something!" Eva declared. "You must have spent hours making it! Such fine craftsmanship! I didn't know you were so talented."

"Well, gee, thanks, Eva. Turns out I'm not too talented at being sneaky, though. I'm afraid I scared your mother half to death last night. I snuck away from the party to put it up, but I didn't know your mother was there."

"Yes, she told me about that."

Daniel blushed.

"But she understands now."

"That's good." Daniel grinned at her. "Hey, do you want to take a swing?"

"Sure! It's been a while." Eva scrambled up the haystack, and Daniel swung the rope to her. Eva had just launched herself when Violet entered the barn.

"Hello, Eva!" she called with a wave. "Mrs. Lewis said that they gave you a ride here. I've been looking for you."

"I was going to find you in a minute," Eva yelled as she swung back and forth. "But I had to come and thank Daniel first."

"For what?" Violet asked, turning her head from side to side as she watched Eva swing.

"The beautiful gift he made me. Didn't he show you?"

"No, but he has been very secretive about something the past couple of months. What is it?"

"Daniel! Can you please stop me?" Eva called. "All of this yelling and swinging is making me dizzy."

Daniel caught hold of the rope and slowed it to a stop.

"Thank you," Eva told him, straightening out her skirts as she released the rope. She explained about the plaque to Violet, going on about the fine job Daniel had done.

Embarrassed by the praise, Daniel shoved his hands in his pockets, trying not to blush.

"I'll have to look at it the next time I come over," Violet promised. "Gee, all he gave me for Christmas was a handful of penny candy."

"It's hard to know what to get for your sister," Daniel protested with a shrug. "I only did it for Eva because I ruined her other one."

"Nothing's wrong with candy," Eva said, smiling at him. "At least you can eat it."

Daniel grinned at her.

"I wasn't complaining about the candy," Violet insisted. "In fact, why don't we going enjoy some right now?"

"Fine with me," Eva said. "But first, I brought each of you a gift." She extracted two small packages from her pocket.

"Really? You have something for me?" Daniel asked in surprise.

"Well, I just grabbed it before I left," Eva admitted. "I felt that I should give you something in return for the plaque."

"Aww, you don't have to give me anything," Daniel protested.

"I insist," Eva said, pressing it into his hands.

Daniel accepted it.

"I suppose that boys don't really like pretty things," Eva spoke as he opened it. "But I thought you might like it. It's a shell that my mama found back when she lived in Boston. She had a whole collection. She gave each of us one once, and I'd like for you to have mine."

"Wow, Eva, this must be really special to you. Are you sure you want me to have it?"

"Positive."

"Thank you very much. I'll promise I won't break it."

Eva and Violet laughed.

"Come on, let's go get some candy now," Violet suggested.

Eva grabbed her friend's hand and they ran down the hill together with Daniel right behind them.

This has turned out to be a good Christmas after all, Eva told herself. She had thought it would be a lot harder without Joy. But just because Joy wasn't in their lives anymore, didn't mean that there couldn't be any joy. Some unexpected - but pleasant - things had happened that Christmas, and Eva was happy.

Chapter 31

Brotherly Bonding

~*~*~

Time passed. Life went on.

Summer of eighteen forty-nine was quite hot. Eva spent every spare moment with her mother, trying her best to keep the fevers down. Unfortunately, Eva wasn't a very good nurse. At least, that's what she thought.

Midwife Stevens had given Eva different herbs to help, but Eva felt she must be using them wrong, for nothing seemed to help Rose.

Eva feared that this would be her mother's last summer.

~*~

Late August, Daniel Baker stopped by the Remington house. Eva hadn't seen much of the Bakers all summer since she didn't seem to have free time anymore. She had even stopped going to church to stay with her mother. Violet - and sometimes her brothers - came by occasionally but said that they didn't want to be a bother to her. Eva had assured her friends that they weren't a bother, but she did appreciate that they were being considerate - even though she missed having company.

"Morning, Eva," Daniel greeted her. "How have you been?"

Eva smiled tiredly.

"I'm getting by. I just wish that there was something I could do to help Mama that would actually work."

"This must be terribly hard on you, but you're a strong girl, Eva Remington. You'll find a way to help your mother eventually."

"Thanks for believing in me, Daniel. Are you here to see Teddy?"

"Yeah, I was going to ask him if he wanted to camp out in our barn tonight. If that's all right with you."

Eva chuckled. "I'm sure he'd like that. And you don't have to get my permission. Teddy is nearly two years older than me."

"I know. I just thought there might be some reason you wouldn't want him to be gone tonight. Where is Teddy?"

"In the loft. And thank you for valuing my opinion."

"Any time, ma'am," Daniel replied, tipping his hat playfully. He strutted towards the ladder leading to the loft.

Shaking her head, Eva giggled as she watched him go.

~*~

Later that evening, Teddy and Daniel lay in beds of straw in the second story of the Baker's barn. They had just finished taking turns swinging on the rope. They could have gone on for another hour, but it had grown dark. And they decided that it was dangerous to continue.

"You know something, Ted?"

"Yeah?"

"Even though I have two brothers, I think of you as my brother."

Teddy propped himself up on his elbow and looked at his friend.

"Well, sure, pal. I feel the same way about you. I mean, we've known each other most all of our lives. We fit into each other's families real swell like. Our families our pretty similar if you think about it. We both have two brothers and two sisters. Well, I guess I *used* to have two sisters." Teddy sighed. "I still miss Joy, even though she's been gone for over a year. Is that wrong?"

"No," Daniel replied. "Of course not. I know that if I lost either of my sisters, I would miss them for the rest of my life."

"I suppose you're right. I still miss Johnny, even though I barely remember him. Sometimes I even forget about him. Is *that* wrong?"

Daniel shrugged, causing the straw around his shoulders to shift away.

"I don't know, Ted. I guess I never really thought about it. How old were you when he died?"

"About six, I'd guess."

"You were pretty young. That was almost nine years ago. I'd say that it's all right if you forget about him sometimes, just so long as you don't completely."

"Makes sense," Teddy agreed. He lay back down.

There were several moments of silence as both boys lay deep in thought.

"Hey, Dan? Can I tell you a secret?"

"'Course."

Teddy propped himself up again.

"I like Violet."

"Everybody likes Violet," Daniel murmured.

"You know what I mean. I *like* her. A lot."

Daniel popped his right eye open and looked at his friend.

"Well, I've known that for quite some time. You're not very good at hiding your feelings."

"Then you must know that it's just as obvious that you like Eva."

"What!" Daniel exclaimed, sitting up. "What are you talking about?"

Teddy snickered.

"Oh, come *on*, Dan. It's written all over your face every time you look at her."

"Do you think she knows?" Daniel asked, running a hand through his hair.

"She might. And don't you want her to know?"

Daniel raised an eyebrow at his friend.

"Do *you* want Violet to know?"

Teddy's cheeks turned crimson.

"'Course not. Not yet, anyway."

"See?" Daniel buried his face in his hands. "Oh, we're a couple of hopeless fools. I'll bet both girls know how we feel."

"You sure can say that again!"

"We're a couple of hopeless fools," Daniel obliged.

Both boys burst into laughter, rolling around in the straw. When they sat up and saw what a mess they were, they cracked up again.

"You look like a scarecrow!" Teddy cried, pointing at Daniel's head.

"You look like a scarier scarecrow!" Daniel shot back.

It took a while for the boys to settle down.

~ 179 ~

"Ya know, Dan?" Teddy spoke once they were lying quietly again.

"Yeah, Ted?"

"If you married Eva... and I married Violet, we really would be brothers."

"Yeah," Daniel agreed, smiling into the darkness. "Twice over."

Chapter 32

Birthday Party

~*~*~

Eva began her eighth and final year of school with both enthusiasm and disappointment. She knew that all life outside of home would end along with school. While other girls would start courting, she would begin full-time care of her family. She had seen what that had done to Joy and was determined not to let it happen to her. Only time could tell, however. Joy had probably never imagined she would turn out the way she had.

~*~

Late October was Violet's birthday. A week before, Violet invited all of the school children over to her house for a party.

"It's going to be a very grown-up party," Violet told Eva on the walk home. "Papa is going to play his fiddle so we'll have music to dance to. Wouldn't that be something, Eva? If we danced with boys?"

"That's all there is to dance with, I suppose," Eva replied, smiling at her friend's excited chatter. "Unless we dance with each other."

Violet giggled.

"Remember, we did that at the Christmas party last year? We must have looked so silly."

"But we had fun."

"Yes, we sure did. You are coming to my party, aren't you?"

Eva laughed.

"Violet! You already asked me that a hundred times. And I already told you; I wouldn't miss it for anything."

Violet also laughed.

"Sorry, Eva I'm just so excited."

"*Really*?" Eva said sarcastically. She nudged her friend playfully. "I understand. I'm excited, too. Well, looks like we've reached my house. See you on Monday."

"I sure wish you could come to church again," Violet said, touching Eva's shoulder.

Eva sighed.

"So do I. But Mama needs me whenever I'm not at school. Well, she's needs me even more often than that. I know that she wants me to keep going to church, but that just isn't practical for me right now. And if I stay, that means Papa can go. I think Mama understands that. Besides it's not as though I'm pushing God out of my life. Every morning I read the Bible to Mama, and we pray together. Sometimes, though, I wonder if God doesn't answer prayer."

"Why, Eva, what do you mean?"

"Every day, when I pray with Mama and before bed, I ask Him to heal Mama of her illness. But she's just as sick she's always been. I know that God hears my prayer. Sometimes it seems as though He doesn't care enough to answer them."

"Eva, you know that isn't true."

"I know, but it feels that way sometimes."

"I understand that, Eva. You just have to put your faith in Him and trust that He has a plan for you and your mother."

"I do trust that, Violet. But it sure would be nice if He would hurry up a bit. I never told this to anyone, but I thought Mama was going to die this summer."

"Oh, Eva!" Violet brought a hand to her cheek. "Was she really *that* bad?"

Eva nodded grimly.

Violet pulled Eva into a warm embrace.

"Oh, you poor darling! I can't believe you lived under that pressure all summer! I should have been there more for you. I just thought that you wouldn't want me in the way because you had so much to do."

"That's all right, Violet. I completely understand."

"What I *should* have done was spend *more* time with you. I could have helped you with your responsibilities."

"That's very thoughtful of you, Violet. But I know you have plenty of chores to do at home."

Violet shrugged. "But I still had plenty of time for my best and dearest friend. I promise that next summer I will come by nearly every day to help you."

"I'll hold you to that," Eva said with a grin. "Now I'd better get inside and check on Mama."

"Of course. I shouldn't have been holding you up."

"Not your fault. And besides, you helped me feel better."

"That's what friends are for!" Violet called as she continued on home.

~*~

The next Saturday, Eva donned her best green dress and carefully tied her hair back with a matching ribbon. Eva liked green best for her dresses since the color brought out her eyes.

Frank, Teddy, and Peter had also been invited to the party. Frank, however, declined the invitation, saying he had made previous arrangements. Everyone knew he was going to spend the day with Sarah Quant, even though he hadn't said. So Eva walked to the Baker farm with her other two brothers.

Several of the other children from town joined them, making the walk quite lively as they chattered in excitement about the party.

The seven Bakers were waiting on the front porch when the guests arrived. Violet and the boys rushed to greet their friends while Mary and her parents remained on the porch, smiling at the children.

After greeting the others, Violet found Eva and grasped her hands.

"Oh, Eva, I'm so glad that you could come!"

Eva laughed.

"I told you I would."

"I know, but I was afraid that your mama might have a bad spell or something, and you wouldn't be able to make it."

Eva gave Violet's hands a little shake.

"Oh, Violet! You know how my mother is! Even if she was feeling terrible, she'd still make sure I wouldn't miss your thirteenth birthday party!"

"I suppose not!" Violet agreed with a laugh. "Come on, everyone! There's food inside."

The children rushed into the house.

"Hello, Mr. and Mrs. Baker," Eva said as she climbed the front steps. "Hello, Mary."

Mr. Baker grinned.

"I thought I told you to call me Michael, little lady."

"Sorry. I guess I forgot... Michael."

"That's better."

"How are you, Eva dear?" Mrs. Baker asked.

"Fine, ma'am."

"And your mother?"

Eva was accustomed to people asking after her mother.

"She's doing much better now that the weather is cooler again."

"Of course. We did have a dreadfully hot summer, didn't we?"

"Yes, ma'am."

"Well, I'll let you run along and get your food now, dear. I'm glad that you mother is feeling better."

"Thank you, Mrs. Baker. I'll see you later." Eva went in though the front door and stood in line behind the other children.

"I sure hope there's some food left by the time we get to the front," Thomas Crews joked from his place just in front of her.

"Yes, indeed," agreed Eva.

The line moved quickly. Although most of the food had been picked clean by the time those in the end of the line reached it, there was still plenty. Eva heaped her plate full.

While they ate their food sitting out on the lawn, Michael tuned up his fiddle.

"You children all ready to dance?" he called once the fiddle was perfectly tuned.

"Yes!" came the unanimous response. The children rushed to put their dishes inside the house where Mary and Mrs. Baker were washing them as fast as possible to avoid buildup.

Mr. Baker began playing a lively tune, and the young people grasped hands and began whirling about.

Eva and Violet danced with each other for a while; Emma and Grace Kline joined their circle. And the four girls giggled uncontrollably as they spun about.

Mr. Baker slid the bow across the strings one last time to end the song. The children all applauded him loudly.

"Did you all like that one?" Michael asked. "It sure looked like you were having fun. Ready for some more?" The response was positive, and Michael began another song.

Emma and Grace both left to get a drink of water. Eva and Violet watched as the others began dancing again.

"It is fun to dance together," Eva said. "But I kinda wish some boys would ask us. Then I'd feel really grown up."

"Me too," Violet agreed.

"Wish granted," Daniel said, stepping up to his sister. He held out his hand. "May I have this dance?"

Teddy approached Eva.

"Eva, will you dance with me?" he asked.

"Well, Teddy. How nice of you to offer, but maybe I don't want to dance with my brother," Eva said slyly.

Teddy winked at her and then Violet.

"I think I can solve that problem." Teddy grasped both of Daniel's upper arms and moved him so that he stood in front of Eva. He then was in front of Violet. "Miss Baker, may I have this dance?" Teddy asked, bowing gallantly.

Violet giggled.

"Oh, Teddy. You're so silly. Of course you may." Violet took his hand and let him lead her a short distance away.

Daniel looked at Eva and winked.

"Looks like I'm stuck dancing with you."

"Very funny, Daniel. You two had that all planned out before you even came over here."

Shrugging, Daniel said, "Maybe we did; maybe we didn't."

"I'll dance with you anyway," Eva said with a heavy sigh, as though it would be quite a task to dance with him.

"I should hope so," Daniel replied. Eva felt a thrill run up her arm when he told hold of her hand. "Teddy and I missed out on fishing to be here today. It's worth getting dressed up if I can dance with you."

Eva shook her head, laughing.

"Well, Daniel Baker! I'm glad to know that I come one step higher than fishing on your list of priorities!"

Chapter 33

A Town in Flames

~*~*~

Time passed. Life went on.

The next summer was even warmer than the previous one. It hadn't rained since the end of May, and August was nearly over.

Frank was lying in bed, unable to sleep because of the humidity of the loft. He was amazed that both Teddy and Peter were sleeping.

Thoughts of Sarah Quant entered his mind. It seemed as though she was always on his mind lately. Frank had turned seventeen that year. He planned on asking Sarah to marry him one day soon. He just had to figure out when. It had to be the perfect time. When everything was just right. He would have to ask her father for his blessing first, however.

Oh, if only I could work up the nerve.

Frank told himself that it shouldn't be too hard. He and Sarah had been courting seriously for over a year now. He was certain that she loved him as much as he loved her. She shouldn't say no.

But what if her father does?

But Frank knew that Glenn Quant liked him very much and had even mention once that he would make a good husband for Sarah.

Peter shifted his position in the middle of the bed. Frank had wished a long time ago that the boys each had their own beds - especially on hot nights such as this one - but in the winter he didn't mind. Peter was a nice little heater; his skin was never cold to the touch - even in winter.

Suddenly, there was the loud clanging of church bells. All three boys sat upright abruptly. That could only mean one thing.

Fire.

The brothers leapt out of bed and raced for the ladder. Peter reached it first and nearly missed the first three rungs.

Harold, Rose, and Eva were all in the parlor, preparing to go outside.

"Where's the fire?" Teddy asked.

"I don't know," Harold replied, pulling his suspenders on over his shoulders. "Come on, boys, we need to go help."

Frank had thought to grab a pair of trousers on his way down, but neither of his brothers had. While Teddy and Peter went back up, Frank followed his father out the door.

Looking up the street, Frank caught his breath when he saw which house was ablaze.

"Sarah!" he shouted, racing towards the building. "Papa, it's the Quant's house!"

Harold was right behind his son.

There were already several men and boys tossing water onto the flames when father and son arrived. A couple of buckets were tossed in their direction, but Frank didn't pick his up. He needed to make sure that his Sarah was safe first.

Frank asked everyone he passed if they had seen Sarah, but most people were concentrating too much on putting out the fire to give him a straight answer.

"Sarah! Sarah!" Frank shouted over and over. He finally gave up his search amongst the crowd, deciding that she was trapped inside somewhere.

Frank raced towards the burning building.

"Hey, son! You can't go in there!" Joshua Kline grabbed him by the arm, pulling him back.

"But Sarah's in there!" Frank cried desperately. "I've got to go get her!"

"Do you know that for sure?" Mr. Kline asked with concern.

"Well, no, but I haven't seen her out here."

"I saw Glenn and Ruth over there with some of their younger children a minute ago. Why don't you ask them before you foolishly go headfirst into a burning building?"

"Yes, sir." Frank dodged through the crowd until he came to where the Quants were huddled, watching their home burn.

"Mr. Quant!"

Glenn Quant looked in Frank's direction.

"Oh, Frank! Have you seen Sarah?"

"No, I was going to ask you that!"

"We're not sure if she got out. She had gone to grab young Benjamin just after we were awakened by the smoke. We haven't seen her since."

Frank nodded and raced around to the back of the building. He knew that Mr. Kline hadn't actually meant that he should go inside if Sarah wasn't out yet. But his worry for Sarah was greater than his fear for his own life.

Frank was just about to enter the house when he noticed some blankets hanging out on the line.

Just because I'm running headfirst into a building, doesn't mean I have to do it foolishly, Frank told himself. He grabbed a blanket from the line and dropped it into a barrel of drinking water. He wrapped the blanket around his shoulders and plunged inside the burning building.

~*~

Rose joined a small group of women watching the men fight off the flames.

Martha Black shrieked in horror when she saw a blaze lick out at a neighboring house.

"I've said before that building these houses so close together is not wise. When one catches on fire, it spreads more quickly," Rose commented.

Jacob Henning must have heard her, because he rounded up some teenage boys. And they began wetting down the neighboring houses.

"Oh, Lord, please help us," Rose whispered a prayer.

~*~

Frank was grateful at that moment that all of the mill worker's houses were identical. Even though the building was thick with smoke, he moved about as if he was in his own home.

There was a coughing sound from somewhere in the kitchen.

"Sarah?" Frank called.

"Here," came the weak reply.

Frank crawled along the floor and found Sarah hiding under the table.

"Frank!" she cried in surprise. "You came here for me? I can't beli..." A rasping cough cut off her sentence.

"Of course I came for you, Sarah. I love you. Now let's get you out of here before you suffocate."

"I can't leave yet, Frank! Benjamin is still inside!"

"I'll come back for him!" Frank promised.

"No, Frank. I can't let you risk your life again."

"Let's just get you out, and then we'll worry about Benjamin."

Sarah nodded and let him drag her out from under the table. Frank wrapped the blanket around her and helped her out the door.

"Sarah! Oh, Sarah!" Ruth Quant exclaimed when Frank carried Sarah over to her family. "Frank, you saved our daughter!"

Glenn shook Frank's soot-covered hand.

"You're a good boy, Frank. How can we ever thank you?"

"By letting me marry her," Frank replied half teasingly.

"You certainly proved that you love her tonight. You have my blessing," Mr. Quant declared.

Sarah blushed when she heard this.

Frank was shocked. *Well, that was easier than I had thought it would be.*

The burning building let out a groan.

"Mama! Papa! Benjamin is still inside!" Sarah screamed.

Ruth fainted in her husband's arms, and Glenn nearly dropped her as he looked frantically towards the house, hoping to see his two year old son.

The other six Quant children huddled near Sarah as some men dropped their buckets to search for the boy.

"Fire!" the shout came again. This time, however, the young boy who called was pointing to a house across the street.

The women deserted their places at the sidelines, grabbed anything that would hold water, and joined in the fight.

The search for young Benjamin persisted while the rest of the townsfolk continued to toss water on the seemingly unquenchable fire.

Frank had decided with the men looking for Benjamin, he would be more useful filling up buckets. He positioned himself by the nearest well and began filling up the empty pails tossed in his direction and handing them to the next person in the fire brigade.

The flames continued to spread. Houses on both sides of the Quant's and the one across the street were burning.

Women screamed as they watched their homes engulf in flames.

"The well is drying up!" Frank yelled, terror edging his voice.

"The whole town will burn down!" Martha Black cried insanely.

"God save us!" a woman exclaimed.

As soon as the words left her mouth, the skies opened, and rain came pouring down.

"Hurray!"

"God be praised!"

"Thank the Lord!"

Cries of joy filled the air.

Frank whispered his own prayer of thanks.

In a matter of minutes, the last flames sizzled and were gone.

The Quant's house now mostly consisted of a pile of charcoal, and the others were past repair. But the fire was no longer spreading. At the moment, that was enough to be thankful for.

Frank found Sarah and embraced her tightly. She clung to him as tears streamed down her face.

"Oh, Frank!" she cried. "I was so frightened... and then you were there... You saved me, Frank darling. You saved my life!"

Frank ran his hand along her rumpled hair, trying his best to soothe her.

"I'm glad I could do it, sweet Sarah - with God's help. For yours is truly a life worth saving."

~*~

Benjamin's funeral was held that afternoon. He had been found under an iron bed frame, suffocated by smoke. Frank would miss the little fellow, whom he had become quite fond of.

Chapter 34
Needless Worries

~*~*~

On the second day of September, in the year eighteen fifty, Eva sent Peter off too school by himself for the first time. Peter, being his outgoing self, was not at all nervous. He was now the oldest pupil in the entire school and quite proud of that fact.

"Me and Angelina are the oldest now," Peter had said before he left. "Isn't that special?"

Eva knew that Peter had had a crush on Angelina for the longest time. She also knew that Thomas Crews was in love with Angelina. Poor Peter would have his heart broken someday in the future.

Now, alone in the parlor, Eva wondered what she should do. She had become so accustomed to doing her household chores around school hours that she had rushed through cleaning up after breakfast. Of course, in the summer she didn't have to work around school, but that was when her mother needed more attention.

Rose had been doing well ever since the fire. Eva guessed that was because it had been raining non-stop, and the air was cool and moist.

Looking out the front window, Eva saw Michael Baker coming into town on his wagon.

Eva hadn't seen Violet in several days. And now that neither of them were in school, she wouldn't be seeing her friend very often anymore.

Swinging open the front door, Eva waved to Mr. Baker.

"Good morning, Eva!" Mr. Baker called, halting his team.

Eva raced down the path and rested her hands on the whitewashed gate.

"Good morning, Michael. How are you?"

"Dandy, just dandy. And yourself?"

"Just dandy," Eva replied with a grin. "Is it Violet's turn to bring the eggs into town this week?"

"Well, actually it is Samuel's turn. But I suppose you'd like to see Violet, wouldn't you?"

Eva nodded eagerly.

"I could have Violet trade this Friday with Sam. Would that be all right."

"Yes," Eva agreed. "Oh, wait a minute. That wouldn't work. I'm going to do a big house cleaning on that day."

"I'm sure Violet wouldn't mind helping you."

"I know she wouldn't. But I want her to come over so that we can have a pleasant visit - not a working one. Could she come Saturday instead?"

"I suppose that could work," Mr. Baker said, rubbing his chin thoughtfully. "I could still have Samuel come on Friday then. We don't sell eggs every day because we like to keep plenty for ourselves - as you know - but sometimes we have a lot more than we need. Yep, that should work if Sam comes Friday, and Violet comes Saturday. I'll tell her when I get home."

"Thank you, Michael. I hope that's not too much trouble for you. I mean, Violet doesn't even have to bring eggs to come into town, does she? Couldn't she just come for a visit? Won't you need those eggs?"

"Like I said, sometimes we have more than we can eat. And, of course, Violet can come into town without eggs to sell. But we could use the extra money anyway. Well, I'd best get along to Luke's Mercantile; Ellen has a nice long list of supplies for me to pick up."

"I'll let you go then. See you later, Michael."

"So long," Mr. Baker said with a wave as he signaled for his team to start walking again.

Eva went back into the house. Now she had something to look forward to.

"Mama, how are you doing?" Eva asked quietly, entering the dark bedroom.

"Kind of tired. Also a little hungry," Rose said. She was lying in the bed, running her fingers along the top of the comforter.

"What would you like to eat?"

"Is there any soup left from last night? And some of your delicious biscuits?"

"There certainly is. I'll bring some right in."

"And some water, too, if you would please, dear. My throat is quite dry."

Eva left to prepare a tray.

When she stepped out onto the back porch to retrieve water from the drinking barrel, Eva noticed a small cluster of Black-eyed Susans growing in the lawn.

Setting down the dipper, Eva moved down the steps and picked three of the flowers.

"These might help brighten Mama's day," she mused aloud.

Returning to the kitchen, Eva grabbed a jar and filled it with water. She then carefully arranged the food and flowers on a tray.

Rose smiled when Eva placed the tray on the bedside table.

"Flowers. How thoughtful, Eva. Thank you."

Eva smiled as she helped her mother into a sitting position.

"Do you want me to help you with the soup, or can you manage?"

"I'll be fine, dear. But I'd enjoy your company. That is, if you're not busy."

"Not right now, Mama. And besides, my main priority is looking after you."

"A girl your age should have different priorities," Rose said with a sad smile. "But I must say that I am proud of your attitude. You've taken all of these responsibilities with stride."

"Oh, Mama, I certainly wouldn't say that."

"I would. I must say that you are doing much better than Joy was when she was your age. I truly believe that keeping you in school helped."

"But Joy was also younger when she started caring for you," Eva protested. "I haven't even done it for three whole years yet."

Rose spooned some soup into her mouth. Once she swallowed, she spoke again.

"I have to admit that I'm slightly worried. Oh, I know this is silly, but you are just about one year younger than Joy was when she..."

"Eloped?" Eva finished.

Rose nodded.

"Mama, you know that I would never leave you."

"That's what I thought of Joy, too… It's terrible of me to think this, I know, but there's just this tiny little fear in the back of my mind."

Eva laid a hand over her mother's.

"You needn't worry about me, Mama. I have absolutely no reason to leave. I love my family so much, and I have such wonderful friends. Joy felt shunned by Marta and Willa because they gave up on her. Violet would never to that to me."

"I know, dear," Rose said, covering Eva's hand with her other one. "I don't mean to sound as though I doubt you. I'm sorry. I don't want my words to discourage you."

"They haven't, Mama. I promise. In fact, I do believe they made me feel stronger."

Chapter 35

And all was Still

~*~*~

That Saturday was the seventh of September.

Violet Baker woke at the crack of dawn. She wanted to spend as much time with her best friend as possible before she had to be home for the evening chores. She had done Samuel's morning chores the previous day so he was doing hers that morning.

The day was bright and clear; Violet only needed a light shawl to help fend off the cool morning breeze. She retrieved a basket from the kitchen and went out to gather the eggs.

The chickens squawked loudly when they saw her coming. Expecting grain, they rushed up to her and began pecking at the ground.

"Oh, you silly birds!" Violet laughed.

"'Morning, Violet!" Daniel called from the mow where he was forking hay down to the cows and horses. He had the barn door wide open, letting in the fresh morning air.

"Good morning, Daniel!" Violet replied.

"Say hello to Eva for me!"

"Will do!" Violet waved as she headed up the back porch to wash the eggs. She knew that Daniel liked her best friend. *If they get married when they grow up, Eva and I will be sisters!* she thought with excitement.

Ellen Baker stepped out onto the porch to get some water for coffee.

"Hello, Violet. All ready to go to town?"

"Yes, Mama. I'm so excited to spend the day with Eva. We have a lot of catching up to do."

"Well, have fun." Ellen went back inside then popped her head out the door. "Did you eat breakfast?"

"I have some bread and jelly."

"That's hardly enough. Why don't you drink a glass of milk first?"

"Yes, Mama." Violet followed her mother inside. She climbed down into the cold cellar where they kept the milk and other food that would spoil if it got warm. When she came back up, Samuel was in the kitchen.

"Hey, Violet. I gotta eat a big breakfast so that I can handle all off those extra chores this morning," Samuel teased.

"You weren't complaining yesterday morning when I did your chores," Violet replied. She grinned at her little brother. "Would you like some milk?"

"Sure. Pour me a big glass full...please."

Violet poured the milk and quickly downed her glass.

"I'll be going now," she told her mother.

"Be safe. I love you," Ellen said.

"Goodbye, Sam," Violet said as she walked out the back door, picking up the basket of eggs on the way.

"Bye, Vi," Samuel replied. Violet knew that he liked to say that because it rhymed.

Before heading out to the road, Violet stopped by the barn to say goodbye to the rest of her family.

Joe and her father were milking the cows. Mary was feeding the pigs. Daniel was still in the mow, forking hay.

"Goodbye, everyone! I'm leaving for town now," Violet called from the doorway.

"Goodbye, Violet!" replied the three in the lower level. Daniel hadn't heard her.

Violet waved but didn't get a response since everyone's hands were occupied.

Adjusting her shawl with one hand and carefully holding the basket of eggs in the other, Violet walked to the end of the drive and turned east towards town.

There were birds flitting about, chirping pleasantly. Violet knew that they would soon be heading south for winter. She would miss their cheerful songs, but she certainly wouldn't miss trying to scare the birds away from the wheat. It seemed as if the creatures thought that it was grown just for them to eat.

Closing her eyes for a moment, Violet listened to the sound of the breeze rippling through the long prairie grasses. It was a sound that she never tired of. It was extremely relaxing and often put her to sleep.

"But I can't sleep now," she reminded herself.

Violet began humming her own little tune. She picked up her pace a little and gently swung the basket in her right hand.

A white and gray rabbit darted across the road in front of her. Violet startled, nearly dropping the eggs.

Once she her heart slowed down, she laughed.

"Sorry, little guy. I probably scared you more than you scared me."

Violet began strolling along again. She softly sang *Amazing Grace*, for that was the first hymn that came to mind. It had always been her favorite.

When Violet ended the last verse, she realized that the birds had stopped chirping.

"Couldn't compete with me, huh?" she jokingly called out.

The prairie was silent.

Violet felt a chill run up her spine.

It was quiet.

Too quiet.

Even the breeze had died down.

Another rabbit ran across the road. This one nearly went over Violet's feet.

Violet clutched the bodice of her dress. She rubbed her fingers along the buttons, trying to relax.

She let out a nervous laugh and started on her way again.

But something didn't feel quite right.

Even the grasses were still.

The entire prairie was still.

Suddenly, there was a deep shadow cast across the land.

Violet turned around slowly.

Her eyes grew wide with horror.

A massive funnel cloud was ripping across the prairie. Headed straight for her.

The wind grew stronger as the twister came closer to Violet, who was frozen in fear.

She let out a shriek of terror.

The basket slowly slid from her fingers. It crashed to the ground.

On the prairie lay egg yolks and shattered shells.

Chapter 36

Sorrow

~*~*~

Eva and her family hunkered down in the cellar while they waited for the tornado to pass.

Eva prayed that the house would still be there when they opened the trap door. She was huddled next to her mother who had been carried into the cellar by her father. Eva thought that that must have been quite a challenge, carrying a person down a ladder.

Frank was leaning against a wall, listening intently to the howling of the wind above them. Peter sat on the floor, absentmindedly drawing pictures in the dirt. Teddy sat on a crate, bouncing his knee up and down and tapping his fingers on his knee.

Harold was halfway up the ladder, occasionally peeking out the trap door.

"I hope Violet's all right," Eva fretted. "She might have left for town before the tornado hit."

"I'm sure she's fine," Rose said, trying to sound comforting. "She's in the Lord's hands."

"I'll go with you to look for her once it's safe to go outside," Teddy promised. Eva could see that he was also quite concerned.

"I think that it's gone," Harold said. He moved higher up the ladder and listened for a minute. "I'm going to look around. Once I decide it's safe, I'll let you know so that you can come up."

"I'm coming with you," Frank said. He went to the bottom of the ladder, looking up at his father expectantly.

"You're a man now. Come on, Frank."

"Me too?" Teddy asked.

"Just wait a couple of minutes, Ted, all right?"

Teddy nodded, although he was obviously disappointed.

Eva and the others waited impatiently, listening to the footsteps above them.

"All right. You all can come on up!" Harold yelled.

Teddy helped Rose to her feet and up the ladder.

"See, Teddy, I needed you down there to help me," Rose said, trying to make him feel better. "You're just as much a man as Frank is. You have a kind and gentle heart."

Teddy managed a smile.

"No major damage down to the house," Harold told his family. "Now we should go and see who needs help."

"And find Violet," Eva added.

"Let's go," Teddy said. He grabbed Eva's arm and headed for the front door.

It seemed as if everyone in town was rushing about the streets.

Jacob Henning was running along, yelling, "Has anyone seen Angelina?"

"Oh, Teddy, Angelina's missing." Eva clutched Teddy's arm tightly. "I have a bad feeling about Violet."

Teddy sucked in his breath.

"Me too."

~*~

Teddy ran north of town towards the river. There were many people milling about, searching for Angelina Henning. Once Teddy informed them that Violet might have been headed to town when the twister hit, they promised to be on the lookout.

Teddy and Eva had split up in front of the school, deciding that it would be better so that they could cover more territory and tell more people. Teddy had run into Frank shortly after parting with Eva. Frank had promised to help look for Violet once he made sure Sarah and her family was safe.

When he reached the bank of the Little Platte River, Teddy paused to catch his breath. He wondered why he had even come this way. He should be looking along the road Violet would have taken. He didn't even remember deciding to go to the river. It was as if some strange force had pulled him there.

Perhaps God was leading him.

Teddy scratched his head, trying to decide if he should go upstream or down.

"Well, God. If you led me this far, I suppose you'll take me the rest of the way."

Closing his eyes, Teddy spun around a few times. When he stopped, he took a big step forward, saying, "This is the way I'm going."

Splash!

Teddy fell headfirst into the river.

Moaning, Teddy pushed himself up, shaking off the water.

"Well, *that* was foolish."

Teddy wiped his eyes and slowly opened them. There, about twenty feet upstream, lay a person.

A girl.

Violet.

"Violet!" Teddy screamed.

He splashed through the water, halting when he was just three feet away.

Violet lay sprawled out, her hair flowing out in the water. Her dress was ripped and missing the left sleeve. One leg was bent out awkwardly. Blood trickled from a cut on her head.

Teddy fell to his knees. The river was extremely rocky right there, but he didn't feel any pain - in his knees. His heart, however, felt as if it had been ripped from his chest.

Pulling Violet into his arms, Teddy pressed his cheek against her wet hair and let the tears fall freely.

"Violet! Oh, my sweet, Violet! I never got to tell you that I love you!"

~*~

Eva's tears seemed to be frozen in her eyes that afternoon. She stood trembling next to her family and the Bakers as they stared at the fresh grave before them.

Angelina Henning had been found safe and was standing alongside her parents. Eva was grateful that the girl had survived. A small part of her wondered why Violet hadn't. Was God trying to tell her something? How many of the people she loved would die before her?

Although she tried to listen to Reverend Lewis's words, Eva's mind was a whirlwind of emotions. She simply couldn't believe that she would never see her best friend again. Not on this earth, anyway.

Reverend Lewis began reading the verses from the beginning of the thirteenth chapter of first Corinthians. The ones about love. They had always been Violet's favorites. Eva could remember her quoting them many times.

"Love is patient, love is kind. It doth not envy, it doth not boast, it is not proud. It is not rude, it is not self-seeking, it is not easily angered, it keeps no records of wrongs. Love doth not delight in evil, but rejoices in the truth. It always protects, always trusts, always hopes, always perseveres. Love never fails."

When Reverend Lewis closed his Bible at the last verse, Eva fell against Frank who was nearest to her, unable to stand on her own any longer.

Frank squeezed her tight and kissed the top of her head.

On the other side of Frank stood Teddy. He was standing stiffly and had tried to plaster an emotionless look on his face, but Eva could see the tears sliding down his cheeks.

Teddy had been the one to find Violet. Eva couldn't imagine what that must have been like for him. She knew that he had loved Violet for a long time now, even though he had never actually said so. Eva wondered how - or if - he would even get over her.

Breaking free from Frank's arms, Eva moved closer to Teddy and gently took both of his hands. Even though she was still lost in her own grief, she felt that Teddy needed to be comforted more than her at the moment.

Teddy looked down at her and forced a sad smile. He eased his hands away from hers and shoved them in his pockets. Then he turned and slowly walked away.

Eva watched him go with depressed eyes.

A gentle hand rested on her shoulder.

Eva turned around and saw Daniel Baker standing there. His expression probably matched her own.

"Daniel!" Eva cried. She fell into his embrace. It seemed as though she was hugging everyone she encountered. "I'm so sorry for you. I can't even express how much."

Daniel rubbed her back and whispered, "Eva, you don't have to say anything. Violet was your very best friend. You're practically one of the family. I know you feel the same way I do."

"Maybe, but I suppose it must be sort of different. After all, she *was* your sister. Oh dear, it's so painful to speak of her in past tense."

"The last thing..." Daniel choked on his words, "I said to Violet was, 'tell Eva hello for me' and she said 'will do'. Looks like I beat her to you. That's the only promise she's ever broken."

Eva wiped her eyes and pulled out of his embrace.

"I don't even remember the last thing I said to her. 'Goodbye' I suppose." Eva sniffed.

"I guess it doesn't really matter," Daniel said, not wanting her to become obsessed trying to remember.

"No, I suppose it doesn't," Eva agreed with a sigh. Suddenly she gasped. "I just realized something horrible!"

"Try to forget it," Daniel suggested.

Eva shook her head.

"Violet was on her way to see me, on a day she normally wouldn't have come to town because I specifically requested. Don't you see, Daniel? Violet wouldn't have gotten swept away by the tornado if she hadn't been on her way to town. And she wouldn't have been on her way to town if I hadn't asked that she visit me. Violet is dead... because of me!"

Chapter 27

Visit from a Friend

~*~*~

With trembling hands, Eva prepared supper that night. Her earlier conversation with Daniel raced though her mind. She had practically killed her best friend. How could she ever live with herself? The only comfort she had was that Violet was now in heaven. Of that, Eva had no doubt.

Teddy hadn't come in to help her as he usually did so Eva began to set the table herself. She picked up a bowl of potatoes and started for the table. Her hands were shaking so much, however, that the bowl slipped from her fingers and crashed to the floor.

Frank dashed into the kitchen; Peter was right behind him.

"Are you all right?" Frank asked.

Eva stared blankly at the shattered china mixed in with the potatoes. She blinked a few times as tears began to fall.

"I'm sorry. I'm sorry!" she wailed, falling to her knees. She started to pick up the pieces. "I ruined our supper! I'm so sorry!"

"Eva, stop! You'll cut yourself!" Frank rushed to her side. He grasped her upper arms and pulled her to her feet. "I'll clean this up. You put the rest of the food on the table. On second thought, Peter will do it. You just sit down." He helped her to the nearest chair.

Peter quickly moved to do as his brother said.

Eva sat for a moment then stood up again.

"I'm not very hungry. I think I'll just go to bed," she said.

Frank looked at her with concern.

"Sure, Eva. If that's what you want to do. Pete and I will clean up after supper. You go on and get some rest." Frank hugged her tightly. "This has been a hard day."

Eva nodded and murmured something too quiet for anyone to hear. She pulled out of her brother's embrace and slowly walked to her room.

After closing the door behind her, Eva fell across the bed and let the tears fall freely. She didn't know how long she cried, but finally she must have run out of water, for her eyes began to dry. That was when her mind went wild. A million thoughts rushed through her, and a great feeling of guilt seized her conscience.

Old feelings arose - the ones she had felt after Johnny's death. Eva didn't try to stop those feelings. She knew - deep down inside - that she wasn't to blame for Violet's death. Not completely, anyway. But she made herself believe that she was for some reason - perhaps because it was safer to wallow in guilt than face the truth and move on with life.

Eva didn't want to move on. She wanted Violet to be alive again. She hated change. Why couldn't things stay the same?

~*~

A few days later Daniel came to visit Eva and Teddy. He found them both in the parlor. Eva was mending one of Frank's shirts, and Teddy was half-heartedly sharpening his pocket knife.

"Good morning, Eva, Teddy," he greeted them as cheerfully as he could.

"Mornin'" Teddy mumbled.

Eva didn't reply.

"Uh, mind if I sit down?" Daniel asked, gesturing to the empty space next to Eva on the sofa.

Eva shook her head ever so slightly.

Daniel sat down. He twiddled his thumbs as he looked at both of his good friends.

"I know," he began, "That you both miss Violet very much. I certainly do. After all, she was my sister. But I'm trying - the best I can - to move on and live my life as normal as possible. I can't stand to see you two the way you are. It breaks my heart. I know that we all have to take our own time to get through this in our own way. I'm still working on myself." Daniel paused for a moment and let out a small laugh. "I'll admit to you that I was asked to come here and talk to you. Frank stopped by the farm yesterday. He told me that the both of you

~ 206 ~

are… well, depressed. I thought up a whole speech on the way over here, but now that I'm here I've forgotten half of it. I hope what I said was enough to help. At least a little bit."

"Do you blame me?" Eva said quietly.

"For what?" Daniel asked, looking at her in surprise.

"For Violet's death. Remember, like I told you at the funeral?"

Daniel gently took her hand - the one that wasn't holding the needle - and looked her right in those bright green eyes.

"No, of course I don't blame you. Don't ever think such things. It's nobody's fault. God decided that it was time for Violet to be with Him so He took her. In a painful way, I must say. But we know that she's happy now. And she'd want us to be happy, too. Don't you think so?"

"I suppose." Eva withdrew her hand and continued working on her stitches.

The three of them sat in silence for several moments.

Having finished patching the hole, Eva knotted and snipped her thread. She shook to shirt out and let out a moan.

"What's the matter?" Daniel asked.

Eva showed him.

"I sewed the cuff of the sleeve together!" she cried in great annoyance. She threw the shirt on the floor and exclaimed, "I can't do anything right anymore!"

Daniel reached down and picked up the shirt. He pulled it on and held out his arms. Frank was taller than him so the sleeves were too long.

"Say! This is a right clever idea, Eva! Sew up the other sleeve and I won't have to wear any mittens!"

Eva smiled slightly and even let out a giggle.

"Don't be ridiculous, Daniel. Give that back so I can rip out those stitches."

Daniel slipped off the shirt and handed it to her.

"At least I got you to laugh," he said with a grin.

Eva concentrated on removing the stitches. It had been somewhat relieving to laugh. Suddenly, the sound of Violet's laugh echoed though her mind, and she became sad again.

Daniel noticed her changed expression but didn't say anything.

"Teddy," he said, turning to his friend, who hadn't spoken since Daniel had first come in.

"Hmm?"

"I know that Violet's death is especially hard on you. I remember that you told me you loved her."

"Love her, Daniel. I still love her, and I always will. There will never be another girl for me. Not ever."

Chapter 28

Mothering

~*~*~

Rose couldn't stand to see her children in the state they were in. The visit from Daniel a few days ago had seemed to help a little bit, but there was still a lot of sorrow that had to be worked through before her children were truly happy again.

Rose decided to have separate talks with both Eva and Teddy. She would do her best to offer words of comfort to help them get through these troubling times. At least that was one thing she could still do as a mother.

~*~

"Eva, your mother wants to see you," Harold announced one morning shortly before he was to leave for work.

"I'm in the middle of scrambling your eggs, Papa."

"I can do that." Harold took the spoon from her. "You go on; Mama's waiting."

Eva obediently went.

"Eva dear, come and sit by me," Rose invited, patting the bed.

"What did you want to see me about, Mama?" Eva asked as she sat. "Are you feeling well?"

"It is how *you* are feeling that I'm concerned about."

"Oh."

"I know, Eva, what's it's like to lose a good friend."

"Do you really, Mama?" Eva asked skeptically.

"I certainly do. When I was just a year younger than you, my best friend died of fever."

"I suppose you took it a lot better than I am."

"Now hold on there; I certainly wouldn't say that."

"But you don't seem like a person who lost their best friend."

Rose smiled sadly.

"Do I seem like a person who lost a son and a daughter?"

"No, I suppose not. How do you handle death so well?"

"Well, after Penny - my friend - died, I was just like you. I moped about, not wanting anything to do with anyone. I cried all the time, and I pushed away the people I loved, not letting them help me. But then I realized what a horrible life that was. I was afraid to love again because I was afraid that I would lose whoever I did."

Eva nodded, knowing exactly what her mother meant.

"I thought, what's the point of living if I do not love? So I started loving again. I opened myself up and made new friends."

"But I don't want new friends," Eva interrupted. "There will never be anyone else like Violet."

"That's true. I'm not asking you to replace Violet. Keep her in your heart and treasure the memories you have together. But also be willing to get out there and give other people a chance."

"How can I do that, Mama? I'm supposed to care for you."

Rose closed her eyes as she pondered the question. She hadn't considered this before sending for Eva.

"Well, I guess if you can't go out to make friends. You'll have to let them come to you."

"Who would want to be friends with me, Mama? Everybody knows my situation. No one wants to be friends with the girl stuck at home caring for her mother - except Violet. And even she was my friend long before I had to care for you."

"I think it's safe to say that all of the Bakers are your friends. That's a good start. Just be patient and trust that God will work this all out for good. That is another thing that helped me get through the loss of loved ones. Trusting God."

Eva pictured the plaque hanging on the kitchen wall in her mind. She hadn't paid it much attention lately, but she would give that verse more thought from now on.

"I think I'm beginning to understand now, Mama."

Rose smiled.

"I'm glad."

"Thanks for being the best mother ever." Eva stood and kissed Rose on the cheek. "I love you."

"I love you too, darling."

~*~

Teddy arrived home from work shortly before five. Ever since he had finished school, he had worked at Luke's Mercantile, stocking shelves.

"Mama wants to talk to you," Eva informed him.

"All right, I'll go right in." Teddy was surprised to notice a sense of peace in his sister.

"Hello, Teddy. How was work today?" Rose asked when she saw her son enter.

"Pretty terrible. Luke said he might have to let me go."

"Why?"

Teddy shrugged. "Probably because I keep knocking stuff down and forgetting to wait on customers."

"Because you're sad and miss Violet?"

"I guess so," Teddy muttered, shrugging again.

"You know that you can't live in your sorrow forever, don't you? I know it hurts to lose someone you love. Especially someone you love so deeply."

Teddy looked at his mother in shock.

"How do you know I love Violet?"

Rose smiled.

"It's easy for a mother to tell - even if she is stuck in bed all day. Over time you will find another sweet girl to love and make your wife."

Teddy shook his head adamantly.

"No, not me. There will never be another girl like Violet."

"She doesn't have to be like Violet, son. Maybe you'll meet some spirited girl with fiery red hair."

Teddy snorted.

"Well, maybe not," Rose admitted with a grin. "But I'm sure that God has someone out there waiting for you."

"I don't think so, Mama. I feel that if I would - if I ever could - fall in love with someone else, that it would be... I don't know, disloyal, to Violet somehow."

Rose shook her head.

"I don't think so, son. Violet wouldn't want you to live the rest of your life longing for her. She would want you to be happy."

Teddy managed a smile.

"That's what Daniel said."

"And he was right."

"I just don't know that I could be happy with someone else."

"You'll never know unless you open your heart and give someone a chance."

"I suppose you're right, Mama. What really bothers me though is that I'll never know whether or not Violet loved me."

"She did. You can be sure of that."

"How do you know, Mama?"

"As I said before, a mother knows these kinds of things."

Teddy raised an eyebrow incredulously.

"Even though you're not Violet's mother?"

Rose laughed.

"Of course. And I'm sure that Eva could also confirm Violet's feelings for you if you don't believe me."

Teddy patted Rose's hand.

"I believe you, Mama. Thanks for making me feel better. I suppose I've been an awful trial to you and the others these past days. I promise that I'll try harder to sort out my feelings."

"Good for you, Teddy. Just make sure you don't try too hard. We all have our own ways of getting through our sorrows. Be sure to do a lot of praying. And as I told Eva, trust that God will work this all out for good."

"I will." Teddy leaned down and kissed Rose's forehead. "I'd better go help Eva with supper now. I haven't been much help to her lately, I'm afraid."

"Go on then," Rose told him, smiling.

Teddy quietly closed the door on his way out. He found Eva in the kitchen.

"Supper's almost ready," she informed him.

"I'll set the table," Teddy offered.

Eva looked at him and smiled.

"Talking with Mama is good for the soul, isn't it?" she asked.

Teddy met her gaze and grinned.

"It sure is."

Chapter 39

A Wedding

~*~*~

Time passed. Life went on.

Eva peeked through the doors of the church and saw Frank nervously waiting up front with Joe Baker by his side.

"They're ready," she announced, turning to Sarah who was being escorted up the steps by her father.

"Oh dear me, the time has come at last. I'm so nervous and excited at the same time," Sarah whispered.

The spring day was perfect for a wedding. Eva was honored to be chosen as Sarah's bridesmaid, especially since Sarah had three sisters of her own. The two girls had become quite close during the time of Franks and Sarah's engagement. Sarah was the closest thing Eva had had to an older sister since Joy had left. Eva hadn't realized how much she had missed having that relationship.

Teddy and Peter each opened one of the church doors, and Mrs. Lewis began to play to organ.

Eva clutched her bouquet as she slowly began walking down the aisle. She felt eyes on her but kept her focus straight ahead. Even though Eva knew it wasn't her wedding, she decided to cherish the moment since she would probably never walk down the aisle as a bride.

Frank grinned briefly at her when she reached the front, then quickly turned his eyes onto his lovely bride.

Sarah was a perfect vision in white as she glided down the aisle on her father's arm. She was beaming at Frank who seemed to be frozen in awe of her.

Joe had to nudge Frank when father and daughter reached the alter.

Frank reached out to shake Glenn Quant's hand. Then he took Sarah's, and the couple turned to face Reverend Lewis.

"Dearly beloved, we are gathered here today to unite these two young people in holy matrimony."

Eva did her best to stand still and pay attention as Reverend Lewis preformed the ceremony. Her eyes wandered to the people seated in the pews. Her entire family sat in front on the right, and Sarah's family was behind her. The Bakers sat behind the Remingtons. Every time Eva glanced at Daniel, he was watching her.

He must be paying more attention to me than the bride and groom, she thought. *I wonder why. Probably because I'm so fidgety.*

Eva decided to ignore him.

Turning her attention back to the couple, Eva listened as they each recited their vows. It made her heart ache to know that she would never get to stand up here and promise to love and cherish someone for the rest of her life.

"I now pronounce you man and wife. Frank, you may kiss your bride."

Frank grinned as he took Sarah in his arms.

Eva wondered what it felt like to be kissed. She supposed she would never know.

The new Mr. and Mrs. Frank Remington started back up the aisle.

Joe offered his arm to Eva. He leaned down and whispered in her ear, "Daniel's jealous because I get to escort you."

Eva looked at him in confusion but didn't reply.

Everyone gathered out in the yard, congratulating the newlyweds. After heartily shaking his brother's hand, Teddy found Eva.

"Hey, sis. You did a great job up there."

Eva laughed. "Teddy, I didn't do anything."

"You just stood there and looked pretty. That's good enough. It's a good thing Joe was up there with Frank. I probably would have tripped on the walk out." Teddy had first been asked to be the best man, but he had politely declined.

"You sure do look pretty," Daniel agreed, coming up behind Teddy. He slapped his friend on the back. "And I've no doubt that you would have made a fool of yourself, Ted."

"Now that you two are here to keep Eva company, I'm going to find Natalie. If you don't mind," Joe said, scanning the crowd for his girl.

"Go on, Joe. Don't feel obliged to stay with me," Eva said.

"Thanks, Eva. You're swell." Joe kissed the top of her head and gave her a squeeze. Eva knew that he had always thought of her as a little sister, and he had grown even more protective of her after Violet had died.

"Are you going to dance with me later, Eva?" Daniel asked once his brother had left.

"If you want me to," replied Eva.

"I wouldn't have asked if I didn't want to." Daniel seemed surprised by her answer.

Eva smiled at him.

"Of course not. Sorry, I guess I'm feeling a bit melancholy."

"Why? This is a happy day."

"I know. It's just… Oh, never mind. I'd love to dance with you later."

Daniel beamed.

"That's what I wanted to hear! We shall dance every song together!"

"Now hold on there, pal!" Teddy protested, grabbing onto Daniel's shoulder. "I can't let you have the prettiest girl all to yourself. Save at least one dance for me, sis."

"I'm very flattered. Don't worry, you can each have half of my dances. I highly doubt anyone else will ask me anyway."

"That's fine with me," Daniel declared. "But I must say that anyone who doesn't want to dance with you is a blind fool."

Eva blushed.

"I'm going to see if Mama's still doing well. I'll see you two later," she said, glad for a reason to excuse herself. She wasn't used to such compliments and wasn't sure how to deal with them. She didn't think herself to be as pretty as they had implied. She knew that there were circles under her eyes, and her skin wasn't nearly as smooth and fair as the other girls.

Eva found her parents talking to Glenn and Ruth Quant.

"Ah, here's the lovely bridesmaid!" Harold announced.

Rose smiled at Eva and embraced her.

"You were a perfect bridesmaid, dear."

"Yes, indeed," Mrs. Quant agreed. "Your dress turned out beautifully."

"Thank you, ma'am," replied Eva politely. She turned back to her mother. "How are you feeling, Mama?"

"Wonderful! My oldest son has gotten married. Sure, I'm a little teary-eyed, but they're happy tears. Mostly."

Eva smiled and shook her head.

"You know what I mean, Mama."

Rose chuckled and patted Eva's arm.

"Yes, dear, I know. I honestly feel fine. Not tired at all. I think that the excitement of the day has made me feel quite energized."

"I'm glad to hear that."

"Why don't you go on and spend some time with people your own age, Eva?" Harold suggested.

"Yes, please do, Eva," agreed Rose. "This is one of those rare chances you have to be a "normal" young person. Go enjoy yourself, and don't even think about me."

"I'll try," Eva promised. She grinned at both of her parents. "I'll see you later." Eva strolled across the grass, wondering who she should find to talk to. She used to automatically look for Violet - not that her friend had even been far off.

Even though only close friends and relatives had been invited to the ceremony, the entire town was invited to celebrate with the couple afterwards. Eva said hello to Grace and Emma Kline but didn't stay for a conversation since she knew they were both shy. She passed behind Maria Henning and Adelaide Haynes. From what she briefly heard, Eva guessed that the two girls were coming up with a plan to get Thomas Crews to dance with Maria. Eva didn't even bother to say hello.

Feeling lonesome, Eva walked across the road and past the schoolhouse. Maybe a stroll along the river would help her feel better.

"Hey, Eva! Where are you goin'?"

Eva turned to see Daniel running towards her.

"The party's thataway," he said, pointing over his shoulder.

"I know," Eva said with a shrug. "I just wanted to be alone for a while. I miss Violet. She's the one I usually talk to during these rare occasions I'm out of the house."

"Oh, well, I can leave if you want to be alone," Daniel offered.

Eva could tell that he didn't really want to go. She was surprised to find that she also wanted him to stay.

"I was going to walk along the river until it's time to eat. You can come... if you want."

Daniel's eyes lit up.

"I'd love to! If you're sure, that is. I don't want to be a bother if you'd rather be alone."

"No, it's fine. I... I want you to come."

The two of them walked in silence. Eva was certain that he wasn't talking because he knew she wanted to enjoy a time of peace. She was surprised to find that walking with Daniel was quite peaceful. She felt a new sense of respect for him because of his thoughtfulness.

Chapter 40

Frank's Farm

~*~*~

Ever since he had finished school, Frank had been working for the Carvers. The Carver family owned several hundred acres and had a nice herd of cattle. Right from the beginning of his employment with the Carvers, the arrangement was that Frank would work for half salary, and the Carvers would give him fifty acres once he had worked there for five years. The Carvers were nice enough to give him the land a year before the wedding so that he could have a house and barn ready to bring his bride to.

Frank was quite proud of his home. Harold, Teddy, Joe, Daniel, Mr. Baker, Mr. Carver, and Carver' two sons had all helped him. Eva, Sarah, and Sarah's sisters and mother had come often in the weeks before the wedding to "make the house livable" Sarah had said. The women had brought quilts, curtains, pillows, doilies, flowers, and other such things.

Now, a week after the wedding, Frank was unhitching his mule after a long day of plowing. He planned on starting to plant corn the next day. He didn't want to go into the wheat business as most of the other farmers did. He didn't want that sense of obligation that came with any job wheat-related in Smithville. He had nothing against the wheat industry. He just wanted independence. The freedom to sell his crops to whomever he wished.

Frank put the mule into her stall and hung up the tack. He swept his gaze around the inside of the barn. There were four stalls on the south end. The mule in one, a milk cow in another, and two empty ones he hoped to have horses in eventually.

There was a stack of loose hay and also baled straw on the west end, near a small door. The main door opened to the east, facing the house. On the north side of the barn was a small pen intended for chickens. The wall to the right of the pen was covered with pegs for saddles, bridles, and other tack.

It wasn't a large barn, but it was enough for Frank. He could always add on or build a bigger one in the future.

Stepping outside, Frank took a deep breath of fresh air and stretched his arms. Sarah should have supper waiting for him by now. He started for the house.

Joe and Teddy had helped him whitewash the house. They had painted the shutters blue at Sarah's request. Frank had to admit that the blue gave the house a charming look. The womenfolk had planted flowers around the house. The daffodils and lilies were just starting to bloom, making it even more charming. Frank thought that the house looked its best, however, when his Sarah was standing on the porch, smiling at him as she was now.

"Supper's ready!" she called.

"I hoped it was," Frank said with a grin. He stopped at the middle step so he was the same height as her to give her a kiss.

Taking his hand, Sarah led him inside. The main room was large. When you walked in, the kitchen area was to the right, and the sitting area was to the left.

Frank followed his wife to the table, and they sat down to eat. Mr. Baker had helped him make the table. It was large enough to seat six. Frank hoped that one day there would be children to fill each of those chairs, and, perhaps, he'd have to build more.

That night Sarah had made biscuits and gravy with sausage. Sarah's cooking was fair, but it didn't hold a candle to Eva's. Frank never complained though. He didn't want to hurt her feelings. Sarah's mother had done most of the cooking in the Quant house while Sarah had taken care of the sewing and knitting and such. Frank figured, with time, she would improve.

Even though Frank was enjoying life out on the open prairie, he did miss his life back in town. He had moved to the farm a month before the wedding but went back home every day for the noon meal. Now Sarah prepared all of his meals, and he had no reason to go to town, except for church and to get supplies, which he hadn't needed to do yet.

Frank wondered how Eva was doing. He hadn't seen her since church last Sunday. He hoped that she and the rest of his family were doing well. He was certain that he would be notified if they weren't.

"You're awfully quiet tonight, Frank. Did you have a hard day?"

Frank glanced up from his food and smiled at his wife.

"Yes. Well, it was a long day, but I kept going. Because I knew that once the day is over, I can come home to you."

Sarah blushed as she smiled.

"That's a very sweet thing to say, darling. I look forward to when you're done working, too."

"I was just thinking. Could we stay in town for a while after church tomorrow and visit with my family?" Frank asked. "I'm sure Eva wouldn't mind making food for us."

"Oh. Well, I was just going to suggest to you that we invite your family over here to eat dinner with us tomorrow," Sarah said.

Frank was surprised.

"You really want to do that?"

Sarah laughed.

"Why not? They're just as much my family as they are yours. Well, you know what I mean. Why shouldn't I want them to come visit?"

"Would you be fine with cooking for all of those extra people?"

"Not a problem. Eva will probably want to help; wouldn't you say so?"

"I'm sure she would." *And maybe she could give you some pointers*, Frank added to himself as he bit into a dry biscuit. "But don't be disappointed if my ma can't come. And if she's not well, Pa probably won't come either."

"I know. I understand. If you would rather, we can go to their house if you want to see your mama."

Frank smiled.

"That's very thoughtful of you, dear. We'll see how Ma's feeling tomorrow and make our plans from there."

~*~

It turned out that Rose was quite weak the next day. Both she and Harold insisted, however, that the young people all go on to Frank's place and not worry about them.

So Teddy, Eva, and Peter walked home with their older brother and sister-in-law.

"What did you plan on making for dinner?" Eva asked as she walked alongside Sarah. "I'd be glad to help with whatever it is."

"Bread and stew. I know it's not much, but it's what I have the ingredients for. I'd be glad for your help" Sarah leaned over to whisper in Eva's ear. "Just between you and me, I'm not a very good cook. I think Frank has to force himself to eat my cooking."

"What are you two whispering about up there?" Frank called from behind them.

"Girl stuff," Sarah replied. "It's a secret."

"They're probably talking about us," Teddy said jokingly.

"You can tell by the way they're grinning," Frank agreed.

Sarah nudged Eva and winked. Both girls laughed.

Once they arrived at the house, Eva and Sarah set right to work in the kitchen. Eva showed her sister-in-law a few tricks she had learned for making bread and also the proper time to add different vegetables to the stew so that everything would cook thoroughly.

After the meal, Frank honestly announced that everything was delicious. Sarah strengthened her confidence in her cooking skills when Frank praised her after she told him that. While Eva had told her what to do, she had made everything by herself.

"Well, dear, even if we have stew and bread for the rest of our lives, I'll be happy if it tastes this good!" Frank declared.

Sarah laughed.

"I doubt you'll be thinking that after a week, darling, but we can give it a try! Eva, you really ought to teach me how to make other foods better. Would it be all right with you if I come over sometime this week?"

"Certainly! Drop by anytime. I love it when we spend time together." Eva was excited at the prospect of being with her sister-in-law more often. It was nice to have a girl close to her age to talk to. Sarah was the one she had shared her secrets with since Violet had died - although Eva hadn't yet mentioned her fear of never getting married. She felt that she wasn't quite close enough to Sarah to bring up such a delicate matter. Maybe she would soon, after a few cooking lessons. Perhaps Sarah could think up some way that Eva could care for her mother without having to live with her. In the mean time, Eva would just have to keep praying that Mama would get well so that she could have her freedom.

Chapter 41

Just a Dream

~*~*~

It was the very next day when Sarah came for her first lesson. Eva showed her the correct amount of lard to add to biscuits and how to make a roast nice and tender. Frank rode into town after he was done planting to share the meal.

"It is sort of strange to teach someone nearly four years older than me how to cook," Eva said to her mother that evening.

"I suppose so," Rose replied with a chuckle. "Aren't you glad, though, that you have the experience to show Sarah those things?"

"I guess I am. I really do enjoy spending extra time with her. It reminds me of back when I used to help Joy in the kitchen. Is that wrong, Mama? That I'm letting Sarah take Joy's place?"

Rose had to think about that for a minute.

"Well... I would say that she isn't really taking Joy's place. I would imagine that you two would have the same relationship even if Joy was still here. It's comforting for you to have Sarah around in a similar way as Joy. An older sister is a great role model... that is if she doesn't... elope... and whatnot." Tears filled Rose's eyes.

Eva patted her mother's hand.

Wiping her eyes, Rose forced a small laugh.

"I'm sorry, dear, I'm getting a little sidetracked. I think it's wonderful that you're helping Sarah with her cooking skills. All of the things you do for us now will make you a great wife and mother one day."

Eva opened her mouth to speak but closed it right away. She had never voiced her concerns to her mother about not being able to get married. Violet was the only one she had told. Eva wondered if her mother had even thought about it. It didn't appear that she had.

"Sarah's coming again on Thursday," Eva said instead. "I'm going to show her how to make meatloaf and garlic potato slices. Those are Frank's favorite. We're going to surprise him with them."

"Sounds like a good plan, darling. If you don't mind, I'm feeling a bit tired and would like to go to sleep now."

"Sure, Mama. I'll leave now. Good night. I love you."

"Love you too, darling. Get some good rest yourself now."

"I will, Mama." Eva quietly closed the door behind her.

Harold was sitting in his chair in the parlor, carving something with his pocket knife.

"The boys already went to bed?" Eva asked.

"Yes. Teddy has to go in to work extra early tomorrow, and I don't think Peter could keep his eyes open a minute longer. He and some of the other boys played a wild game of something or other for three hours straight after school."

"Ah, yes," Eva said as she perched on the edge of the sofa. "I believe he told me they were having a war. He's always been interested in wars and soldiers ever since he was young. Remember the toy soldiers he always played with? Well, he told me today that he was too old for toys, and he was going to be a solider himself."

"Just as long as he's never a real one," Harold said jokingly, but Eva could tell he was slightly troubled at the thought. "My father - your grandfather - fought in the war of eighteen twelve. He was badly wounded and never fully regained use of his left leg. It turned him into a sour, hate-filled man. I wasn't born until after the war had ended. But my mama told me that he had been a very loving and kind man before he was wounded. I would surely hate for such a thing to happen to any of my sons."

Eva smiled sadly.

"Well, hopefully we'll never have to worry about such things. There probably won't be another war for at least a hundred years!"

"I hope you're right, darlin'. I would like to say that there will never be another war again, but the Bible tells us that there's gonna be a lot of wars and other terrible things before the end of time. And I know that there are some people getting pretty riled up about slavery. Wouldn't be surprised if some sort of war breaks out because of it."

Eva nodded even though she wasn't paying much attention anymore.

"I'd like to keep you company longer, Papa, but I'm getting pretty tired myself. Good night."

"'Night, Eva. Pleasant dreams."

Eva nodded again as she rose from the sofa. She went to her room and shut the door. After changing into her night gown and brushing out her hair, she climbed underneath the warm covers. It seemed as though sleep was the only place she could have pleasant dreams.

~*~

Eva spun around slowly in front of a full length mirror, admiring her lovely gown. Her hair was piled upon her head with ringlets hanging around her ears.

"Oh, Eva, you look beautiful," said a girl with dark hair and violet eyes. "You are most certainly the prettiest bride ever."

"Yes, indeed," agreed the other bridesmaid who was older than the first.

"Eva, it's time to go," Harold said, peeking into the room.

Eva walked over to him and placed her hand in the crook of his elbow.

"I'm ready, Papa."

"You look ready, sweetheart."

"You are most certainly ready, Eva darling," Rose said from nearby. She looked healthier than Eva had ever seen her. Her cheeks were red and full instead of sunken, and her eyes were clear and bright.

The two bridesmaids led the way down the aisle. Eva and Harold followed. As they walked, Eva recognized everyone sitting in the pews. But try as she might, she could not see the groom standing in front by Reverend Lewis.

Harold and Eva were nearing the front of the church. The first bridesmaid was blocking Eva's view of the groom. Eva peered around her to get a look, but the other bridesmaid also moved in the way. Suddenly, both of the girls stepped aside. Eva caught a glimpse of the man just before a bright light hit her eyes.

Eva opened her eyes and found herself lying in her bed. The bright morning sunshine was streaming in through the window.

With a moan, Eva flipped back the covers and crawled out of bed.

"I can't even get married in my dreams," she muttered.

Even though she had caught a glimpse of the man before she had awoken, she hadn't recognized him. She couldn't even tell if he had been handsome or not.

Eva pulled her night gown over her head and slipped into her everyday dress. Then she moved to the dresser to brush and fix her hair.

As Eva was twisting together a braid, she realized with a start that Violet and Joy were the two bridesmaids in her dream.

Does that mean something? she wondered to herself. *Violet and Joy can certainly never be my bridesmaids. Does that mean that I'll never be a bride?*

Chapter 42

Sweet as Eggs

~*~*~

Eva was preoccupied with her dream as she prepared breakfast. She knew that she shouldn't let it bother her. Dreams didn't necessarily mean anything. And if they did, Eva had no idea what this one meant.

"I just have too many different thoughts on my mind these days," Eva murmured to herself. "I really ought to forget about that dream."

"Aw, sis, don't give up on your dreams," Teddy said from behind her.

Eva startled. She had been so lost in thought that she hadn't heard him come up.

"What dream are you giving up on?" Teddy pressed.

"It's nothing, Teddy. Just a dream I had last night... in my sleep."

"Oh, I see. It really seems to be bothering you. Do you want to talk about it? Might make you feel better."

"Why would you say it's bothering me?" Eva asked as she salted the scrambled eggs.

"Well... you burnt the bacon to a crisp for one. And that's sugar you're putting on the eggs."

Eva's fingers froze. She looked at the container she had taken a pinch of what she thought was salt from. Sure enough, it was sugar.

"Oh, goodness! I'm so sorry, Teddy! I've ruined breakfast! I'll have to throw all of this out. It looks like we're having oats."

"Wait a minute!" Teddy exclaimed, grabbing the pan from her. "Let me try them first. I might like sweet eggs."

Eva raised an eyebrow at him as she released the pan.

"You sure are an odd one, Teddy Remington. Go ahead and try them if you like."

Teddy put the pan on the table and looked into her eyes.

"Do you want to talk about it?" he asked again.

Eva shook her head firmly.

"It's nothing, Teddy. Really. Just a silly old dream. Forget about it."

Although he didn't look convinced that everything was all right, Teddy sat down to eat his eggs.

"Not half bad," he said after a couple of bites.

Eva wasn't sure whether he just said that to make her feel better, or if he really did like the eggs.

"If you say so," was all she said.

Peter entered the kitchen.

"What's for breakfast?" he asked.

"Burnt bacon and sugared eggs," Eva replied sourly.

"Huh?" came the confused reply.

Teddy laughed as he stood up.

"Sorry, bro. No eggs left. See you two later. I have to get into work early."

"Goodbye, Teddy," replied Eva and Peter.

"I can't believe he ate all of those eggs," Eva muttered as the door closed behind her older brother.

"Were you joking when you said what's for breakfast?" Peter asked, slightly concerned.

Eva chuckled.

"Yes and no. I'll made oatmeal for us."

Peter simply shrugged and helped himself to a glass of milk.

Eva decided that his reaction suggested he was accustomed to strange behavior from his sister. Smiling to herself, Eva figured that all boys think that their sisters are strange.

"Better hurry up and eat, Peter. Or else you'll be late for school," Eva advised her brother as she set a bowl of oatmeal before him.

"Like I care," Peter muttered.

Eva rolled her eyes. Peter didn't seem to be as interested in an education as she was.

"I care, and you should, too. This is your second to last year of school, Pete. You should try to make the most out of it."

"I know. I just wish that I could hurry up and finish school so that I can get a job like Ted."

"That time will come soon enough. I sure wish that I was still in school."

"You can go for me then," Peter said in all seriousness.

"Very funny, Pete. I finished the seventh grade two years ago and I don't need to learn it over again."

"I know. You still want to go to college, don't you?" Peter looked at her expectantly.

Eva was surprised that he would remember that. It must have showed because he said, "You still have the acceptance letter, don't you?"

Eva nodded mutely. Besides getting married, furthering her education was her biggest dream. The only problem was that she knew she couldn't have one if she got the other. But both of them were so unlikely to happen that she figured she didn't need to worry about that.

"Well, I'd best be goin' then. I'll learn as much as I can for you, sis." Peter pushed back his chair and stood.

"Thanks, Peter." Eva was touched by his new attitude and embraced him.

"No need to get mushy now," Peter moaned, pushing her away. "I'll see you when I come back for dinner."

"See you later," Eva replied. She followed him to the front door. "Don't forget your books."

"Right here." Peter showed her his primer.

Eva stood in the doorway and watched him trot down their path and hop over the gate. She shook her head and smiled.

Just as she was about to close the door, Eva spotted Daniel Baker walking past.

"Good morning, Daniel!" she called to him.

Daniel beamed when he saw her.

"Morning, Eva! How are you today?" he called back, stopping by the gate.

"Fine! Won't you come in for a minute?"

"I'd love to, but I'm on my way to take these eggs into Luke's. Can I stop on my way back?"

"Sure. Oh! Wait a minute!" Eva rushed into the kitchen and grabbed a paper sack. She dashed back outside and met Daniel at the gate.

"Here's Teddy's dinner. He left so early I forgot to give it to him. You don't mind bringing it, do you?"

"Not at all. It's not like it's out of my way or anything." Daniel took the sack from her and pretended to nearly drop it. "Oh my! It sure is heavy though! What did you pack in here?"

Eva knew that he was teasing, for the sack didn't even weigh three pounds. But she told him the contents anyway.

"Sounds good. Well, I'd best get moving. Mama says that it shows good manners to deliver things on time. And I know Luke likes to have his eggs by eight o'clock."

"All right, Daniel. I'll see you on the way back. I planned on making some cookies. You can test the first batch if you want."

"The whole batch?" Daniel joked, raising his eyebrows.

Eva giggled.

"I'm sure that they'll be wonderful if they're made by you. But it would probably be best if I gave you my expert opinion on them," Daniel told her in all seriousness. He grinned at her and patted the top of the gate. "Can't wait to try those cookies." Then he continued on his way.

Chapter 43

Conversation and Cookies

~*~*~

Daniel pushed open the door to Luke's Mercantile and stepped inside. Teddy was behind the counter, stocking shelves. He had his back to Daniel and didn't turn around at the sound of the bell above the door.

Grinning, Daniel quietly set down the basket of eggs and paper sack. He crept over to a display for women's hats and shawls - made by some of the townswomen. He picked up a straw bonnet with a blue ribbon and placed it on his head. Then he grabbed a shawl and wrapped it around his shoulders.

Stooping over like an old lady, Daniel tipped his head down to hide his face and walked towards the counter.

"You there, sonny!" he screeched in the best old lady voice he had. "I need fifty pounds of flour, three hat pins, five spools of purple tread, and one milk cow!"

"Milk cow?" Teddy asked, spinning around. He burst out laughing when he saw the person standing before him. "Daniel, you crazy duck! What on earth are you doing in that getup?"

Daniel chuckled and threw the clothes on the counter.

"I just thought I'd have a little fun with you, pal." Daniel retrieved the eggs and sack. "I brought today's eggs, and Eva sent your dinner along."

"Oh, did you stop by the house?"

"Sorta. Eva was seeing Pete off to school when I happened by. She said she'd let me stop on the way back to try the cookies she's making."

"*Did* she now? Well, just be sure to save me at least *one* cookie. Eva sure does like your company, it seems."

"Seems so," Daniel agreed, nodding thoughtfully. "Do you think she likes me?"

Teddy shrugged.

"Can't say. It's hard to tell with Eva. She was acting mighty peculiar this morning. Put sugar on our eggs."

Daniel made a sour face.

"How did that taste?"

"Honestly, not half bad. I ate all the ones she made."

Chuckling, Daniel said, "That sounds like something you'd do."

"Do you think when you stop on your way back you could talk to her? I think that something was bothering her this morning. You seem to have a way about you that's good for straightening these kinds of things out."

"Sure I'll talk to her. Do you have any idea what might be bothering her?"

"Nope," Teddy shook his head. "She's acting a lot like Joy did when Joy was Eva's age. Well, she's not nearly as bad as Joy was. But she's only a few months younger than Joy was when she eloped with Jack Green. I sure would hate to see that happen with Eva. She might get ideas and elope with Harvey."

Daniel's eyes grew wide.

"You don't think she would? Not really?"

Teddy shrugged.

"I never thought Joy would have either."

"Don't worry, Ted. I'll talk to her. I'm going to marry Eva when we get a little older. She can't elope! She just can't!"

~*~

Eva pulled the first batch of cookies out of the oven. She smiled proudly at their golden color and sweet smell. Onto the table went that pan, and into the oven went the next batch.

There was a tap on the doorframe that separated the kitchen from the parlor. Eva looked up and smiled at Daniel.

"Hope you don't mind that I let myself in," he said.

"Not at all. You're practically family."

"Those cookies sure do smell good."

"Just sit yourself down, and I'll get you a glass of milk to go with them."

Daniel sat across from where she was working and grinned at her.

"Thanks, Eva," he said when she placed a glass of milk and a plate holding two cookies in front of him.

"You're welcome." Eva clasped her hands together and waited eagerly for his reaction.

After giving the cookies an extra minute to cool, Daniel picked one up and took a bite. He chewed slowly, a thoughtful look on his face. He frowned, scrunched up one eye, and took another bite.

"They're... edible," he finally concluded.

"Daniel!" Eva exclaimed. She knew he was teasing, but she still grabbed a nearby towel and wacked his arm with it.

"Hey, now! Don't get violent!" Daniel cried, holding out his hands in defense. "I was just kidding!"

"I know," Eva said with a laugh. "I'm sorry. Did I hurt you?"

"'Course not. I've been hit with harder things than a towel. The cookies really are delicious, Eva. I like them a whole lot. I just enjoy getting you riled."

"And why is that, Daniel Baker?" Eva demanded, planting her hands on her hips.

"Because you look so cute when you do," Daniel replied with a cocky grin.

Eva blushed deeply and dipped her head. She busied herself in scooping the next batch of cookies.

Daniel moved up behind her and placed his hands on her shoulders.

"I'm sorry, Eva. I shouldn't get you worked up the way I do. You look cute even when you're not riled."

Eva felt her entire face heat up. She turned away from Daniel so he couldn't see her embarrassment.

Daniel also blushed slightly.

"Sorry. I shouldn't have said that, either - even though it is true. I've embarrassed you now, too."

"That's all right, Daniel. I... I need to check my cookies." Eva slipped away from his hands and went to the cook stove. She opened up the oven door and saw with dismay that they had turned dark brown. She moaned slightly and reached for a towel to remove the pan.

"Here, let me do it," Daniel said, taking the towel from her. He pulled the pan out of the oven and set it on the table. "Sorry they got burnt. It's my fault."

"No, it's not." Eva moved to look closer at them while Daniel slid the other pan into the oven. "I don't suppose that they're edible, though. I'll have to toss them."

"Don't you dare! It's my fault that they got burned. I'll do my part and suffer though eating them."

Eva laughed, glad to have the Daniel she was comfortable with back.

"You boys sure are something. Eating burnt cookies and sugared eggs. I never." She shook her head in wonder.

Grinning lopsidedly, Daniel joked, "I guess as long as its food, we'll eat it."

"Well, then. If you're sure you want to eat them, I'll put those burnt cookies in a sack once they cool for you to take home. That way you don't spoil your dinner by eating them all now."

"I sure do want to eat them. Thanks for thinking of that. I wouldn't want to fill myself up. Mama's making fried chicken and baked potatoes for lunch. Say! Would you want to come home with me to share the meal? I know that Mama wouldn't mind." Daniel looked at her expectantly, eagerly awaiting her answer.

Eva smiled sadly.

"Oh, Daniel, you know that I'd love to. But I have to stay here in case Mama needs me."

"Oh, right," Daniel muttered, shoving his hands in his pockets and staring at the floor in disappointment. "I sorta forgot there for a minute. Maybe some other time then," he added hopefully.

"We'll see," was all Eva could promise.

Chapter 44

Reasons to Love Me

~*~*~

As planned, Sarah came into town for her next cooking lesson that Thursday. Eva had gotten all of the ingredients out beforehand so the two girls set right to work.

"I've never actually made a meatloaf before," admitted Sarah.

"Don't worry, it's not very hard," Eva assured her.

"That's good," Sarah replied with a laugh as she added some spices to the ground beef. "If it is Frank's favorite, it would only be right that I learn to make it. And I certainly want to be good at making it so I'm glad it's not hard!"

Eva also laughed. She could see why her brother had married this wonderful girl. She was easily delighted and always carried a positive attitude. It made Eva wonder what a man might see in her some day that would make him want to marry her.

"What are you thinking about, Eva?" Sarah asked, seeing that Eva was lost in thought.

"Oh!" Eva blinked and looked at her sister-in-law. "I was just thinking about how much I admire your cheerfulness and positivity."

"Why thank you, Eva," Sarah said with a smile.

"I know that those features in your personality are some of the reasons Frank married you. It kind of made me wonder what I have about me that would make someone fall in love with me."

"Well, Eva, it isn't very hard for me to think of some. You're kind and generous. You're a hard worker. You accept changes - no matter how difficult they may be - without complaint. When you had to take Joy's place caring for your mother, you stepped right in and gave it your best. You do such a wonderful job caring for your family. I mean, here you are, teaching me to cook. Any man would want to marry you just for your cooking."

"Wow, you sure came up with a lot of things fast," Eva said in surprise. She had never considered some of those traits belonging to her.

Sarah laughed.

"And I'm not done yet."

Eva stared at Sarah in amazement as she began pressing the meat mixture into a pan.

"These things are obvious, but I'll say them anyway. You're sweet and charming. You're very pretty."

"Sarah! You're going to make me vain!" Eva interrupted with a laugh.

Grinning, Sarah replied, "I'm sure you don't get told those things nearly as often as you should." She slid the meatloaf into the oven and set to work slicing the potatoes Eva had just washed.

Eva just shook her head, not sure what to think of all the compliments.

Knowing that this was the perfect time to bring up her worries, Eva opened her mouth to speak.

"Hello, everyone! I'm home!" There was the sound of the front door shutting.

"Why, Papa, you're home early," Eva said as Harold entered the room.

"Mr. Farnsworth said it would be fine for me to leave a little early when I told him that your mother wasn't doing very well these past few days." Harold gave Eva a hug and then turned to Sarah. "Why, here's my favorite daughter-in-law! Nice to see you, Sarah."

"Good to see you too, Harold," Sarah replied pleasantly as she embraced her father-in-law.

"It was nice of Mr. Farnsworth to let you get off early, Papa. Weren't things very busy at the mill today?"

"It was kinda slow. We're waiting for some of the farmers to bring in more loads of wheat for us to grind. Mr. Farnsworth said that he and Yankee Smith were talking about also grinding corn to make corn meal."

"That would be interesting," Sarah said.

Harold shrugged. "I honestly don't think anything will come of it. Most folks around here seem to like growing their wheat. Mmm, something smells good! What are you two making?"

"Meatloaf and garlic potatoes," Sarah informed him. "Eva tells me that they are Frank's favorite."

"Yum! Mine too. Well, one of my favorites, that is."

Eva snorted and turned to Sarah. "Every night Papa says that what I'm making is his favorite."

Harold chuckled and kissed the top of Eva's head.

"That's because you made it. My favorite food is whatever I'm eating. That way I have nothing to complain about."

"Good way of looking at it," Sarah said. "I'll have to remember that."

"Frank already knows that rule," said Harold, grinning.

"What rule?" Frank asked as he entered through the back door. "I was told to come here for supper, not a school lesson."

"It's nothing to do with school, dear," Sarah told him. "We're talking about food."

"Well, personally, I'd rather eat food than talk about it. What are we having?" Frank inhaled deeply. "Oh, hold on. I know! Meatloaf and potatoes! Oh, wait! With garlic! My favorite! When will they be ready?"

"In about ten minutes," Eva guessed. "Why don't you go find Teddy and Peter?"

"I saw Teddy coming from the opposite direction when I was coming into town. He should be here any minute. Is Peter in the house?"

"No, he was playing some kind of game with his friends in the school yard. I told him to be home for supper, but he probably lost track of time."

Frank nodded and left to find his youngest brother. He passed Teddy on his way out the door.

"I'm going to talk with your mother for a little while before we eat," Harold said. He gave Teddy a friendly slap on the shoulder in greeting as he passed his son.

"Hello, Sarah. Hey, sis," Teddy greeted the girls. "Food sure smells good. Do you want me to set the table or something?"

"Sure. I already set the dishes out on the counter," Eva responded.

Within fifteen minutes, everyone was gathered in the kitchen, and the food was on the table. The family enjoyed the meal thoroughly, causing Sarah to grow even more confident in her cooking skills.

After supper, Frank and Sarah visited with the family for only a half hour before heading home. Eva didn't get another chance to speak with Sarah alone. She wasn't sure if she would ever have a good opportunity to bring it up again.

Chapter 45

Regrets

~*~*~

Time passed. Life went on.

It was a pleasant Saturday in June, eighteen fifty three. The sun was shining brightly and there were only a few puffy white clouds in the brilliant blue sky.

Eva stood on the back porch, staring out onto the prairie, wishing that she could go for a stroll by the river. Any other girl could have simply put on her bonnet and left, but not Eva. Eva wasn't free to leave whenever she wished.

Over the years, Eva had become accustomed to her lot in life. She had to, knowing that there was nothing she could do to change it. But on a day as lovely as this one, it was hard to stay indoors.

"Good morning, Eva. Beautiful day, isn't it?"

Eva looked to her right and saw Daniel standing at the bottom of the porch steps.

"Yes, it is. I just wish that I could go out further than the porch to enjoy it."

Daniel leaned against the railing and looked up at her.

"It is a shame. If you didn't have to stay near the house, I would ask you to take a walk with me. But since you can't go anywhere, would you want some company?"

"That's nice of you to offer, Daniel. But you don't have to stick around just because you feel sorry for me. I'm used to it."

"That's not it at all, Eva. I honestly want to keep you company. Shall we sit down?" He gestured to the steps.

Eva nodded and sat next to him on the second to top step.

"How's your mother doing today?" Daniel asked after several minutes of silence.

"Not very well. Her health has been at such a low these past few years. I have no idea how she manages to hold on."

"She certainly has enough reasons to stay alive," said Daniel.

Eva looked at him curiously.

"What do you mean?"

"She has you... and the rest of your family. Don't you think that's a good reason to stay alive? So that she can watch all of you grow up and have families of your own? Frank and Sarah already have two children. I'm sure that your mother is eagerly awaiting more grandbabies. Don't you think so?"

"I suppose," Eva agreed hesitantly. "But after the trouble Sarah had with little Joseph, Midwife Stevens advised them not to have any more children, at least not for a while."

"Well, that's just Frank. What about Ted? He's nineteen, same as me. That's old enough to get married."

"You know that Teddy says he'll never marry. Violet was his only love."

"He'll probably change his mind eventually."

"Teddy will likely convince you otherwise."

"I know that Peter still has a ways to go before he gets married, but what about you, Eva?"

"What about me?" Eva asked, not liking the direction this conversation was headed.

"You'll be sixteen in a couple of months. Don't you have plans to... court anyone?" Daniel was watching her intently.

Eva propped her elbows on her knees and rested her head on her hands.

"I honestly don't think anyone would be interested in courting me."

"That isn't true! Not at all! Why would you say such a thing?"

Eva shrugged, not wanting to share her deepest fears with him.

"Do you... is there... someone... that you wish would court you?" Daniel asked tentatively.

"No," Eva replied without hesitation.

Daniel appeared both relieved and disappointed at the same time.

The two of them sat quietly for what seemed like an eternity. Daniel was the one to break the silence.

"Eva, I..."

Eva leapt up.

"I just heard Mama calling me!" she exclaimed, rushing up the steps and into the house. "I'll be back in a minute!"

Eva quietly pushed open the door to her parent's room and found Rose fast asleep. She hadn't really heard her mother call. But it was the best excuse she could come up with to leave before Daniel could say whatever it was he had planned on saying. Eva wasn't quite sure what he had on his mind, but she was certain it was something she didn't want to hear.

~*~

Heaving a sigh, Daniel stood and took a few steps away from the house. He shoved his hands in his pockets and kicked at a clump of dirt. He had come so close to finally confessing his feelings for her, and she had gone and run away.

Daniel hadn't heard Rose calling to Eva. He knew that she had just made that up to get away from him. He simply couldn't understand why though.

Does she know how I feel about her? Daniel was almost certain that she did. *It's as if she's scared of me. Scared of acknowledging what we could have together if she would just give me a chance. But why? Why is she scared?* That was the part Daniel couldn't figure out. Perhaps it was because they had always been friends, and she wasn't comfortable becoming more.

Daniel glanced towards the house. It didn't appear that Eva would be returning any time soon.

She must be hiding from me, Daniel figured.

Walking back to the porch, Daniel placed his hand on the railing and debated going inside. He had walked into that house unannounced often enough, but he wasn't sure that this would be a good time.

Tapping once on the railing, Daniel pushed off of it and walked away.

~*~

Glancing out the front window as she passed by on her way to the kitchen, Eva saw Daniel walking in the direction of home.

A sinking feeling entered her heart. She had stayed inside too long, and he had given up on her returning. She had no doubt hurt his feelings.

Rushing to the front door, Eva flung it open. She started to call out to Daniel but stopped herself. Silently, she stood there and watched him walk away.

When I was out there with him, all I wanted to do was leave. But now that he's gone, I want him to come back. Funny, isn't it?

Eva remained in the doorway long after Daniel had disappeared. Regret filled her as she wished that she had gone after him. She would have to apologize for being so rude the next time she saw him. For she certainly had been rude running off on him the way she had. All because she refused to listen to what he had to say, and she didn't even know why.

Chapter 46

Disastrous Apology

~*~*~

It was two weeks later, and Eva still hadn't seen Daniel. He usually stopped by every few days, but he was apparently avoiding her. Eva realized with great shame and regret that she must have hurt him more than she'd thought.

Unable to live with herself any longer, Eva decided that she was going to have to go to Daniel if he wasn't going to come to her. That would be quite hard to do, however, since she couldn't leave the house. Rose was even weaker than she had been two weeks ago, and Harold had told Eva to remain within earshot of her mother at all times.

"I'll just have to find someone to stay with Mama," Eva decided. She supposed that she could wait until her father came home, but lately he was always tired and stressed. Peter was an option, but he wasn't very responsible. Besides, he would be staying at a friend's house that night. Teddy was good at caring for their mother, but he had been spending the last few weeks at Frank's house, helping him build an addition for their house.

Cracking open the door to her parent's room, Eva peeked at her mother. Rose was sleeping fitfully. Her face had been quite pale of late - nearly white, and her eyes had sunken in more than ever before. She was mostly skin and bone since she hadn't been able to keep much food down for nearly a month now. Eva wasn't sure what to do. She didn't admit it aloud, but she believed that her mother was dying.

Taking a shaky breath, Eva shut the door. She moved across the parlor and looked out the window. Her eyes lit up when she saw Mrs. Lewis walking down the street.

"Mrs. Lewis!" Eva called as she swung the front door open.

"Why, good afternoon, Eva. How are you?" Mrs. Lewis stopped by the Remington's gate.

"Would you please come in for a minute?" Eva asked.

Mrs. Lewis pushed the gate in and rushed towards the house.

"Is something wrong with your mother?" she asked in concern.

"She's no worse than the last time you visited. I was hoping that you would do me a favor."

"Anything, dear. What do you need?"

"I really need to speak to a friend of mine. But as you know, I can't leave the house..." Eva began.

Mrs. Lewis smiled.

"I'd be happy to stay with your mother, dear."

"Really, Mrs. Lewis?" Eva exclaimed in delight. "That would be wonderful! I mean, unless you have something else to do."

"No, I was just on my way back from a quilting bee. You go on and speak with your friend." There was a twinkle in Mrs. Lewis's eye. Eva couldn't help but wonder if the lady knew where she was headed.

"Thank you so much, Mrs. Lewis. I promise I won't be gone long."

"Take all the time you need, Eva dear. I don't have anything waiting for me to do."

"Thank you!" Eva cried again as she dashed out the door, not even bothering to grab her sunbonnet.

West down Mill Workers Lane, Eva ran, ignoring the looks people gave her. Once she was about a mile out of town, Eva slowed to a walk, wondering why she was in such a hurry to see Daniel. She decided to take her time and enjoy the time she had out of the house.

As she neared the Baker farm, Eva saw a horse and rider approaching. She thought at first that it was Daniel but realized as the pair got closer that it was Samuel Baker.

"Hello, Sam!" Eva waved to him.

"Eva? Is that you? Never thought I'd see you outside again. Ah, sorry, I didn't mean it like that."

Eva chuckled.

"That's all right. Sometimes I feel that way myself. Is Daniel home?"

"Yeah. He's training our new horse in the paddock behind the barn."

"Thanks, Sam. See you later."

Samuel waved and continued on his way.

As she walked across the farmyard, Eva smiled at Mary's four children who were playing a game of tag. Mary, Mary's husband, Clark, and Ellen Baker sat on the front porch watching the children. The three of them greeted Eva, who stopped only briefly to say hello.

Eva found Daniel in the paddock just as Samuel had said she would.

"Daniel!" she called to him from the gate.

The bay mare was on a lunge rope, running in circles. Daniel stood firmly, opposite end of the rope in on hand and a whip in the other. He turned at the sound of her voice. A grin flashed across his face before he replaced it with a pained look. He turned his back to her and snapped the whip to urge the mare into a faster trot.

Eva watched as he continued to lunge the mare. She wondered if he was purposefully putting off talking to her, or if he simply wanted to finish his training session.

"Daniel! I just wanted to tell you that I'm sorry!" Eva yelled.

Daniel spun quickly to face her. As he did, the whip snapped across the mare's hind legs.

The mare reared.

"Daniel! Look out!" Eva screamed.

The right hoof shot out and struck Daniel on the back of the head. He fell to the ground. The mare landed - trampling Daniel's legs as she did - and galloped to the far end of the paddock. She swung around and raced back across the enclosed area, jumping over the fence and disappearing around the barn.

Chapter 47

Discovery in the Chest

~*~*~

Time passed. Life went on.

Nearly a year had passed since Daniel had gone. Every day Eva relived that horrible moment. She could clearly picture Daniel lying unconscious on the ground. She could still feel the way her heart had stopped beating.

She hadn't run to him right away - which she sorely regretted. Instead she had remained frozen by the gate, barely breathing. When she had snapped out of her state of shock, she dashed across the paddock and fell on her knees by his side. The back of his head had been bleeding, and his left leg turned at an odd angle.

It had been that moment - as she knelt by his still form - that Eva realized she loved him. And not as an older brother, the way she had made herself believe. Eva realized that she was *in love* with Daniel Baker.

"Eva, you're going to burn those eggs."

Peter's voice brought Eva back to the present.

"Oh! I'm sorry, Pete." Eva quickly removed the eggs from the pan. "I guess I was kind of distracted."

"You're always distracted lately," Peter informed her. "That's all right... about the eggs. It gives them better flavor when they are darker."

Eva smiled at her younger brother. She knew that he just said that to make her feel better.

Peter quickly devoured the eggs.

"I'm off to work. See you later, Eva."

"'Bye, Peter. Don't hurt yourself now."

"Gee, sis, you worry too much. I promise to be careful,l though." Peter had joined a construction company that was temporally in the area building a few storage sheds for the wheat the mill produced.

"I'm sorry. I guess that's what big sisters do. Don't forget your noon meal."

"I sure won't!" Peter flashed a grin at her as he grabbed the sack with the dinner she had prepared for him.

Once Peter had left, Eva filled a glass with water and brought it to her mother.

Rose had improved over the winter months as she always seemed to, but now that the warm weather was approaching again her health was once again slipping.

"Good morning, Mama. How are you feeling today?" Eva handed the water to her mother and opened the curtains to let in the morning sunlight.

"Better now that I've seen a pleasant face." Rose took a sip of the water. "How are *you* feeling today?"

Eva smiled. Her mother's first concern was never for herself.

"I'm fine. Are you hungry?"

"Not really. I suppose I should eat something, though. Maybe some oatmeal?"

"I'll have it ready in ten minutes." Eva left to prepare the oats. She returned within the promised time.

"Mama?" Eva spoke once Rose was situated with her bowl.

"Yes, dear?"

Eva perched on the edge of the chair next to the bed.

"I was wondering... I don't really know how to put this. But I've been thinking lately and got to wondering; how come you're not as healthy as you used to be. I mean, when Joy was still taking care of you, you would occasionally be well enough to get out of bed. But now you are always too weak. Am I doing something wrong?"

Rose looked at Eva in shock. She set the bowl on the nightstand and took Eva's hands.

"Oh, my no, dear. It's not your fault at all. Not in the least. It's just that I'm... getting older. This sickness I have has taken a toll on my body over the years. It's been what? Five years since Joy's been gone?"

"More like six."

"See, dear? That's more than enough time for my heath to get worse."

"But it could have gotten better," Eva protested. "If I had cared for you better."

"Now, Eva, I don't want to hear another word about this," Rose said firmly. She moved her eyes towards the window. "It's such a lovely day. Why don't you take a walk? Get some fresh air?"

"Mama! You know very well that I can't leave you here alone."

Rose smiled.

"I won't be alone."

Eva raised an eyebrow at her mother.

"God is with me," Rose finished.

"*Mama*," Eva said in exasperation.

"What? Don't you trust that God will take care of me while you're gone?"

"Of course, but..."

"No 'buts'. Go put on your bonnet and enjoy this beautiful day."

"All right, Mama. If you insist."

"I do."

Eva grinned and kissed her mother's forehead.

"I promise that I won't be gone long."

"Don't you worry now, darling. I'm in good hands."

"Yes, Mama," Eva said with a smile.

After securing her bonnet atop her head, Eva stepped outside and took a deep breath of fresh air. She decided to walk to the school and then go north from there.

As she strolled along, Eva thought once again about Daniel. At that moment, when she had realized that she loved him, she had also finally acknowledged that he loved her. Sure, she had known - deep down inside - for a long time. But she hadn't allowed herself to believe that he truly did. Because she was afraid. Afraid that she would break his heart when she told him that she would never be able to marry him.

Eva supposed that it didn't matter anymore anyway.

~*~

As soon as Eva left, Rose pushed back the covers and struggled into a sitting position. She reached under her pillow and pulled out a set of embroidered napkins. She had been working on them whenever she felt up to it. It had taken nearly two years, but the set was finally complete.

Unable to stand, Rose crawled along the floor, out of her room and into Eva's. She moved to the hope chest and struggled to open the lid.

Once the lid was opened, Rose was surprised to find the chest barely half full. She didn't recognize anything new. Everything in the chest Eva had shown Rose after she had finished making them. The most recent item - a tablecloth - had been made three or four years ago.

Rose was curious to know why Eva had stopped filling her hope chest but knew she couldn't ask her daughter without giving herself away. She wanted the napkins to be a surprise. Rose wasn't sure that she would live until Eva got married, and she wanted to make sure she had something special for her girl.

Lifting up a stack of linens, Rose was about to place the napkins underneath when she noticed a piece of paper.

Curious, Rose pulled the paper out from under the linens. When she got a better look at it, she realized that it was actually an envelope. Turning it over, she looked at the return address.

"Georgia Female College. What in the world..?" A million thoughts rushed through her mind.

With only slight hesitation, Rose pulled the contents out of the envelope and unfolded the paper.

"Dear Miss Eva Remington, We at the Georgia Female Collage are pleased to inform you that you have been accepted..." Rose mumbled the following lines under her breath. "And we are especially excited to inform you that you have won the scholarship..." Rose gasped. The letter trembled in her fingers. "Oh, Eva," she whispered. "Why didn't you tell me?"

Rose would definitely have to give herself away now. No surprise napkins were worth not talking to Eva about this.

Chapter 48

Promotion

~*~*~

Eva returned to find her mother lying on the floor next to her bed.

"Mama! Are you hurt? Did you fall out of bed?"

"Not exactly, dear. I just couldn't get back up."

Eva hurried to help Rose into bed.

"What happened?"

"I have a confession to make, but apparently, you do too."

"Huh?"

"Well... I went into your room when you were gone."

"Mama! You know that you shouldn't be out of bed. Whatever did you do that for? Why were you in my room?"

"That's my confession. I've been making something for you - for your hope chest - during the times I don't feel as weak. I wanted to make you something special. In case I'm not around when you get married."

Eva wanted to say something but kept her mouth shut.

"I was going to hide them in the bottom when I found this." Rose held up an envelope. "Now it's your turn to do some confessing. Why didn't you tell me about this?" Rose asked as she handed the envelope to Eva.

Eva gasped when she realized what it was.

"Oh, my! I had completely forgotten about that!"

"Eva, not only were you accepted, but you also won the scholarship! You should have told me. Does your father even know?"

Eva shook her head.

"You could have gone on to college and furthered your education. Why didn't you?"

Eva looked at her mother in confusion.

"How could I have possibly gone, Mama? You needed me here."

"You still should have told us, darling. We could have worked something out."

Eva picked at the corner of the bedspread.

"Yeah, you say that now. But honestly, at the time, it wouldn't have worked."

Rose remained silent for a long time.

"Even though I feel terrible for being the reason you couldn't accept the scholarship..."

"Mama, it's not your fault," Eva interrupted.

Rose held up her hand.

"Let me finish. I want you to know that I'm very proud of you."

"What for?" Eva asked, confused.

"Because you gave up your dream for your family. That takes a lot of courage. Shows good character and a sense of responsibility. Now my respect for you is even greater than it was before."

Eva beamed with pleasure.

"You respect me?" she asked.

"Of course. With all the things you do for us, you deserve respect."

"Hmm," Eva was thoughtful. "I guess I kinda always thought that you only respected people who were older than you."

Rose laughed.

"I suppose that is the way it is most of the time. But in special cases, it can be the other way around."

Mother and daughter shared a smile.

"Now, Eva, there is one thing that confuses me," Rose spoke after a moment.

"What's that?"

"Your hope chest. It's half empty."

"Actually, it's half full," Eva said jokingly, hoping to steer the conversation to a different direction.

"Eva, I'm serious. Why did you stop making things to put in it?"

"Oh, I don't know," replied Eva with a careless shrug.

"I had mine stuffed full when I was fourteen."

"I don't have much time to sew except the things we need now. Besides, I don't have a suitor. It's not as if I'm going to be getting married soon so I'm not very worried about filling it up."

"But don't you want to get married? Don't you dream of that? I remember when I made linens and whatnot for my hope chest, I would always dream of my life with my future husband. I suppose that my life hasn't turned out exactly the way I had planned, but I wouldn't change anything."

"Really, Mama? Not even your health?"

"Nope," Rose shook her head and smiled. "Things may not have turned out the way *I* planned, but everything turned out *exactly* the way *God* planned. I am content."

"I'm glad, Mama. I'm content if you're content."

"But you still want to get married, don't you, Eva? You will make such a wonderful wife and mother. I know you wanted an education, but being a wife and mother is even better than that. That is what God intended for women. Not that we can't learn and have careers as men do, but caring for and loving others are the greatest things we can do."

"I think so too, Mama. And yes, I do want to get married." Eva decided not to ask how she could still care for her mother if she did get married.

"You seem to be quite worn out, Mama. Why don't you get some rest now?"

"I am tired." Rose adjusted herself with Eva's help. "I'm glad we had this talk, Eva."

Eva smiled softly and kissed her mother's pale cheek.

"Me too, Mama. Me too."

~*~

"Ted."

Ted Remington glanced up from his dusting. He had made it clear nearly a year ago that the childish name of "Teddy" shall longer be used. He preferred the shortened version of his name that Daniel had always used, as it made him sound more his age.

"Yes, Luke?"

"You've been working for me for a good many years now, haven't you, my boy?"

"Since I finished school," Ted replied.

"Well, as you know, I'm getting up there in years. And it's getting harder for me to keep up with everything the way I used to."

"I think that you're doing a fine job, sir."

"Why, thank you, my boy. Nice of you to say so, but what I said is true. Anyway, my point is that I need a manager for the store. To place orders, run the store, and things like that. And, Ted my boy, you would be the perfect manager."

"Really, Luke?" Ted exclaimed in delight. "You mean it?"

"Of course. I want to warn you that it will be a lot of work, and you'll have to put in more hours than you currently do."

"I can handle it."

"I know you can, my boy. Otherwise I wouldn't have offered you the position."

"Thank you! I promise that I'll make you proud."

"I know you will. I'm proud of you already. You understand that this higher position also comes with higher pay?"

Ted's eyes lit up. He hadn't yet thought of that. His family could surely use the extra money.

"I hadn't thought of that! Thank you, Luke! When do I start?"

"Why don't we say next Monday?"

"Fine with me," Ted nodded.

"Good!" Luke slapped Ted on the back. "I'd say that you're done dusting. Why don't you run on home and share the news with your family. I can see that you are just bursting to tell someone."

"Gee, thanks, Luke!"

Ted grabbed his hat and dashed out of the store. He could hear Luke laughing from inside.

"Say, Ted! Ted Remington!"

Ted slowed his pace and looked around to see who had called him.

Fred Waters was running towards him waving an envelope.

"This came for you on the stage today," Mr. Waters told Ted. "Driver gave it to me when he switched horses at the livery."

"Thank you, Mr. Waters," Ted said as he took the envelope.

"See you later, Ted."

"See ya."

Ted glanced down at the envelope. His eyes widened when he saw the sender's name.

Clutching the envelope in his fist, Ted made a mad dash towards home.

~*~

After her mother had fallen asleep, Eva gathered the dishes from the bedside table and carried them into the kitchen. As she set the dishes next to the wash basin, her eyes drifted to the wall next to the back door. The plaque Daniel had made her still hung proudly.

"Trust in the Lord with all thine heart, and lean not unto thine own understanding," she read the verse in a whisper.

As she reached out to trace the smooth edges, tears filled Eva's eyes.

Chapter 49

Wonderful news

~*~*~

"Eva! Eva!"

Eva could hear her brother calling for her before he even entered the house. She rushed to the front door and flung it open seconds before he burst inside.

"Teddy! What's wrong?" Eva and her mother were the only ones who still called Ted that.

"Nothing! At least, I don't think anything is. Look at this letter I got!"

"Who's it from?"

Ted showed her the return address, and she gasped.

"I wanted to wait until I was home to open it. Let's sit on the sofa, and I'll read it to you."

Eva and Ted made themselves comfortable in the parlor.

"Hurry up and open it," Eva said. Her foot was tapping on the floor as she nervously waited to hear the contents of the letter. She smoothed out her skirt with trembling hands and then clasped them together in her lap in an effort to relax.

Ted tore the envelope open and extracted a piece of paper. He slowly unfolded it.

"Dear, Ted," Ted began. He tried to steady his shaky hands so that he could focus on the words. "I'm sorry that I did not write to you before. I admit that it took a lot of courage to write this letter. I only worked up the courage because it contains good news. I just finished writing my family a similar letter. All right, here's the good news... After months of therapy, I'm finally able to walk again..." Ted choked on the last words and then trailed off. Eva could see tears in his eyes.

Reaching up to wipe tears from her own eyes, Eva felt her entire body fill with joy. This was the best news she had ever heard.

Once Ted had had a moment to gather himself, he continued.

"For the longest time, the doctors didn't think that there was any hope for me, but I showed them what I was made of. I'll be arriving home by stage on the twentieth of May. I hope to see you all then. Love, your friend, Daniel Baker."

Eva flung her arms around her brother. Ted squeezed her tightly, and they both wept tears of joy.

"The twentieth of May! That's tomorrow!" Eva exclaimed when Ted finally released her. "Oh! I don't think I'll be able to sleep tonight!"

"Me neither. Boy, it'll be good to see ol' Dan again."

"It sure will!" Eva replied. Her entire face was glowing. She forgot for the moment that she wouldn't be able to marry Daniel - even if he did still love her.

"I'm going to make a cake to celebrate!" Eva exclaimed, jumping up from the sofa.

"Great idea! Are we going to eat it tonight?" Ted also rose. He looked at her expectantly.

Eva frowned at her brother.

"It's to celebrate Daniel's homecoming. Don't you think we should save it for him?"

"Why don't you make two? We can have one tonight and one tomorrow. Besides, I'm sure Mrs. Baker is making all sorts of goodies right this minute. I've no doubt that we'll be invited to supper at the Baker's tomorrow evening."

"I'll bet that you're right. We don't have enough ingredients to make two cakes, however. And if we *do* get invited over, I should bring something. So we'll save the cake."

"I'll go get some things from Luke's quick. He trusts me to pay if I need something after the store is closed. Hey, speaking of which, I got a promotion today!"

"Really?" Eva had started for the kitchen but stopped and turned to her brother in surprise.

"Yes. Luke made me store manager."

"Oh, Teddy! That's wonderful!" Eva embraced her brother. "I'm so happy for you."

"Thanks, sis. It comes with a raise too. We won't ever have to worry about not having enough money again."

"Don't you want to save your money for when you start a family?" Eva asked even though she knew the answer.

"Violet was the only girl I've ever loved. I'm destined to be a bachelor so I might as well spend the money on family."

"If you say so."

Ted left to get the ingredients.

Sitting back down on the sofa, Eva's mind flashed back to Daniel's accident.

Having seen the mare appear from behind the barn while sitting on the porch, Mrs. Baker, Mary, and Clark came running to the paddock only moments after Eva had fallen to her knees beside Daniel.

"Is he dead?" Mrs. Baker whispered, grasping Mary's arm. Both women's eyes filled with terror.

"He's unconscious," Clark informed them as he dropped down next to Eva. "It looks like one of his legs is broken, and the other one is also injured. Mary, go get help."

Mary nodded and raced off.

Eva clutched Daniel's hand and wept.

"It's my fault!" she cried. Her hair ribbon had come untied, and her light brown locks fell over her face, covering her reddened, tear-stained eyes.

"Now, dear. Of course it's not," Mrs. Baker comforted, patting Eva's shoulder. "Let's get you inside."

Daniel's hand slowly slipped out of Eva's as Clark helped her to her feet. Mrs. Baker put her arm around her and led her out of the paddock.

"It is my fault. It is," Eva muttered. "I startled the horse." She looked back one last time at Daniel's still form.

Daniel had still been unconscious the next day when Michael and Ellen Baker left with him in their wagon to take him east to a hospital. Daniel had never written to Ted or her until the letter they had received that day. However, the Bakers had kept the Remingtons informed. For the longest time the doctors were certain that Daniel would never walk again. And now, here he was, coming home, fully recovered.

Eva's feelings were mixed. While she was certainly glad he was recovering, and she was eager to see him again, she didn't know what she would say to him... now that she knew she loved him.

Deciding to let her mother know the news before starting on the cakes, Eva pushed herself up from the sofa and quietly slipped into her parent's room.

Chapter 50
Broken Hearts

~*~*~

Eva was so excited and nervous the next morning that she barely managed to dress herself.

Wanting to look her best for Daniel, Eva wore her green Sunday dress and carefully pinned up her hair. She also made sure that her shoes were nicely shined - even though no one could see her feet from beneath her floor-length skirt.

"You sure look pretty today," Harold greeted her with a smile as she entered the kitchen. "Perhaps could it be because a handsome young man is coming home soon?"

"Perhaps," Eva replied with a sly grin.

"I can't wait to see Daniel again," Peter declared as he came up behind Eva.

"Well, aren't you up early?" Eva said to him. "You don't even have to work today."

"Well I don't want to miss Daniel's stage."

"None of us do," Ted agreed. He was sitting next to Harold at the table. Both men were drinking coffee.

"I'll have breakfast made shortly," Eva promised.

"That's good. I'm starved," Ted announced.

"Me too," Harold added. "Breakfast doesn't get made in time when the cook is busy worrying about her looks."

"You are all perfectly capable of scrambling an egg," Eva retorted. She knew that her father was teasing her, though.

"Yeah, sis. You sure are fancied up today," Peter said, noticing Eva's attire for the first time.

"You look nice," Ted told her with a sincere smile.

"Thank you." Eva returned the smile and went on to make breakfast.

The stage was to arrive at nine o'clock. Eva and the rest of her family - save Rose - headed down to the depot at eight forty.

The Bakers were already there. The two families greeted each other. There was much laughter and excited chatter.

"You all must come for supper at our house," Ellen Baker declared.

"I'd love to, but I'm going to have to stay with Rose," Harold told her. "The children can all go, though. That includes you too, Eva."

Eva beamed at her father.

"Thank you, Papa."

Frank and Sarah came walking up with their two young children. Ted had borrowed Harold's horse from the livery the previous night to let them know the news.

As nine o'clock neared, more of the townsfolk arrived. Word had spread fast, and everyone was eager to welcome the boy home.

Reverend Lewis led the group in a prayer that the stage would arrive safely and on time, and that God be with the family as they reunited.

Eva clutched Ted's arm, digging her fingers into his skin. She stood on her toes as though she would be able to see the stage coming from a higher point.

"Eva, not so tight please," Ted said, prying her fingers loose.

"Sorry, Teddy," she apologized. "I'm just so excited - and nervous - all at the same time."

"Me too. You can hold onto me, just don't rip off my skin."

Eva blushed slightly and took hold of his hand instead.

"Here she comes!" a boy hollered.

Grabbing onto Ted with both hands now, Eva bounced up and down.

"He's coming! He's coming!" she exclaimed. For a brief moment she thought that the only thing that could possibly make this moment better was if Violet was there.

The stage came to a halt in front of the depot about fifteen minutes after nine. Daniel had his head out the window and was waving at the crowd.

The Baker family crowded by the door. Michael opened it and helped his son out.

Eva remained off to the side in order to let the family have their time together. She watched with pleasure as Daniel went from one person to the next, hugging and kissing his parents and siblings and saying how much his nieces and nephews had grown since he'd been gone.

Daniel said something and pointed into the stage coach.

Michael reached inside and pulled out a cane.

Eva's eyes widened. She had noted that Daniel had a slight limp, but did he need a cane? Would he always need one?

Daniel happened to look at her just then. He saw the shock on her face, and his smile faded.

Feeling awful that Daniel's first glance at her hadn't shown him the way she really felt, she started through the crowd towards him. She wanted to greet him properly.

Just as she was almost to him, however, Reverend and Mrs. Lewis took their turn welcoming Daniel home. The rest of the crowd pressed in. Eva couldn't even see Daniel anymore.

With a sigh, Eva turned around and went home.

~*~

Once Reverend Lewis and his wife had left, Daniel looked around for Eva. His face fell when he caught sight of her walking away. He remembered the look on her face when their eyes had first met. Surely she wouldn't think less of him because he needed a cane. Maybe the shock of seeing him again after such a long time was too much for her to handle at the moment.

Daniel wanted desperately to go after her. But more friends were greeting him, and he didn't want to be rude. His mother had already told him that she would be coming for supper along with her siblings. He would have to wait until then to speak with her. He had spent the whole trip figuring out what he would tell her. But now that he had seen her, he wondered if he could work up the courage to say those things.

~*~

Eva and her two brothers left for the Baker's around four that afternoon. Frank and Sarah would meet them there, along with the Lewises and a few of the Baker's other close friends.

All the way, Eva tried to think of what she would say to Daniel. She desperately wanted to tell him that she loved him, but there were too many reasons why she couldn't. It would be hard, however, to act as though nothing had changed from before.

Daniel, Samuel, and Joe were seated on the porch when the Remingtons arrived. Samuel immediately invited Peter to look at his new calf in the barn.

Ted shook hands with both Joe and Daniel, and then he turned to Eva.

"I had my turn to catch up with Dan earlier. Now I'll let you have a chat with him."

Ted left with Joe. Eva was almost certain that the fellows had planned this previously.

"Do you want to go for a walk?" Daniel asked her once they were alone.

"Don't you think we ought to just sit here?"

"I'm not a cripple, Eva." Daniel rose from his chair and grabbed his cane. "This here cane is mostly to help me balance until my legs get stronger. I won't need it forever." He finished, looking directly into her eyes.

Eva felt a chill run down her spine as their eyes locked.

Daniel took a step closer to her. Eva quickly turned away.

"Where shall we walk to?" she asked.

"Nowhere in particular. Let's just walk."

Daniel carefully made his way down the steps; Eva remained by his side.

"I'm not going to fall," Daniel said as he reached the ground.

Eva meekly took a step back.

Daniel smiled softly at her.

"But I like having you by my side."

Eva smiled back and matched his pace again.

The two of them walked silently. Eva didn't pay much attention to where they were going so she was surprised when they stopped by the paddock behind the barn.

"This is where it all happened," Daniel said, gesturing inside the fence. He leaned against a post and looked down at her. "If I remember correctly, you came to tell me something."

"I was going to apologize for being so rude to you that day." Eva rested her arms on the fence, placed her chin on the backs of her hands. She stared into the empty paddock, remembering that horrible day. "I should have never come here that day."

"But if you hadn't, we wouldn't be here right now."

"We're only here now because we're celebrating your homecoming. You would have never left home if that horse hadn't trampled you near to death. Daniel, she could have killed you!" Eva burst into tears.

Daniel was quick to gather her into his arms.

"But she didn't," he said comfortingly. "I'm all right."

"I was so frightened!" Eva wept against his chest.

"Of course you were." Daniel ran his hand down her back.

"Don't you wish we could go back and change the past?" Eva asked once she had calmed down some. "If I hadn't come here that day, you wouldn't have had to spend nearly a year in the hospital."

"I'm glad I spent that time away," Daniel said.

Eva pulled away from him and looked up into his face.

"You are?" she asked in confusion.

"Sure. It gave me lots of time to think."

"Oh? And what did you think about?"

Daniel grinned and touched her cheek, wiping the tears away.

"You," he whispered.

"Me?" Eva murmured, choking on the word.

"Who else? Eva, I don't know how you feel about me, but I love you. I have for as long as I can remember. I... I understand that... with my leg... you might not be able to love me anymore. If you ever did."

"If anything, I thought that you might not love me anymore," Eva admitted before she could stop herself. "It was my fault that you were injured. I know that you said that you were grateful for the time you had away, but I thought that you might hold some kind of a grudge against me for it."

"Oh, Eva, I could never have a grudge against you. I'm glad that you were the last person I saw before I was knocked out," Daniel chuckled slightly then returned to his serious state. "Don't blame yourself for my accident. You've blamed yourself for more things than you ever should have. If anything, it was my fault. I was careless with the whip."

Daniel trailed his fingers down her arms and took hold of both of her hands.

"What you said before, about you being afraid that I wouldn't love you anymore. Does that mean that you love me?"

Eva trembled. The moment that she dreaded most had finally arrived. If she told him the truth that she did love him, but that she couldn't marry him, it would break his heart. And if she lied and said she didn't, it would break his heart.

"Oh, Daniel, I can't!" she exclaimed, pulling her hands away from his.

"Can't what? Can't love me?" Daniel's face fell.

"No...yes... I don't know! I just can't!" Eva broke into a fresh round of tears and ran off, leaving Daniel at the fence, shedding some tears of his own.

Chapter 51

The Problem

~*~*~

Daniel left Eva alone for a few weeks, giving them both time to think. Daniel was almost certain that she loved him. But there was something holding her back, and he couldn't figure out what it was.

It was early June when he finally worked up the courage to go see her.

"It's my day to take the eggs into town," Daniel declared, entering the kitchen where his mother was making breakfast.

"No, it was your turn last week," Samuel reminded him.

"Well, I'll switch you, pal. All right?"

"Sure, Dan. I know you just want to see Eva." Sam grinned at him.

Ellen Baker smiled gently at her son.

"Take things slow with her, Daniel. She's had a rough life. I can see that she loves you. Give her time, and eventually she'll come around."

Daniel grinned and kissed Ellen's cheek.

"I will, Mama. Thanks for the advice."

"That's what mothers are for," she replied with a chuckle.

Daniel also laughed. As he stepped out the door, however, her words echoed in his mind.

"Of course!" he exclaimed, snapping his fingers. After quickly gathering the eggs, he picked up his pace and walked briskly to town.

~*~

Eva was washing the breakfast dishes when Ted entered the kitchen through the back door.

"Since I don't have to work today, I thought that I'd stay with Mama for a while so that you can go get some fresh air," Ted said, grinning at her.

Eva raised an eyebrow at him.

"Is this some kind of a joke?"

"Of course not, sis. You need a break every once in a while, and today, I'm the one to give it to you."

Eva smiled.

"That's very nice of you to offer, but I have a lot to do today. After I finish the dishes, I'm going to clean the entire house."

"I can do that for you."

"Really?" Eva asked skeptically.

Ted took the dish rag from her hand, looking right into her eyes.

"Really."

Eva beamed and threw her arms around him.

"Oh, thank you, Teddy! You're the best brother ever!"

"I know," Ted replied teasingly.

Eva playfully punched his upper arm.

"Go on now and enjoy your day off." Ted pushed her out of the kitchen.

"I'm going! I'm going!" Eva cried. She quickly told her mother of Ted's generous offer.

"That was very kind of him," Rose agreed with a smile. She had been doing a bit better in the past week and was sitting up in bed, working on a sewing project. "Have a good time, dear."

Eva nodded and left the room. She called out to Ted that she was leaving and went to retrieve her bonnet.

There were four pegs by the door to hold hats, bonnets, coats, and other such things. Eva had to remove three items before reaching her bonnet.

"Just shows how often I get out of the house," Eva muttered to herself.

Stepping out into the fresh morning air, Eva took a deep breath and exhaled slowly. Then she headed down to Luke's Mercantile to thank Luke for giving her brother the day off.

~*~

"Coast is clear," Ted called out the back door.

Daniel came out from his hiding place beneath the porch.

"Thanks, Ted," he said, slapping his friend on the back. "This means a lot to me."

"Yeah, well, you really owe me one. I have to clean the whole house now."

Daniel laughed.

"Don't worry, I'll help you once I'm done talking with your mother. Are you sure that she's well enough to see me?"

"Yes, she's been doing a lot better. You go on now in case Eva decides to come back."

Daniel nodded. He went through the kitchen and across the parlor. Then he knocked on the bedroom door.

"Come in," Rose Remington called.

Daniel could tell just by her voice that she was stronger than the last time he had seen her.

"Why, Daniel Baker! What brings you here?" Rose asked when she saw who it was.

"I was hoping to talk to you... if you're up to it. I need some advice."

"Of course. Sit down in this chair right here."

Daniel removed his hat and settled into the chair.

"What are you making?" he asked, pointing to her sewing. He wasn't quite ready to bring up his dilemma yet.

"A shirt for my little grandson. But I assume you didn't come here to talk about sewing. Unless you want to learn how to, that is." Rose grinned at him.

Daniel grinned back.

"No, that's not it."

"It's about, Eva. Isn't it?"

Daniel nodded, glad that she had guessed it.

"I noticed that she's been rather down lately. She was quite happy when she learned that you were coming back. But after supper at your place, her attitude changed. She never told me what happened. I don't suppose you would care to enlighten me?"

Daniel gave her a very brief explanation.

"I just don't get it, Mrs. Remington. I believe that she loves me. But something is holding her back, and I can't figure out what. It's almost as if she's scared."

Rose leaned back and closed her eyes. For a moment Daniel thought that she had fallen asleep, but then she spoke.

"I think I know what it is. I should have seen it sooner."

"What, Mrs. Remington? What is it?" Daniel asked, leaning forward.

"It's me." Rose opened her eyes and looked at him. "I'm holding her back."

"How so?" questioned Daniel, still not seeing what she meant. Then it hit him. "Oh!"

Standing up, Daniel ran a hand through his hair and began pacing the floor.

"Everything makes perfect sense now. I know the problem now, but how on earth am I going to solve it?"

Chapter 52

The Solution

~*~*~

Eva was surprised when she returned home just less than two hours later to find a clean house.

"A friend helped me," Ted explained when she asked how he had managed to finish so quickly.

"Daniel was here?" Eva asked, knowing whom he meant.

Ted nodded.

Eva felt slightly hurt that Daniel had stopped by and not waited for her. She supposed that he wasn't ready to see her yet, after the things she had said to him. She wasn't sure if she was ready yet herself.

"Well, you did a good job. I'll make some cookies, and you can give half to Daniel."

Ted grinned.

"Great! I love your cookies, and I know Dan does too. I can help you make them if you wouldn't mind."

"No, I wouldn't mind at all." Eva smiled at him. "In fact, I think that that would be very nice."

~*~

Daniel took a long walk by the river after he left the Remington house. He needed time to think of what to do next. The Platte River was always where he went when he needed to clear his head. The gentle sound of running water calmed him, and the shade from the trees was refreshing, for the June day had turned quite warm.

Daniel walked about a mile befor he turned around and headed back. In the distance he could see the flour mill.

"Of course!" he exclaimed, snapping his fingers.

Eva's mother had found the problem. Perhaps Eva's father could find the solution.

Daniel ran as fast as he could with his cane. He was out of breath by the time he arrived at the mill.

A large group of men exited the building as Daniel walked towards the doors.

Looking up at the sun, Daniel saw that it was dinner time.

Perfect, he thought. *Now if I can just catch Harold before he goes home to eat.*

It was Harold, however, who first saw Daniel.

"Hello, Daniel!" the man called. "What brings you here?"

"I wanted to talk to you... about Eva."

The two men walked a distance away from the others.

"What about Eva?"

"Well, sir. I'm in love with her, you see..."

"Mmm." Harold grinned at him.

"So I want to marry her, of course, but there's one problem."

"Oh, and what's that?"

"Your wife." Daniel blushed and caught his breath. "Sorry, I didn't mean for it to come out that way."

Harold chuckled.

"That's all right, son. I know what you mean."

Daniel let out his breath.

"Thank you, sir. I didn't mean any disrespect."

"None taken. Go on."

"You see, sir, I believe that Eva loves me as much as I love her - even though she says that she doesn't. I think it's because she has to care for her mother and doesn't feel that she can get married... because it wouldn't be fair to me."

"I understand completely. I believe that I have the answer to your problem."

"What's that?"

"Well, Ted is intent on using most of his pay to help support the family, and I recently got a raise, as well. I think that with only four mouths to feed, we could afford to hire someone to take care of my wife. That way Eva could get married and not have this responsibility anymore."

Daniel's eyes widened.

"Really? You would do that for me? And Eva?"

"Eva's worked very hard these past years. She's done her share. Now it's time for her to make her own life... with you."

"Thank you, sir!" Daniel gripped Harold's hand and shook it firmly. "I promise that I'll be the best husband I can be."

"I know you will, Daniel. I'll let you tell her when you're ready. I promise that I won't say a word."

"Do you want me to court her for a while first? Or can I go right ahead and propose?"

Harold chuckled.

"I already gave you my blessing - in case you missed that. I think that you and Eva have known each other for such a long time that you don't have to go through the courting process. Just make sure she's ready."

"I'll be patient with her. I promise. You can trust me."

Harold patted him on the back.

"I know I can, son."

~*~

Daniel was nervous the next morning as he prepared himself for church. Harold had told him the day before that he would stay with his wife so that Eva could attend church. Daniel was then to ask her to go for a walk. On the walk he was to explain to Eva what he and her father had decided on the previous day.

Straightening his tie around his neck, Daniel cleared his throat as he assessed himself in the mirror.

And then he was to propose.

With shaking hands, Daniel picked up his hat and placed it on his head. Then he joined his family on the walk to church.

~*~

"Get yourself ready for church, Eva."

Eva looked at her father in surprise.

"What did you say, Papa?"

~ 272 ~

"I believe you heard me correctly, darlin'. Go get yourself prettied up. I'll stay here with your mama today."

"Thank you, Papa!" Eva cried, flinging her arms around Harold. "This means so much to me."

"You're welcome." Harold patted her back. "Hurry up now. You don't want to be late."

"Yes, sir."

Eva felt a thrill run up her spine as she stepped into her green Sunday dress. It had been months since she had gone to church. Yesterday Teddy had stayed home so that she could go out, and now her father was staying with her mother. Life was good at the moment. Eva even forgot about her troubles with Daniel.

~*~

After the service, Eva was stopped by the Kline twins who were quite happy to see her. She chatted with the girls for a couple of minutes before greeting Mr. and Mrs. Baker.

"Good to see you out of the house, Eva," said Ellen.

"It's good to be out," Eva replied.

"Daniel's around here somewhere. I think he wanted to speak with you," Michael informed her.

"Oh." Eva ran her gaze over the crowd of people. "I don't see him."

"That's because he's behind you," a familiar voice said.

Eva turned around and smiled at Daniel.

"Why, hello," she said.

"Hello," he replied, gazing into her green eyes. "Care to take a walk with me?"

Eva glanced behind her, but Mr. and Mrs. Baker had vanished.

"I suppose so. It can't be too long, though. Papa will want me home."

"I'm sure he's not worried."

"Huh?" Daniel's reply had confused her.

Daniel grinned.

"Come, we'll walk out on the open prairie." Daniel gestured east of the church.

"All right," Eva agreed after a moment's hesitation.

The two walked in silence until they were a good distance away from town. Eva surprised herself by being the first to speak.

"You're still using your cane, I see," she said, pointing to it.

Daniel waved it in the air.

"I don't really need it anymore."

"Then why do you carry it?"

"I guess I don't exactly know." Daniel shrugged. "I don't always have it with me, but it's a good reminder."

"Of what?"

Daniel stopped walking. He held the handle up for her to see. *Proverbs 3:5* was carved into it.

"That's our verse," he told her, pointing to the reference.

"*Our* verse?" Eva questioned.

Daniel blushed slightly.

"Well, I deemed it our verse. It's the same one carved on the plaque I made you."

"Yes," Eva murmured. "I know."

"Whenever I look at this cane, it reminds me that I can trust God no matter what happens." Daniel looked down at her with serious eyes. "No matter how impossible things seem, I can trust that God will work it out. He has a plan for each one of us, and it will work out one way or another."

Eva knew where he was leading.

"But sometimes what we think might be God's plan, really isn't," she said, hoping to avoid whatever he was going to say next.

"And sometimes we try to pretend that we don't know what God's plan is because we're scared of it," Daniel was quick to respond. "I carved this cane myself. I added the reference a few weeks after I finished it because I knew that I would need the reminder. Besides," Daniel added with a chuckle. "I look quite dapper carrying it around. Don't you think so?" Daniel struck an elegant pose.

Eva giggled.

"Indeed you do."

The two of them continued walking again.

"I have a confession to make," Daniel spoke after several minutes of silence.

"Oh, really? And what might that be?"

"I asked Ted to tell you he would stay with your mother yesterday... to get you out of the house."

Eva looked at him and frowned.

"Why?"

"Because I wanted to talk to your mother."

"Why?"

"Because I thought that she might know why you run like a frightened rabbit every time I try to talk to you about how I feel."

"Oh?" Eva felt her face heat up. "And did she have any ideas?"

"Yes. She made me realize what I should have a long time ago."

Eva took a shaky breath. It was somewhat relieving to know that her secret was out.

"And now you understand why I can't marry you."

"Nope."

Eva halted and turned to stare at him.

"What on earth do you mean, 'nope'? Don't you get it?"

"Yes... and no."

Eva threw up her hands in exasperation and continued walking.

Daniel grabbed her arm to stop her.

"Now wait a minute, Eva. Let me finish."

Turning to face him, Eva crossed her arms.

"Fine."

"After I talked with your mother - and helped Ted clean your house - I went to see your father. Eva, he gave me his blessing... to marry you."

Eva inhaled sharply.

"Doesn't he even understand?" she exclaimed. "Who will care for Mama if I marry?"

"He decided that with his pay and what Ted is chipping in, he can afford to hire a girl to care for her."

"What?" Eva murmured. "Someone else... taking care of my mama? She probably wouldn't even know what to do. No, no, this would never work."

"I'm sure that he would find someone with experience. Don't you see, Eva? This is your chance. You can marry me and be free of the responsibility of caring for your mother. We'll live close by so that you can visit her whenever you wish. Please, Eva, please say you'll marry me."

"I don't know, Daniel. This is all so sudden."

"Not really. I've loved you for years. Haven't you noticed?"

Eva didn't speak.

Taking both of her hands in his, Daniel looked right into her eyes.

"Eva, can I tell you a something?"

Eva nodded, unable to say anything because of the way he was looking at her.

"When I was at the hospital the doctors didn't think that I'd ever walk again. They said that I'd be paralyzed... for the rest of my life. For a while, I gave up hope, but then I thought of you, Eva. I thought, 'What good would I be to Eva if I can't walk?' It was you, Eva. You were my motivation to push myself harder so that I would be able to walk again. And here I am, standing before you. I thought about you every day I was away. I realized that I can't life my life without you." Daniel dropped to his knee. He was still holding her hands. "I need you, Eva Remington. Please, say you'll marry me. I'll be the happiest man alive."

Eva trembled as his words echoed in her head... and then her heart. A warm feeling spread throughout her body from the loving way he gazed at her. She suddenly realized how overflowing her love for him was.

"Yes," she finally spoke, her voice shaky. "Yes, Daniel Baker. I will marry you!"

Chapter 53

Glorious Days of Summer

~*~*~

Eva hadn't known that such happiness existed. It seemed as though all of her worries had blown away, as if they were as light as a feather.

Everyone was thrilled to learn that Daniel and Eva were finally engaged, saying that it was long overdue.

The couple set the date for the first Saturday in September that year. Daniel didn't want to wait much longer. Eva agreed, figuring that that would give her enough time to properly train the girl who would be caring for her mother.

Daniel started building a house on a small plot of land just out of town. Ted, Peter, Frank, Joe, and Samuel were all helping. Harold and Michael also lent a hand on occasion. Daniel figured at the rate they were going, the house would be finished long before the wedding, and that there would also be time to get a good start on a barn.

Sarah came often to help Eva create her wedding dress. Rose helped whenever she felt strong enough. Eva told her not to wear herself out. Rose, however, insisted that the excitement of planning a wedding gave her great strength. She did promise to get plenty of rest in the weeks before the wedding. Neither of the women wanted Rose to miss the special occasion.

Eva had chosen Sarah to be her bridesmaid. She debated having a second one but wasn't close enough to any of the girls in town to ask them. She remembered the dream she had had long ago of her getting married. Joy and Violet had been her bridesmaids in that dream. She wondered if Daniel was the groom she had dreamt of.

In the small amount of spare time she had, Eva began making things for her hope chest. She embroidered hers and Daniel's initials into several of the items. Soon the chest was packed full. Eva couldn't wait until she could decorate her home with them.

In mid-July, Harold finally found a girl to hire. Her name was Susan, and she was the oldest of twelve children. Her family lived on a farm ten miles south of Smithville. She was sixteen years of age and had a pleasant personality. Eva decided right away that she liked the girl, and the two became friends.

Daniel came to visit Eva nearly every day. She had more free time with Susan around so he would often take her for walks or rides outside of town. Eva brought Daniel and the other men dinner on occasion. Daniel eagerly showed her the progress made on the house every time she came by.

Eva loved the way the house was laid out. She couldn't wait until the day she could live there and make it into a home for Daniel and herself. Often she would stand in the main room and plan out how the furniture would be arranged, imagining cozy nights by the fire and times when family and friends would visit. She would also dream of cooking in the lovely kitchen that Daniel had created for her. A large cook stove had been ordered, and there was plenty of counter space. She would take great delight in working in that kitchen.

Over the time Daniel had been in the hospital, Joe and Samuel had finished training the mare Daniel had been working with. She would be one of the first of the livestock that Daniel and Eva would own. While Eva still had uncertain feelings about the horse, Daniel joked that she had helped bring them together - and had also knocked some sense into his head.

Besides the mare, Daniel planned on buying pigs, cows, and chickens for their farm. Eva was pleased that she would have fresh eggs and milk right outside her door every morning. But she made it clear that when the time came, she would *not* be the one doing the butchering. Daniel had laughed at that and said he'd like to see her chasing around a hen with a hatchet.

The house was completed before the end of July. Daniel moved in right away. Sometimes Eva would come see him in the evening. The two of them would sit on the porch and watch the sunset while dreaming about their future.

As the August days slowly passed, Eva felt her excitement grow. She hummed as she went about her daily chores. Her face was a glowing beam of sunshine. Only a few more weeks and she would be a bride at last.

Chapter 54

Another Loss

~*~*~

"How's the bride-to-be this fine morning?" Harold asked his daughter. August was nearly over, and Eva's excitement had doubled in the past week.

"Wonderful, Papa." Eva kissed her father's cheek. "Your breakfast will be ready shortly. Susan went outside to get more wood."

"Mmm. I'm going to miss your cooking, that's for sure. But Susan can certainly hold her own in the kitchen."

"Thank you, Mr. Remington," Susan said as she entered the kitchen from the back way. "When you have eleven younger siblings, you learn to do a few things."

"That's true enough. I can tell by the way you work that you have experience. I'm glad you're the girl I hired."

"Thank you, Mr. Remington," Susan said again beaming. She set her load of wood by the cook stove.

"You can call me Harold if you wish. I know that my wife insisted you call her by her given name. Feel free to do the same for me. After all, we are living in the same house."

Susan nodded. "Yes, sir."

"Here's your eggs and toast, Papa," Eva said, placing a plate before him.

"Thank you, darlin'. Looks good." Harold began eating. Eva and Susan soon joined him.

"Where are the boys?" Harold asked after a while, noticing his sons weren't present.

"They had an early breakfast and left to help Daniel with the barn," Eva informed him. "He's going to put the finishing touches on today, and then he'll be done. Then we can start keeping animals there."

"That boy is going to make a farm girl out of you yet," Harold said with a grin.

"Well, I'm going to be the wife of a farmer, so I'd better learn to be a farmer's wife!" Eva said.

Both Harold and Susan laughed.

"I'd better get off to work before I'm late," Harold spoke as he cleaned the last of the eggs off his plate. "Thanks for a wonderful breakfast."

"You're welcome, Papa. Have a good day."

"I will. See you two later." Harold kissed the top of Eva's head and smiled at Susan.

"Goodbye, Papa."

"Goodbye, Mr. Rem... Harold."

Harold hummed a happy tune as he left the house and headed towards the mill. He was joined by several of his coworkers. The men chatted and joked as they made their way across the stretch of prairie that separated the mill from town.

"Just think, Harold, in a little over a week you'll be walking your daughter down the aisle. How does that feel?" Jacob Henning asked him.

"Wonderful and scary at the same time," replied Harold.

"I know exactly how you feel. It was the same for me when I gave my Sarah away to your son," Glenn Quant said.

"I'm nervous for the day when I have to walk my twins down the aisle," Joshua Kline joined the conversation. "Of course, the two of them are so shy that they haven't let any boys court them yet. I'm kind of relieved because of that, but I also feel bad for them."

"Just give it time, Josh. There are lots of nice boys in this town," Jacob said. "My Maria hasn't found anyone yet that I know of. But I have a feeling that Thomas Crews is going to be asking me for Angelina's hand one of these days."

Harold laughed.

"I know that Peter is disappointed about that. He's had a crush on Angelina for a few years now."

"Seems strange for grown men to be talking about the romances of our children," Glenn spoke. "That's more like what the womenfolk do."

"Well, our children are our future. I suppose we ought to talk about theirs every once in a while," Joshua said.

"That's true," agreed Harold.

Jacob also nodded.

"Well, here we are, boys," Harold announced. "Ready for another day of hard work?"

"Always," Jacob said.

The four men laughed.

~*~

It was about ten o'clock that morning when Eva heard yelling outside. She and Susan raced out into the yard to find out what was going on.

"There's been an accident at the mill!" Virgil Jones hollered. Virgil was the teenage boy who ran errands for Mr. Farnsworth.

Eva flew out the gate and joined the gathering crowd.

"What happened?"

"Was anyone hurt?" Questions fired from every direction.

Virgil waved his hands to quiet everyone down. His gaze swept the crowd. It rested on Eva.

Eva sucked in her breath sharply. She grasped onto Susan's arm and squeezed tightly.

Susan could feel the blood drain out of her arm, but she didn't pull away.

Silence filled the air.

"It's my father, isn't it?" Eva asked in a loud whisper.

Virgil walked towards her. His face was expressionless.

Eva could feel the eyes of the entire crowd on her.

"Yes," Virgil finally spoke.

Eva felt her knees buckle. She braced herself, preparing for the worst.

"He was carrying a sack of flour when he tripped over a lever. His arm got... caught... in one of the stone grinding wheels..."

The entire crowd gasped in unison.

Eva began to get lightheaded. She started to sway. Susan and Virgil both reached to steady her.

"…He lost a lot of blood," Virgil continued. "He… he didn't… didn't make it."

A silent scream escaped Eva's lips. She felt Susan's arms wrap around her. The crowd had gone blurry.

Reaching up, Eva touched the spot where her father had kissed her that morning.

Just that morning he had been alive and as strong as he had even been. And now he was gone… forever.

Chapter 55

A Rock of Strength

~*~*~

"What do you say we head back to your house for the noon meal?" Daniel asked. He gave the nail he had just driven into the wall an extra tap.

"Sounds good to me," Ted agreed.

"I sure am starved," Peter chimed in.

"Then let's go. We can finish putting up these boards after we eat."

The three men neatly piled their tools and started for town. The streets were strangely empty, but none of them thought much of it.

Peter was the first one to enter the Remington house. Daniel was right behind him, and Ted brought up the rear.

"Eva, what's the matter?" Peter asked, as he was the first to spot his sister.

Eva was curled up on the sofa, sobbing uncontrollably. Susan was trying her best to comfort her.

Daniel dashed to her side and knelt by the sofa.

"Eva darling, what's wrong?" he asked, smoothing the hair back so that he could see her face.

Slowly, Eva raised her head. Her eyes were red, and her face was pale.

"Oh, Daniel!" she cried, flinging her arms around his neck. "It's awful! Just awful!"

"What?" Ted asked. He and Peter moved closer to the sofa.

Eva cried into Daniel's shoulder. He rubbed her back gently, waiting until she was ready to speak.

"There was an accident at the mill... Papa..."

Daniel's hand froze on her back. He could hear Ted and Peter both gasp from behind him.

"He's going to be all right, though. Isn't he?" Peter asked desperately.

"No, he's not, Peter! He's... he's... dead! Peter! Papa's dead!"

Daniel pulled Eva completely into his arms and held her tight.

Ted collapsed on the sofa and buried his face in his hands, covering his sobs.

Peter stood in shock for a moment.

"No, he's not! Papa's not dead!" he yelled. Then he ran out the front door.

Susan sat quietly, observing the scene through her own tears.

~*~

After several minutes, Ted peeked through his fingers.

"How's Mama?" he asked softly.

"She's... doing as well as can be expected," Eva replied. Her crying had given her the hiccups.

"I'll go check on her," Ted said. He stood on shaky legs and made his way to his parent's room. *Well, I suppose it's just Mama's room now,* he thought sadly.

Quietly, Ted opened the door a crack and peered in.

"You may come in," Rose said softly.

Ted opened the door wider and slipped inside.

Rose was sitting up in bed. She held Harold's pillow in her lap and was stroking it lovingly. Ted could tell that she had been crying even though she wasn't presently.

Perching on the edge of the bed, Ted reached out to take his mother's hand.

Slowly, Rose raised her eyes to meet his. She smiled half-heartedly.

"How are you doing, Mama? Do you want me to get you anything?"

"No, thank you, Teddy. Just stay here with me for a while. Will you?"

"Sure thing, Mama."

Rose returned her gaze to the pillow. She didn't speak for a long time. Ted sat by her patiently.

"I've lost countless friends in my lifetime," Rose finally spoke. "I lost a son, and I lost a daughter. I've managed - fairly well - to move on. But this time, it is my husband. I don't know, I just don't know how I can live without him. He was my rock. He was always there for me. He treated me kindly. He never would have left me, not even my sickness scared him away. I don't know what I'll do without him, Teddy."

Teddy wrapped both of his hands around his mother's pale, fragile ones.

"Don't worry, Mama. We will all take care of you, just as we always have. I'll be your rock."

~*~

Back in the parlor, Eva was finally beginning to calm down.

"Daniel," she said, pulling herself away from him.

"Yes, darling?" Daniel trailed his fingers around her tear-stained face.

"There won't be a wedding next Saturday."

"That's all right, Eva. I understand that you need some time. We can postpone it."

"No, Daniel. We're not going to postpone. There won't be a wedding next Saturday… or ever."

"What do you mean?" Daniel asked in shock. He grabbed her arms and searched her eyes for an explanation. "I understand that you're feeling very depressed right now, but there is no need to cancel the wedding. Surely you're not thinking straight. Please, Eva, tell me this is a joke."

"Do you think that I would joke at a time like this?"

Daniel let his fingers slip off of her arms. He stood and began pacing the floor.

"Then explain it to me, Eva. I don't understand." Daniel ran a hand through his hair and stared at her.

"Don't you see, though? With Papa gone, there will only be half of the income entering this house than before. We can't afford to keep paying Susan. And when Susan leaves, I'll have to go back to caring for Mama, just like before."

Daniel froze as her words hit him. What she said made sense.

Susan had been watching the scene in silent shock. But when she heard Eva's last remarks, she was quick to speak.

"Please, don't let me be the reason you don't get married. That makes me feel awful. I'll be happy to stay on just for room and board."

"But you need to money to send home to your family," Eva reminded her. "That's a very generous offer, but it wouldn't be fair to you."

Susan nodded meekly and left the room to give them privacy to talk.

"I don't have a solution right now, Eva," Daniel said after a moment. "But give me time, and I will figure something out. Please, Eva. Please say that you'll still marry me. I'm willing to wait until you're completely ready. Promise me, Eva. Please."

Eva looked at him with sad eyes.

"I'll think about it, Daniel. That's all I can promise."

Chapter 56

Forever in Our Hearts

~*~*~

The funeral for Harold Remington was held two days later. Rose was carried out to the cemetery by Ted. She leaned on him and Frank during the service. All three were dressed in black along with the others who had come to pay their respects.

Daniel's arm was supportively wrapped around Eva's shoulders. She had quickly let out the hem on her own black dress, as she hadn't worn it for several years. Her hair was pulled back in a tight bun, and she had a black shawl wrapped around her head, despite the warm weather.

Reverend Lewis solemnly conducted the service. Eva's mind flashed back to the glance she had taken at her father in his casket the day before. He had been covered with a blanket. Only his face was in view. Eva could tell from the way the blanket fell around his form, that his left arm had been completely amputated.

Now, Eva stared at the closed casket resting on boards above a freshly dug grave, waiting to be lowered inside.

Letting her eyes wander, Eva thought about the many times she had stood in this cemetery, saying goodbye to someone she had known and loved.

Once the service had concluded and the grave was covered, everyone except the family left.

Ted helped Rose down next to the grave. Eva watched as her mother rested a hand on the soil and whispered something that none of them could hear.

Turning her back to her father's grave, Eva walked a few yards away and laid a hand on the cross with Violet's name carved into it.

Daniel had followed her. He also rested a hand on his sister's cross.

"I still miss her so much," Eva whispered.

"Of course you do. So do I," Daniel said softly.

"She will forever be in our hearts." Eva then moved on to Johnny's grave. "I sometimes forget about Johnny. I was so young when he died. Let's go pick some flowers for them."

"All right," Daniel agreed. He took her hand and led her to a patch of wild flowers. "Those ones over there are pretty."

"Yes, they are." Eva picked a handful and gave them to Daniel so that she could pick more.

Once they had two large bouquets, the couple returned to the cemetery. Eva carefully arranged the flowers around first Violet's, then Johnny's cross.

Ted and Frank had already taken Rose home. Daniel and Eva walked back to the house, neither one spoke.

Sarah and Susan had prepared dinner for everyone. The family ate together in silence. Each was lost in his or her own thoughts.

Eva kept looking at her father's place where Frank now sat. What would it be like, eating meals with only Ted, Peter, and herself at the table? It would be terribly empty for sure.

After cleaning up the meal, Susan left to pack. Ted would be taking her home the next day. Eva would miss the girl.

Frank helped Rose back to her room and then joined the rest of the family in the parlor.

"I suppose," Frank began as he leaned against the mantel. "That we ought to think about what will happen next."

"I will support the family," Ted spoke up. "I can afford to with my pay. And Pete has been good about sharing his money."

"At least the situation can't get any worse," Peter said.

Frank looked over at his sister.

"I'm sorry, Eva, that this affects your wedding. We'll make sure it happens as soon as possible."

Eva nodded but didn't say anything. She could feel Daniel's eyes on her.

There was a knock on the door.

"I wonder who that could be," Frank muttered as he went to open it. "Why, Mr. Farnsworth."

"Hello, Frank. May I come in?" Mr. Farnsworth asked solemnly.

"Sure." Frank opened the door wider and stepped aside.

"I know that this is a bad time, but I can't put it off any longer," began the mill manager.

"What is it?" Ted asked.

"Well, it's like this… I'm going to be blunt… you will have to move… out of this house."

"What!" Eva exclaimed.

"I'm afraid I don't understand," Ted said.

Frank pressed a hand to his forehead.

"I do. This is a company-owned house."

"And that means..?" Eva pressed.

"With none of your family working at the mill, you have no right to live in this house," Mr. Farnsworth explained. "We're giving you a week to pack up your things and find someplace else to stay, but that is all. We need this house for the next worker… who will… replace… your father. I wish it could be longer, but I that is all I could get you."

"Thank you for trying, anyway," Frank said. "We'll figure out something."

"I'm sure you will, Frank. I hate to be the one to bring you such bad news. And I'm truly sorry about your father. He was a good man."

"Yes, he was," Frank agreed. "Thank you for saying so."

Mr. Farnsworth nodded. He bid goodbye to the others and quietly left.

"Frank, what are we going to do?" Eva asked desperately.

"I'm not sure yet. Let's go tell Mama."

Frank, Ted, Peter, and Eva all filed into their mother's room.

"Mama, Mr. Farnsworth just brought us some bad news," Ted was the first to speak.

Frank explained the situation.

Rose sighed.

"I should have seen this coming."

"What do you think we should do?" Eva asked of her mother. Rose always had good advice.

"I'm sorry, dear. This time I can think of nothing."

"What if…" Ted began. "I worked at the mill. Then we could keep the house."

"No, Teddy. You have a good job working at Luke's," Rose protested.

"I could," Peter piped up. "I've just been doing odd jobs since the construction company left."

"No," Rose said firmly. "I want none of my children working at the place that killed my husband. We will have to leave."

"But, Mama," Eva said quietly. "Where will we go?"

Chapter 57

Packing up Memories

~*~*~

"You could all come live with us," Sarah suggested when the four siblings reentered the parlor. "If that would be all right with you, Frank."

"I'm sure that we could make room."

"No," Eva immediately protested. "Your house is full with just the four of you."

"I could rent that little cabin south of the Glenshaw's property," Teddy suggested. "At least until till we come up with a more permanent solution."

"You could marry me this Saturday as planned," Daniel said to Eva. "Ted can rent the cabin. Your mother could live with us. Peter can stay with either Ted or us."

"That wouldn't be fair to you, Daniel. I don't want you to have to start married life with a ready-made family."

"I wouldn't mind. Honest, Eva. I love your mother as if she were my own. What would you say if the tables were turned, and it was my mother who was sick?"

Eva tilted her head to one side and smiled.

"I would insist that she stay with us," Eva replied.

Daniel grinned and clapped his hands.

"Then it's all set!" Grabbing Eva's arms, he kissed her cheek, not minding at all that the entire family was watching. "On Saturday we will finally be married!"

"Hurray!" Sarah exclaimed.

"All right then," Frank said. "Let's get packing."

~*~

Eva wandered about the nearly-empty house. Boxes were stacked in the parlor, waiting to be loaded up and taken to the house that would soon be hers. Daniel and Ted had taken one load that morning before going to help the Bakers with harvesting.

As she strolled across the parlor floor, memories flooded Eva's mind. There were bad ones, but also plenty that were good.

She remembered the times she had sewed and knitted by the fireplace. She remembered playing checkers with her brothers and Daniel. She remembered her father sitting in his chair, reading or whittling.

Eva remembered when Joy had screamed at her and accused her of murder.

Peering into the kitchen, Eva smiled sadly as she remembered the hundreds of meals she had prepared there... and how much her father had enjoyed each one of them.

She remembered when Joy had taught her to cook, and when she had taught Sarah how to cook. She remembered Daniel sitting at the table, eating her cookies.

Moving on, Eva peeked at her mother sleeping in bed. Rose's room had been mostly cleared out. Only the bed and a trunk of clothes remained. It was the same in Eva's room.

Back in the parlor, Eva removed the day-to-day calendar from the wall and set it in a box. Today was the thirty-first of August. Tomorrow was the first of September. The day after that she was to be married.

Entering the bedroom that had been hers all of her life, Eva opened her chest of clothes and gently picked up her wedding dress, which was lying on top.

Eva straightened up and held the gown to her chest. The white satin skirt dusted the floor. She couldn't wait for Daniel to see her in it.

Closing her eyes, Eva began humming and dancing about the room. She remembered Frank and Sarah's wedding when she thought that she would never have one of her own.

Laughing at herself, Eva carefully returned the gown to the chest.

"Only two more days," Eva whispered. "Two more days and Daniel will become my husband."

"Sure is hot out here today," Ted said.

From a few feet away, Daniel nodded.

"You can say that again."

"Sure is hot out here today," Ted repeated.

Daniel chuckled. He reached into his pocket to retrieve a kerchief to wipe the sweat off of his forehead. Then he returned to swinging his sickle. Harvesting wheat was hard work any day, but it seemed three times harder when the sun was beating down on one's back.

"I'm going back to the wagon for some water," Ted said. He set his sickle down and headed for the wagon which was several yards behind them.

Daniel followed, as did Joe who was also cutting the wheat.

Samuel, Clark, and Daniel's father were by the wagon along with Mary, Ellen, and Joe's wife Natalie. Michael was driving. The women were tying the wheat into bundles. And Sam and Clark were tossing the sheaves into the bed of the wagon.

"Tired already?" Clark teased.

"Just in need of a drink," Joe said.

Ted was the first to reach the barrel of water. Daniel and Joe waited patiently as Ted downed four dippers filled with the cool water.

Daniel let his older brother go next, and then he also drank four dippers of the refreshing water.

Just as Daniel was bringing the fourth to his lips, he noticed something strange in the distance.

Dropping the dipper, Daniel's eyes grew round, and he pointed to the west.

"Fire!"

Chapter 58

Thieving Flames

~*~*~

"What are we going to do?" Mary screamed.

Michael pulled a tarp out from under the wagon seat.

"Here! One of you boys get this wet and see if you can put it out. It doesn't look very big."

The flames were coming closer. They stretched across the prairie, eating whatever came into its path.

Joe was the one to reach for the tarp. He dunked it into the water barrel and raced towards the fire.

"Be careful, Joe!" Natalie screamed after him.

"I wish we had a plow to make a fire-break," Michael said as he stared after his oldest son. "You women get into the wagon; I'll see if I can get you to safety. Daniel, Ted, take the water barrel off of the wagon."

The two young men heaved the half-full barrel to the ground. Clark helped the women into the back of the wagon, and Michael gave the frightened horses free reign.

"Ted, help me," Daniel called. "We'll pour the water out in a straight line and see if it will get the ground wet enough to help slow the fire."

Daniel and Ted began to tip the barrel.

"Wait!" Joe hollered, running towards them dragging the tarp. "Let me get this wet again first."

Ted straightened the barrel, and Joe dropped the tarp in it.

"This sure is heavy when it's wet," Joe said.

"Here, I'll help you with it," Clark offered. He took one side, and both men ran towards the nearing flames.

Daniel felt as if he was being roasted alive as he and Ted began slowly pouring the water. It sickened him to be wasting so much water. But it wouldn't be a waste if it helped stop the fire and saved part of their crop.

The fire raged on. Closer and closer it got. The last drops of water fell to the ground.

"Well, this is it!" Ted yelled. "I sure do hope it works!"

Joe and Clark went flying past them as flames licked at the ground only a few feet away.

"Run!" Joe shouted.

Daniel and Ted ran.

A wagon came into view. Michael was driving, and several neighbors were piled in the back. Each one was holding either a bucket of water or a blanket or sack.

The men jumped out of the wagon and rushed to beat at the flames. Soon the last one flickered and snapped as one final effort to stay alive before it too gave in.

There was great rejoicing. Daniel and the others shook the neighbor's hands and thanked them for coming to the rescue.

"There's been several little fires all over the prairie today," Mr. Carver informed them. "But I must say that this was the biggest. I'm glad that no one was hurt. Sorry about your crop, though."

Michael swept his gaze over the singed field and sighed heavily.

"Yes, it is a tragedy. My other fields are already harvested, though. So that is a blessing. I'm just relieved that my family is all safe."

"That is indeed a blessing," Mr. Carver agreed. "Would you like some help with the rest of your field?" He looked to the other men to see if they were willing to lend a hand.

"I'd be much obliged to you all. But you don't have to help if you really don't want to," Michael replied.

"We sure do want to help. What are neighbors for?"

Michael and his sons all looked at each other and smiled.

"Then let's finish harvesting this wheat!" Joe exclaimed.

~*~

It was late that evening when Daniel finally saddled up his horse to go home. He was so tired that he dropped the reigns and rested his head on the mare's neck, knowing that she knew the way home.

"Daniel! I'm glad that you're back!"

Daniel blinked and straightened in the saddle. His back was sorer than it had been before. It wasn't terribly comfortable sleeping on a horse.

Phillip Morris, his next door neighbor, was looking up at him. Daniel could tell from his face that something was wrong.

"What's up, Phil?" Daniel asked, rubbing his back.

Phillip jabbed his thumb over his shoulder.

Daniel looked up.

His mouth dropped open in shock.

There, where his house had once stood proud, was nothing but a pile of charred wood.

~*~

Eva dug around in the kitchen, scrounging up the bit of food that was left to make one of the last meals she would ever prepare in this house.

Most of the basic foods were gone - or very nearly. A cup of flour and a pinch of sugar. She figured it would be easier to use up what they had instead of buying more supplies only to move them to her new house in a couple of days.

Suddenly, Eva heard a fit of coughing coming from her mother's room. She dashed out of the kitchen and to her mother's side.

Rose looked much worse than she had when Eva had last seen her.

"I'm going to get Midwife Stevens to look at you," Eva said.

Rose nodded as she began coughing again.

Eva patted her mother's back and then flew out the door and down the street.

Thankfully, the midwife was at home. She quickly followed Eva back to the Remington house.

"I wish there was a doctor here," Midwife Stevens murmured after she had examined Rose.

Eva's eyes widened in horror. Only a year ago the midwife had strongly protested when it had been suggested that the company hire a doctor. Something must be terribly wrong if the midwife wanted one now.

"What is it?" Eva asked, frightened of the answer.

"I have no idea what she has, and I don't know what to do for her. I'm sorry, Eva."

Eva nodded slightly. She wrung her hands together.

"How much… time…. do you think she has…. left?"

Midwife Stevens looked sadly at Eva. Then she glanced at Rose and shook her head slowly. Then she left.

Eva felt a tear slip down her cheek. She had just lost one parent. Surely God wouldn't take the other one so soon.

There was a knock on the front door.

"Who could that be at this hour?" Eva wondered aloud. She quickly swiped at her eyes.

Perhaps it was Mrs. Lewis or some other lady, coming with an offer to help with packing.

Standing by the door, Eva took a deep breath and made sure her crying had stopped.

She opened the door.

Her mouth dropped open in shock.

There, on the porch, stood someone Eva thought she'd never see again.

Chapter 59

~*~*~

"Joy," Eva whispered, stunned.

"Eva, is that really you?" asked the woman on the porch. "You've grown up so much since the last time I saw you."

"I had to," Eva replied somewhat bitterly.

Joy bowed her head in disgrace.

"Yes, I suppose you did."

"We all thought you were dead. Where have you been all these years?"

Joy glanced up at her.

"May I come in? I'll explain everything."

Eva stepped aside so that Joy could enter.

"What's with all of the boxes?" Joy asked, waving her hand around.

Eva took a shaky breath.

"It's a long story."

"Where's Mama and Papa? And the boys?"

"Frank's married and living on a farm just outside of town."

"Frank's married?" Joy asked in surprise. "Yes, I suppose he would be. I'd imagine that Teddy is too? And perhaps even yourself?"

"Teddy's not. I'm to be married day after tomorrow."

"Really? To whom?"

"Daniel."

"Daniel Baker?"

Eva nodded.

"He always was a nice boy. What about Teddy? He always had a crush on Violet. They're not married yet?"

Looking away, Eva whispered, "Violet... Violet died... a few years ago."

"What! How? Oh, Eva, I'm so sorry!" Joy impulsively hugged her sister. Eva was surprised that, after their long time apart, she didn't mind the embrace. "Obviously so much has changed since I've been gone."

"That's not even half of it," Eva muttered.

"What's that?" Joy asked, releasing Eva.

Eva shook her head.

"I'll explain later. First, let's go find Frank, Ted, and the others, and you can tell us where you've been these past eight years."

"I'd like to see Mama first," Joy protested. "I need to ask her forgiveness for what I did. I'm asking for yours as well."

"Mama is quite ill at this time," Eva said. She didn't mention anything about forgiving Joy, as she wasn't sure whether or not she wanted to. "I think that the shock of seeing you will be too much for her right now. Let's go find the others."

Joy reluctantly agreed.

Eva asked Mrs. Black from next door to stay with Rose.

The two sisters walked down the road towards the house Daniel had built. Thankfully, they didn't run into anyone. Eva didn't want the whole town to know about Joy's return before her family did.

The girls arrived at the site to find Daniel staring blankly at a pile of rubble which used to be their house.

"Daniel! What on earth happened?" Eva cried in shock.

"There was a fire…" Daniel trailed off when he saw Joy. "What in the world..! That can't be… you're not…"

Joy smiled and laughed a little.

"Yes, Daniel. It is me."

Daniel pointed at Joy and looked to Eva.

"She's dead!" he exclaimed.

"Or so we thought," Eva said. "We need to find the others so that Joy can explain to everyone at once."

"Has your mother seen her yet?"

"No, I think that it will be too much of a shock for her right now. She's extremely ill."

There was the sound of running horses coming up the road. It was Ted.

"I just heard about your house," he said as he dismounted. "Oh my, and your barn too, I see."

~ 300 ~

Daniel nodded in dismay. Then he pointed to Joy.

Ted glanced at the young woman. At first he didn't recognize her.

"Joy! I thought you were dead!" Ted slid off his horse and hugged her.

"Not you, too?" Joy said jokingly. "Where are Frank and Peter? And Papa?"

Ted looked over at Eva.

"You didn't tell her?"

"Tell me what?"

Eva avoided her sister's gaze.

"Papa... he's... dead," she finally whispered.

"What?" Joy said softly. "When did this happen?"

"About a week ago," Ted said.

Joy reached out and grasped his arm to steady herself.

"A week?" she murmured. "If I had come just a week earlier, I could have seen him again. Papa dead. I can't believe it. How did it happen?"

Ted briefly explained.

Joy looked as if she were about to faint.

"Let's take her over to Frank's house," Daniel suggested.

Ted swung back onto his horse. Daniel helped Joy up behind him.

Eva found Daniel's mare grazing nearby, still tacked, and led her to Daniel. Daniel mounted the horse, and Eva climbed up behind him.

The two men guided their horses down the road to Frank's farm.

Frank, Peter, Sarah, and the two young ones were all on the porch when they arrived.

"I can't believe it!" Joy exclaimed once the initial shock had worn off. "Frank married little Sarah Quant!"

Sarah laughed.

"I'm only about a year younger than you, Joy. Would you like to meet your niece and nephew?"

"Of course!" Joy smiled at the two children.

"Ruthie is three, and Joseph is almost two," Sarah said, laying a hand on each one as she spoke.

Joy knelt down.

"I'm your Aunt Joy," she said. "I'm sorry that I haven't been around to watch you grow up so far, but I promise that I'm going to visit you a lot more often."

"Then you're going to be staying?" Eva asked.

"Yes, whatever happened to Jack?" Frank questioned.

"Let's all sit, and I'll tell you the whole story." Joy sat on one of the wicker chairs.

The others each found a place and turned their attention to Joy.

"So... the night that I - ranted, we'll say - there was a terrible blizzard as I'm sure you'll remember. I wandered about for, I don't know how long, feeling sorry for myself and whatnot. Finally, I knew that I needed to get inside before I froze to death. I knocked on the first door I came to. It happened to belong to the Greens.

"Jack let me in, and I explained to him what had happened. He told me to go back home, but I was firm in my decision not to. He eventually admitted that he loved me, and it sparked an idea in my head. I suggested that we elope."

"It was you who suggested it?" Ted asked in shock.

"Yes," Joy nodded, blushing. "He was strongly against it at first. He wanted to marry me the proper way. Finally, he gave in, and we decided to go west. Platte City was the first town we came to. It was our intent to purchase stage tickets for as far as we could go and make a life there."

"But you did buy those tickets. Papa said that the clerk had found money lying on his desk," Eva interrupted.

"Papa went after me?" Joy asked with tears in her eyes.

"Of course," Frank answered. "Why wouldn't he?"

Joy shrugged.

"I don't know. He was so angry with me that night."

"That's true. But he was only angry because he loved you."

Joy nodded

"Oh, I am so ashamed of what I've done."

"But, Joy, I don't understand. Papa said that that stage coach crashed, and there were no survivors. That is why we thought you were dead," Eva said.

"That is why I said we *intended* to purchase tickets *west*. We were the ones who put the money on the desk. But after some thinking, we decided to go east instead."

"Huh?"

"Yes. We took the next stage east - that is why we weren't on the one that apparently crashed. We eventually ended up in the Smoky Mountains of Tennessee. Jack and I both fell in love with the mountains, we built our home there. That is where we've been the past eight years."

"And why haven't you contacted us before?" Ted asked.

"Because I was ashamed of what I had done, and I didn't believe that you would forgive me."

"What made you change your mind?" Frank pressed.

"Because of the couple that moved into a house nearby. Their name is Davidson. The wife has a sickness similar to Mama's. They came from a flour-producing town like Smithville. Their doctor sent them to live in the mountains because of the fresh, moist air. It is the flour dust in the air that makes Mama sick. She has an allergy to it."

Eva smacked a palm to her forehead.

"I should have figured that out before! Mama said she was always sick as a girl. It must be because she grew up in a bakery. She told me once that she wasn't sick after she left Boston... until she and Papa moved here! We should have taken her away from this place long ago."

"That is why I came back," Joy said. "It was my responsibility to take care of Mama, and I dropped it onto your shoulders, Eva. Rather abruptly. I thought that I would take Mama to live in the mountains with me and Jack. She will like to get to know her other grandchildren."

"You have children, Joy?" Eva asked, somewhat surprised.

Joy nodded,

"Three girls and two boys."

"Are they here now?" Frank questioned.

"The children are back home staying with a neighbor. Jack is at his parents' house, making amends with his own family."

"I know I should be grateful that Mama will be going to a place where she will have a chance at getting well," Eva said. "But I'm really going to miss her."

"We all will," Frank said.

"You don't have to make up your mind right away," Daniel spoke for the first time. "But now that our house has burnt down..."

"Oh my, I nearly forgot about that," Eva muttered.

"...How would you like to go, too?" Daniel finished.

"Live in the mountains? With Joy and Mama?" Eva tried to wrap her head around the idea of moving so far away.

"It's very different than living on the prairie, but you'll get used to it," Joy promised.

"I trust that I will," Eva said with a smile. "And, Joy."

"Yes?"

"You have my forgiveness."

Chapter 60

~*~*~

Life went on.

Eva spun around slowly as she assessed herself in the mirror. She smoothed the flowing shirt of her gown one last time before turning to the other women in the room.

"Oh, Eva, you look beautiful," said the first bridesmaid with light brown hair and blue eyes. "You're the prettiest bride ever."

"Yes, indeed," agreed the second bridesmaid, a bit younger than the first.

"Eva, are you ready?" Frank asked, peeking into the room.

"Yes."

"You sure do look pretty, sis."

"Thank you, Frank. I'm glad that you agreed to give me away."

"Of course," Frank replied, offering his arm. "What are big brothers for?"

Eva grinned and gently placed her hand over his elbow.

The foursome made their way out of the Lewis's guest bedroom, which had been offered as a place for the girls to get ready, as it was conveniently located next to the church.

Joy and Sarah, Eva's bridesmaids, entered the church first. Eva could hear the music, and her heart beat faster.

"Are you ready for this?" Frank asked.

Eva nodded.

"More ready than I ever thought possible."

The wedding march began.

"That's us," Frank said.

Peter and Samuel swung open the church doors, and Eva saw Daniel for the first time that day. He was standing at the front of the building, Reverend Lewis to one side and Teddy on the other.

"Don't run now," Frank leaned over and whispered as Eva began to pick up her pace.

Eva bit back a giggle and slowed down a bit.

~*~

It had seemed like forever to Daniel as he waited for his bride at the front of the church. He couldn't believe that after all of these years, she would finally be his wife. God had surely blessed him.

Sarah and Joy each slowly made her way up the aisle. The doors to the church were closed, but Daniel knew that Eva was on the other side.

Daniel smiled briefly at each bridesmaid before returning his attention to the back of the building.

The wedding march began.

Samuel and Peter opened the doors in unison and there stood Eva, a vision in white holding onto Frank's arm.

Daniel's eyes froze on her as the pair slowly made their way towards him.

Chuckling, Ted nudged him in the ribs.

Leaning next to his friend's ear, Daniel whispered, "Thanks, I needed that."

As Eva grew closer, Daniel could see that her face was aglow with happiness. Her loving eyes were fixed upon him. He was filled with the greatest joy he had ever known.

~*~

Eva's heart was beating even faster as she came within feet of her beloved.

Daniel was grinning at her the way he always did, except this time she could see his love for her reflecting off of his face.

Before she knew it, Eva and Frank had reached the front.

Frank shook Daniel's hand.

"Take good care of her," he said.

"I will," Daniel promised.

"I love you, sis," Frank whispered in Eva's ear. He kissed the top of her head the way her father always had.

"I love you too, Frank."

Daniel took Eva's hand and led her to face Reverend Lewis.

Eva smiled up at Daniel and took a deep breath as she prepared to make her vows.

~*~

Eva Baker was glowing as her husband escorted her out of the church a short while later. A covered wagon awaited them. Their few belongs - the ones that had still been in the town house when Daniel's had burnt down - were loaded in the back.

Frank carried Rose out of the church and placed her in the bed in the back of the wagon. Those who had attended the wedding rushed out of the church and began their goodbyes.

Eva felt tears of both joy and sorrow spill down her face as she bid farewell to those she had known all of her life. Daniel tried to hold onto her, but they were pulled apart in the crowd as everyone hugged them and shook his hand.

Eva clung to Sarah for a long time.

"Be safe now," Sarah whispered. "Write often."

"I promise."

"Goodbye, Eva. Take good care of my son now," Ellen Baker said. "I wish that you didn't have to rush off right after your wedding."

"Me too, Mrs. Baker."

Ellen laughed.

"You're Mrs. Baker now, as well, Eva. Call me Ellen."

"Of course, Ellen." Eva also laughed.

"You've always called me Michael," Mr. Baker said, coming up behind his wife. "But you can call me 'pa' if you want to."

"I'd be glad to. It's good to have a papa again." Eva embraced the man and kissed his cheek.

"And it's good to have a daughter your age again."

"Ready to go?" Daniel asked, having finally found Eva again.

Eva looked up at him with tears in her eyes.

"I suppose so. This is much harder than I thought it would be." Daniel squeezed her.

"It always is." Daniel reached out to shake his father's hand. "Goodbye, Pa. Bye, Mama." Daniel embraced them both and kissed his mother.

"Goodbye, son. Be good to her."

"I will." Daniel grinned down at his wife.

Eva grinned back at him.

"Now you really are my little sister," Joe said, joining their circle. "Glad to have you in the family, even though you're going to be miles away."

"Thanks, Joe." Eva embraced him. She then found Mary and her family and bid them each goodbye.

Daniel finally managed to pull her away from the crowd. Frank was waiting for them by the wagon.

"Be good to my little sis," he said to Daniel, shaking his brother-in-law's hand firmly.

"You know that I will be."

"And don't wait too long to visit."

"We won't."

Eva flung her arms around her eldest brother's neck and clung tightly to him.

"Goodbye, Frank. I'll miss you. I love you."

"I love you, sis."

Daniel helped Eva up onto the wagon seat and climbed up beside her.

"Ready?" he called into the back.

"We're ready!" Rose and Peter replied in unison.

"Are you ready up there?" Daniel yelled to Jack who was in the wagon in front of them.

"All set!" Jack hollered back. He signaled to his team, and the wagon began slowly rolling forward.

Daniel also started up his team. He and Eva waved at their friends and family as the people of Smithville slowly grew smaller.

Eva let her eyes drift in the direction of the house she had grown up in. It looked exactly like every other house on the street. But that one was special because it had been hers.

"Daniel, stop!" she suddenly exclaimed.

Daniel reigned in the horses.

"What?" he asked.

"Something wrong?" Rose called.

Eva jumped down from the wagon and ran through the gate and up the path.

"Eva, what on earth are you doing?" Daniel yelled, racing after her.

Eva flung open the door, grateful that it wasn't locked. She dashed through the parlor, her footsteps echoing off the walls of the empty house.

Stopping just inside the kitchen, Eva pointed across the room to the wall near the back door.

"I can't believe that I nearly forgot that," she said.

Daniel's eyes followed her finger. They landed on the plaque he had made her with Proverbs three, five carved into it.

"It's been there so long that it has become part of the room. Can we please take it with us?"

"Of course." Daniel walked across the room with Eva right behind him. He removed the plaque and handed it to her.

"Thank you," Eva said, grinning at him. Her eyes fell on something carved directly into the wall. It was a "D" and "E" inside a heart.

"Daniel, did you put that there?"

Daniel blushed.

"I *might have* done that before I hung that up. I wonder what the people who live here next will think."

"They'll think that I married a very sweet man," Eva told him. "Come on, let's go on our adventure."

The newlyweds returned to their wagon and yelled to Jack that they were ready to go again.

Ted rode up alongside them. He had decided the previous night that he wanted to go with them. He said that there was no reason to stay in Smithville if most of his family was leaving. And there would never be anyone else for him except Violet. Eva was glad to have her brother along. Only Frank was staying behind. But that was all right because Eva knew that they would see each other again one day.

The wagons continued east. Eva remembered when she had gone with Daniel to the cemetery the previous day to say goodbye to her father, Johnny, and Violet. They had put large bouquets of fresh flowers on each grave.

Part of Eva was sad to be leaving Smithville. It was the only home she had ever known. She had gained much there, and she had lost much there.

The other part of Eva was excited to go on to a strange new land. She was glad that her mother would finally have a chance to get well. She was eager to begin her life with Daniel.

Eva squeezed Daniel's hand and kissed his cheek. He grinned and kissed her back.

Eva had never felt so complete in her life. Over the years she had regained her trust in mankind. She even trusted Joy again. But she knew where she could put her ultimate trust as they went on their journey.

Looking out onto the open prairie, Eva took it all in, knowing that she would soon have to adjust to a different type of landscape. She was at ease with the changes that were to come, though.

"Because in God... I put my trust."

~*~*~

Let the morning bring me word
of your unfailing love,
for I have put my trust in you.
Show me the way I should go,
for to you I entrust my life.
Psalm 143:8

~*~*~

www.ingramcontent.com/pod-product-compliance
Lightning Source LLC
Chambersburg PA
CBHW060850250626
47159CB00008B/2680